"Here's what we're going to do."

David paused for a moment. "I want to make it clear, right out front, that I'm not changing my mind about selling the inn. But I promise you it will not be sold until after December nineteenth, so if you want to raise the money to buy it, then go for it. I won't stand in your way."

Once he finished laying out his plan, he halfway expected Willow to jump up and down and squeal and throw her arms around his neck. That would have been nice. And also inappropriate and unwise.

Thank God Willow wasn't that kind of woman. She didn't squeal or hug him. She just gave him a killer smile that drew his attention to her mouth, and her plump, kissable lips.

And right then, David had a name for the itch he'd always felt in Willow's presence.

Lust. But not the simple kind. Oh no. This was nuanced and complicated and problematic. He wanted Willow...

Praise for Hope Ramsay's
Heartwarming Series

Last Chance Hero

"Fans will enjoy another visit to Last Chance, the quintessential southern small town. The characters in this town are priceless...Readers can expect to have a whole lot of fun."
—RT Book Reviews

"I love visiting Last Chance and getting to revisit old friends, funny situations, the magic and the mystery that always seem to find their way into these wonderful stories."
—HarlequinJunkie.com

Last Chance Family

"4 stars! Ramsay uses a light-toned plot and sweet characters to illustrate some important truths in this entry in the series."
—RT Book Reviews

"[This book] has the humor and heartwarming quality that have characterized the series...Mike and Charlene are appealing characters—unconsciously funny, vulnerable, and genuinely likeable—and Rainbow will touch readers' hearts."
—TheRomanceDish.com

Inn at Last Chance

"5 stars! I really enjoyed this book. I love a little mystery with my romance, and that is exactly what I got with *Inn at Last Chance*."
—HarlequinJunkie.com

"5 stars! The suspense and mystery behind it all kept me on the edge of my seat. I just could not put this book down."
—LongandShortReviews.com

"An upbeat, empowering, and still sweet novel about balancing community pressure with personal needs."
—*Publishers Weekly*

"Every time I read one of the Last Chance books, it's like coming back to my old family and friends...[In] no time, you will be caught up in the characters lives and flipping the pages madly until you finish."
—FreshFiction.com

Last Chance Book Club

"4½ stars! [A] first-class romance, with compelling characters and a real sense of location—the town is practically a character on its own."
—RT Book Reviews

"Abundant Southern Charm and quirky, caring people. Another welcome chapter to Ramsay's engaging, funny, hope-filled series."
—*Library Journal*

"I love this story...Southern charm at its funniest."
—FreshFiction.com

"Last Chance is a place we've come to know as well as we know our own hometowns. It's become real, filled with people who could be our aunts, uncles, cousins, friends, or the crazy cat lady down the street. It's familiar, comfortable, welcoming."
—RubySlipperedSisterhood.com

"Hope Ramsay heats up romance to such a degree every reader will be looking for a nice, cool glass of sweet tea to cool off."
—The Reading Reviewer (MaryGramlich.blogspot.com)

Last Chance Christmas

"Amazing...These lovely folks filled with Southern charm [and] gossip were such fun to get to know...This story spoke to me on so many levels about faith, strength, courage, and choices...If you're looking for a good Christmas story with a few angels, then *Last Chance Christmas* is a must-read. For fans of Susan Wigg."
—TheSeasonforRomance.com

"Visiting Last Chance is always a joy, but Hope Ramsay has outdone herself this time. She took a difficult hero, a wounded heroine, familiar characters, added a little Christmas magic, and—voilà!—gave us a story sure to touch the Scroogiest of hearts...It draws us back to a painful time when tensions—and prejudices—ran deep, compels us to remember and forgive, and reminds us that healing, redemption, and love are the true gifts of Christmas."
—RubySlipperedSisterhood.com

Last Chance Beauty Queen

"4½ stars! Enchantingly funny and heartwarmingly charming."
—RT Book Reviews

"Grab this today and get ready for a rollicking read."
—RomRevToday.com

"A little Bridget Jones meets Sweet Home Alabama."
—GrafWV.com

Home at Last Chance

"An enjoyable ride that will capture interest and hold it to the very end."
—RomRevToday.blogspot.com

"Full of small town charm and Southern hospitality... You will want to grab a copy."
—TopRomanceNovels.com

Welcome to Last Chance

"Ramsay's delicious contemporary debut introduces the town of Last Chance, SC, and its warmhearted inhabitants... [she] strikes an excellent balance between tension and humor as she spins a fine yarn."
—*Publishers Weekly* (starred review)

"[A] charming series, featuring quirky characters you won't soon forget."
—Barbara Freethy, *New York Times* bestselling author of *At Hidden Falls*

A
CHRISTMAS
BRIDE

A
CHRISTMAS
BRIDE

HOPE RAMSAY

FOREVER

NEW YORK BOSTON

Copyright © 2016 by Robin Lanier

Excerpt from *A Small-Town Bride* © 2016 by Robin Lanier

Cover image © Masterfile
Cover design by Elizabeth Turner
Cover copyright © 2016 by Hachette Book Group, Inc.

Forever
Hachette Book Group
1290 Avenue of the Americas
New York, NY 10104
forever-romance.com
twitter.com/foreverromance

First Edition: September 2016

Forever is an imprint of Grand Central Publishing.
The Forever name and logo are trademarks of Hachette Book Group, Inc.

The publisher is not responsible for websites (or their content) that are not owned by the publisher.

The Hachette Speakers Bureau provides a wide range of authors for speaking events. To find out more, go to www.hachettespeakersbureau.com or call (866) 376-6591.

ISBNs: 978-1-4555-6480-4 (Mass Market); 978-1-4555-6482-8 (ebook)

Printed in the United States of America

OPM

10 9 8 7 6 5 4 3 2 1

*To the independent retailers who
are the heart and soul of every
small town's Main Street*

Acknowledgments

Starting a new series is not easy, so I have many people to thank for helping me get through the ordeal of writing of this novel.

First, to my Washington Romance Writer pals, Carol Hayes, Keely Thrall, and Robin Kaye, for their patience in letting me spin out my plotlines for this book, which started out as a summer story and ended up set at Christmas. Your handholding and sensible advice were invaluable. Your plot ideas involving ice-skating mishaps were mostly hilarious even if they didn't make it into the book.

Thanks also to my dear husband, who chauffeured me on many weekend drives through the Shenandoah Valley as I researched the setting for this book and the Shenandoah Falls series. During one of these drives, I dropped in unannounced on a number of merchants in Berryville, Virginia, who were so gracious and generous with their time, especially when I asked a lot of impertinent questions about rents and zoning and life in a small town dealing with suburban encroachment. I hope I captured some of their concerns in this book and the short story that preceded it.

As always, many thanks to my editor, Alex Logan, who made me rewrite the beginning, thereby saving you, dear reader, from having to wade through something that was utterly impenetrable. Not to mention repetitive and boring.

A
CHRISTMAS
BRIDE

Chapter 1————————————————

Eagle Hill Manor could have served as a backdrop for *Gone with the Wind* except that every one of the grand portico's twelve Doric columns needed a coat of paint. Willow Petersen stood on the front walkway, shading her eyes. The November sun cast sharp shadows across the mansion's dingy facade.

Once the home of a wealthy robber baron, Eagle Hill Manor had been open to the public as an inn for decades. But it had clearly fallen on hard times in the eight years since Willow had last visited. It seemed hard to believe that two years had passed since Shelly had died.

As far as Willow knew, Shelly's mother, Poppy Marchand, still lived here. But why hadn't Mrs. M put up her autumn decorations? Where were the grapevine wreaths with their autumn-gold ribbons? Where were the pots overflowing with purple and gold chrysanthemums? Autumn was one of the inn's busier seasons, with tourists coming from all over the commonwealth to stay at one of Virginia's great old houses and take in the fall foliage along the Skyline Drive.

Willow squared her shoulders and fought down a wave of unease. If Mrs. M had died or moved away, Willow wouldn't have known it; she'd done a bad job of keeping in touch, even before Shelly's death.

She had reached the front door when it opened outward, propelled by a redheaded child who barreled forward and connected with Willow's midsection, knocking her back a step. A sudden, warm mix of relief, nostalgia, and sorrow spilled through Willow like a blessing. She hugged the child to her middle, absorbing a bittersweet mixture of grief and joy. Natalie, her godchild, whom she'd neglected. She clung to the girl's shoulders and hoped time would stand still.

It didn't.

A sharp, utterly male voice shouted from within the inn, "You come back here, Natalie Marie. You're behaving like a brat." Footsteps thumped from beyond the open door, coming in her direction.

- The little girl pushed Willow away, then scampered down the steps, her tangled red hair dancing behind her like a fiery contrail. She took off into the woods adjacent to the inn, her pink jacket and purple leggings soon lost to sight.

An instant later, the owner of the voice came roaring through the door. He took the front steps two at a time and then stopped in the middle of the leaf-strewn lawn, looking right and left.

David.

The years had turned his face hard and gaunt, which

only underscored his stunning good looks. He'd lost none of his presence, either. He took a breath and started to speak, and then pulled up short.

"Willow? Is that you?" His words came out in a cloud of steam in the chilly November afternoon.

Willow jammed her hands into the pockets of her cashmere coat—a relic from better days. "David." Her voice sounded dry and thin.

He cocked his head a tiny bit, assessing her. She'd gotten used to people doing that, ever since her decision to go public with her accusations of fraud against Restero Corporation, her former employer. Restero hadn't taken her charges lying down. Their PR department had publicly painted Willow as a malcontent, a troublemaker, and even worse in numerous press releases that the *Wall Street Journal* had run almost verbatim. Now people stared at her the way they used to stare at her mother, as if she were slightly crazy.

"What are you doing here?" David asked.

"I live here," she said, balling her hands into fists inside her pockets. "I mean I've moved back to Serenity Farm. With Mom," she added, feeling small and broken.

"Really?"

"Yeah, I know, big surprise. Me coming back to Shenandoah Falls and living with my crazy hippie mother."

"Yes, it is."

"David, I'm so sorry about—" He silenced her with a lift of one eyebrow. As a member of the Lyndon family—one of Virginia's most elite—he'd truly mastered that expression. Her heart almost broke. Once he'd been a good friend, but apparently that was no longer true.

She changed the subject. "Natalie went that way." She pointed to the path leading into the woods. "I'm sure she's hiding out in the secret place."

His censorious stare turned into a bona fide scowl. "How could you possibly know anything about Natalie?"

"I don't," she admitted, the pain sharp. "But I knew her mother." Willow managed to keep her voice controlled despite her emotions.

David turned away and marched off toward the woods, head down, hands swinging. His blue suit and dark wing-tip lace-ups weren't exactly the right attire for tromping through the woods on a cold November day. But hand-tailored suits were the uniform of choice for the male members of the Lyndon family. David wore his well.

Willow turned away, wondering if everyone in town would give her this kind of reception. She could almost hear the whispers going up and down the local grapevine: "Yep, that Willow girl sure is a chip off the old block. The apple didn't fall too far from the Petersen tree. Both of those women are troublemakers."

She walked into the inn's lobby, where she drank in the familiar setting, comforted by the fact that nothing much had changed since her girlhood. The place still smelled of beeswax and lemon oil, Persian rugs still covered the hardwood floors, and a pair of Queen Anne chairs still sat by the big fireplace in the lobby. But the furniture was dinged and scratched, the rugs threadbare, and the chairs' upholstery faded. The lobby, which should have been busy at this hour with people arriving for high tea, was dark. So was the dining room.

Shelly would be so disappointed.

The thought settled into Willow's mind the way snow

sometimes settled on the mountains, a cold thing that made her shiver. That last day of her life, Shelly had traveled to New York to meet with an architect about restoring the inn. She'd lost her life on the train coming home in a tragic derailment, and now, apparently, all those plans had come to nothing.

Willow continued through the familiar spaces, down a private hallway, and stopped in front of the closed door that led to the inn's office. She knocked.

"Come," came the answer she'd been hoping for.

Willow opened the door and found Mrs. M sitting behind an oak desk far too big for her. She wore a pair of half reading glasses that required her to tilt her head up as she looked at her computer screen. Her ever-present pearls and heather-gray twinset were like familiar friends. Her hair may have gone from blond to ash gray, but she still wore it in a pageboy, parted on one side.

"Natalie's swim bag is all packed and ready to go. It's on the front table. I know you don't want my opinion, but—"

She looked up from her computer, surprise unfolding across her face like an old-fashioned lady's fan. "Oh my goodness. You're not David...Willow. Oh my. Is that you? Good God, it's been years." Mrs. M jumped up from the desk and rushed forward with arms extended. An instant later, Willow found herself enveloped in an Estée Lauder hug. The scent left a warm, sugary feeling in its wake.

Mrs. M pushed her back. "Let me look at you," she said in her Tidewater accent.

Willow struggled to smile. "Mrs. Marchand, I—"

"Oh, for goodness' sake, you're a grown woman now. Please don't call me that. It reminds me that Craig has gone and left me behind. Which isn't all that newsworthy. That man was always in a hurry."

"I came to pay my respects. Somewhat belatedly for—"

"Oh, hush. There's no need. I got your letter, remember? And I've kept it. It's a comfort to know Shelly had such a good friend. I'm sorry you were so far away when the accident happened. In China of all places. You have become quite the world traveler, haven't you?"

"I guess. Not so much now, though."

Mrs. M waved her hand in dismissal. "No more of that kind of depressing talk. Do you have some time? I was about to go find some ginger snaps and tea. David should be along any moment to pick up Natalie, and then—"

"David has already arrived and made a detour. Into the woods," Willow said.

Mrs. M's blue eyes widened. "Detour?"

"I met him on my way in. I stumbled into the middle of a father-daughter disagreement of some kind. Natalie seemed upset and was running away from him and—"

"Oh, good Lord." Mrs. M bolted through the door. "Natalie," she shouted, "are you still playing in the library?"

Willow followed Mrs. M down the hall into a sitting room off the lobby that had always been called the library because of the big bookshelf filled with dog-eared paperback novels. The room was deserted except for a redheaded American Girl doll and assorted clothing and accessories scattered over the carpet.

"Natalie, where are you?" Poppy's voice sounded urgent.

"I told you, Mrs. M. I interrupted an argument or

something. She ran off into the woods, and David followed after her. I'm sure she's headed for the secret place."

The worry on Mrs. M's face disappeared. "You remember the secret place?"

"Of course I do. Shelly and I spent hours and hours there with our Barbies, planning elaborate weddings." And their dreams for the future.

Mrs. M nodded. "Yes, you did. And Natalie knows that place. I showed her the secret path this summer, and I told her that if she ever needed to talk to her mommy, that was the place to do it." Mrs. M's voice trembled a little as she continued. "At least that's where I go when I need to talk to her."

"Oh, Mrs. M, I'm so sorry. I should have come home sooner. I should have—"

"Nonsense. What happened was an accident. There's nothing you could have done to stop it. I'm just glad to see you. And now that I know where Natalie is, I think I'll let her play hide-and-seek with her father. I'm pretty sure he's forgotten all about the secret place and the hidden path. Maybe if he has to look for it, it will make him late to his mother's Election Day party, and that will be a few more minutes that Natalie doesn't have to dance to Pam Lyndon's tune. Why don't we go find a pot of tea."

"But aren't you worried about—"

"Not in the least," Mrs. M said with a wave of her hand. "Natalie is eight years old. When you and Shelly were that age, you had the run of the place. Remember?"

Willow remembered. Those were some of the best times of her life.

"Good. I'm an old-fashioned grandmother. I think the

term these days is 'free-range granny.' A child needs some space to roam, if you ask me. And it's the least I can do for Natalie, since her other grandmother would like to keep her on a very short leash."

Willow followed Mrs. M into the big, professional kitchen, which was empty of the usual cooks and helpers. Mrs. M busied herself with the kettle and a box of store-bought ginger snaps. She laid out a tray with a vintage china teapot and several mismatched English teacups. One of the saucers had a tiny chip—something Mrs. M would never have tolerated back in the day.

"Let's sit in the solarium," Mrs. M said, picking up the tea tray.

The solarium was a tiny bit cool on this November day. Once upon a time, the windows had provided a view of the Blue Ridge Mountains, but the azaleas in the flower beds outside had grown wild and leggy and now obscured the view on all sides.

They settled themselves on a couple of wicker rocking chairs. Mrs. M poured, and the spicy scent of Earl Grey filled the air.

"When did the inn close its doors?" Willow asked.

Mrs. M picked up her saucer and leaned back into the rocking chair. "Not very long ago. In September."

"Was business that bad?"

Mrs. M rocked back in her chair. "Time marches on, and I couldn't keep up with things like I used to. To be honest, I thought my innkeeping days were over when Craig and I sold the inn to Shelly. But then Craig and Shelly passed, and I ended up back here trying to do it all. It's time to hand the place off to someone else."

"But Shelly had so many plans. I mean, we had lunch

not long before the accident, and all Shelly talked about was restoring the inn. Whatever happened to her plans?"

"I'm afraid her plans died with her." Mrs. M put her cup and saucer down on the table. When she spoke again, her tone was sad and nostalgic. "Willow, I know Shelly had big dreams of restoring the inn, but she was never going to put them into action. David never wanted to be an innkeeper. And sooner or later, Shelly would have had to make a choice between her marriage and the inn. I'm sure she would have chosen her marriage. She loved David very much."

David tramped through the woods, going around in circles yelling Natalie's name. His daughter was being her worst willful self, but after twenty minutes of searching to no avail, a deep worry overtook him.

What if something terrible had happened to her? Maybe she'd fallen down and hit her head. Or maybe some intruder had kidnapped her. David reached for his cell phone and was poised to dial 911 when footsteps through the leaf litter sounded behind him.

He turned, hoping Natalie had come to her senses.

No such luck. Willow Petersen came striding down the path in her black coat, her blond hair all tucked up in a businesslike hairdo. "Poppy sent me to find you, in case you've forgotten the way to the secret place."

Annoyance and resentment prickled along his skin. How the hell did Willow Petersen know anything about Natalie and her secret hiding places? Willow had met Natalie exactly one time, on the day of his daughter's christening a little more than eight years ago. For all of Natalie's short life, Willow had been too busy with her career to give a crap about her goddaughter.

After Shelly's death, he would have expected Willow to make an effort to show up. But there had been nothing. Nothing at all.

He wanted to tell her off. He wanted to read her the riot act for missing Shelly's funeral on that cold December day. He wanted to scream at her because it seemed so damn unfair that Shelly wasn't here anymore.

But he had more discipline than that. So he swallowed down his anger and said, "You have a firm grasp of the obvious." Then he gave Willow his implacable, bulldog scowl—the one he'd regularly used to intimidate people as chairman of the Jefferson County Council. It bounced right off her.

"Come on, I'll show you the secret path." She swished past him and headed down the main path a few strides. He followed as she took a left turn off the main footpath and onto a muddy rut that was most definitely not a regular path.

After a short walk, they emerged from the woods into a small clearing near Morgan Avenue. The meadow looked neglected, as if it hadn't been mowed in some time. The wild grass had grown knee high, and even now, the first week of November, yellow and white wildflowers bloomed everywhere.

Off to the left a few paces stood the tumbled-down limestone church that was known as Laurel Chapel. No one had worshipped there in almost a century, and its sanctuary was now open to the sky, its arched windows broken. Beside it stood the oldest cemetery in town, where a few of David's forebears had been buried. The graveyard was ringed by a dry stone wall that was in good repair. St. Luke's, the Episcopal church in town, took care of the cemetery. Laurel Chapel had once been the Episcopalians' place of worship before they built the big church in town a hundred years ago. The congregation had sold the land up here, along with the old church building, as a means of raising the funds for their much grander place of worship. In the years since, the building had fallen to ruins.

David knew this place, but he'd never walked here from the inn before. He'd always come by car and parked in the gravel lot adjacent to the ruins of the church. Hikers seeking access to the Appalachian Trail frequently parked there, especially in the spring when the mountain laurel bloomed.

The laurel had been in bloom that day, long ago, when Shelly had brought him up here full of ideas and plans for their wedding. She'd wanted to put up a tent on this meadow and hold the reception at her parents' inn.

That wasn't possible, of course. The guest list for their wedding included senators, governors, and the vice president. The meadow by Laurel Chapel wasn't anywhere close to secure enough for a guest list like that. So they'd been married in Washington, DC, with the Secret Service in attendance.

"I know for a fact Shelly brought you here," Willow said as if reading his mind. "I'm surprised you didn't know about the hidden path. The old chapel always was Shelly's secret place."

He didn't respond. What could he say? He should have known this. Instead, he walked past her toward the church and through the empty doorway into the nave. Leaves lay in clumps across the stone floor where once the pews, altar, and pulpit had stood.

"Natalie, are you hiding in here?" he asked.

A little whimper from the corner of the sanctuary was his answer. He moved forward through the gloom and found his daughter sitting in a pile of leaves. She hugged her knees with a pair of grubby hands, and her head rested on dirty leggings.

The pull of muscles across his shoulders eased at the sight of her. He lived in perpetual fear of losing her. He wanted to pull her into his arms and spoil her. But what kind of father would that make him? She needed discipline.

"Natalie," he said in his sternest voice, "I won't tolerate this kind of behavior from you. What were you thinking, running away from me? You could have been injured or worse."

His daughter looked up at him, her chin wobbling while defiance sparked in her deep brown eyes.

"Sweetheart, I know you're disappointed about your swimming time trials, but it's Election Day, and Grandmother's party is important. Not just to her, but to me. Didn't I explain last night that there will be important people at this party that I have to be nice to because I'm thinking about being a congressman? Those people want to meet you too."

"I don't want to meet them."

Of course she didn't. But that didn't change things. Like it or not, Natalie would grow up as a congressman's daughter, like he'd grown up as a senator's son.

"Sweetie, we talked about this, remember? When I

was growing up, there were lots of times when I had to do things that I didn't want to do because Grandfather is a senator. But I did as I was told. Because I am a Lyndon, and Lyndons make sacrifices."

Natalie wiped her nose on the sleeve of her jacket, and he almost corrected her before he remembered that he didn't have a handkerchief with him today because he hadn't been to the laundry in more than a week.

He became acutely aware of his failings as a parent. Natalie did that to him. Often.

"I don't want to go. I want to beat Meghan in breast-stroke. She's always telling everyone she's faster than I am."

"I'm sorry. But there will be another set of time trials next month, and swimming competition doesn't start until the spring. Election Day comes once a year. Besides, you don't want to make Grandmother unhappy, do you? You know how unpleasant that can be."

Natalie's mouth thinned like Shelly's used to whenever they argued about Mother. But this time Mother was right. David needed to be at her barbeque this evening because he was planning a run for Congress next year. Important donors and political consultants would be in attendance, and they all wanted to meet Natalie. Like it or not, she was the candidate's daughter, and the two of them were a package deal.

He folded his arms across his chest. "Do you want a time-out?"

She gave him a mutinous scowl.

"Do you? Because it can be arranged. Honestly, Natalie, I just don't know what I'm going to do with you. I don't like this attitude you've suddenly developed."

The quiver in her lower lip intensified. *Damn*. He hated it when she cried.

"Are you ready to go?" he asked, fully expecting her to either burst into tears, give him the eight-year-old death stare, or pitch a tantrum.

She opted for a version of the death stare, complete with big tears that spilled down her cheeks, leaving dirty tracks on her face. "Yes, Daddy," she said in a forlorn voice as she stood. His heart wrenched when she hung her head and started walking toward the door.

He turned and found Willow Peterson standing behind him, her hands on her hips, her gaze sharp and unforgiving.

"You don't get to judge me," he barked. "I have a career too."

She lifted one shoulder and blinked. "I'm not judging you, David. I was just wondering if it's true what Mrs. M said—that you're planning to sell the inn because you're going to run for Congress."

"I never promised Shelly I would keep the inn. And I wish to God Almighty she had listened to me. Because if she'd listened, she would have given up those silly plans of hers. And if she'd given up those plans, she'd never have gone to New York to meet with an architect. And if she'd never gone to New York, she would be alive today."

And with that he stepped around his wife's so-called best friend and left the ruined chapel behind.

Chapter 2⎯⎯⎯⎯⎯⎯⎯⎯⎯⎯⎯

It was happy hour when Willow strolled into the Jaybird Café and Music Hall in downtown Shenandoah Falls. The scent of beer and French fries jolted her with a wave of deep nostalgia as she took the last open seat at the bar.

Willow's family had owned and managed the Jaybird for more than thirty years, providing farm-to-table menu choices and live music on Friday and Saturday nights. The café was a second home for Willow and her younger sister, Juni, who'd come along a couple of years after the family had settled in Northern Virginia. Many a night, Willow and Juni had eaten their dinners at the café, done their schoolwork at one of the tables, and crashed on cots in the back.

Now the little baby who had once toddled around the place was the café's manager and backup bartender. Tonight she was busy dealing with a larger-than-normal happy-hour crowd, who were drinking and keeping tabs on election results on the television screens scattered around the dining room.

"What have you been up to today?" Juni asked from behind the bar.

As usual, Willow's sister was channeling Mom this evening. She wore a blue East-Indian print dress that she'd probably bought at the Haggle Shop, the local consignment store that had a large section of vintage clothing. Juni had dark curly hair that reached her waist, and even though she and Willow shared a mother, they looked nothing alike. Willow had straight blond hair and eyes that were a mossy shade of green. Juni's eyes were as dark as espresso coffee.

"I spent some time at Eagle Hill Manor. Did you know David Lyndon's selling the place?" Willow asked.

"That's not surprising. The inn's been closed for a couple of months." Juni leaned toward the bar and spoke in a low voice. "If I had the money, I might just buy that old place."

"Since when do you have a burning desire to be an innkeeper?"

Juni shrugged. "Don't know. I just have a feeling, you know?"

Juni was always having "feelings" about stuff. She could also allegedly read auras, tell fortunes with tarot cards, and heal people with crystals. In short, Juni couldn't have been less like Willow if she tried.

"What do you think?" Juni asked. "You're the one with the MBA from Wharton. Could Eagle Hill be a business opportunity?"

"I'd have to do some market research. I know nothing about the hospitality sector."

Juni shook her head. "It's amazing how much time you waste with your research. I say go with your gut this time. My gut says that someone is going to make a pile of money with that place."

"Someone with liquid assets," Willow said. "Which isn't me. Hey, can I beg a beer and one of your bacon cheeseburgers? I'm desperate for comfort food, not Mom's fried eggplant."

Juni gave Willow a madonna-like smile as she pulled a draft. "If you tried eggplant, you might like it."

Willow shook her head and made a gagging noise. "I have tried it."

Juni put the beer in front of her sister. "I'll put in an order for the cheeseburger. I gotta go. It's crazy in here tonight for a Tuesday."

Juni headed off to fill a drink order, leaving Willow alone to brood about the dismal state of her life. She had no job and no prospects.

After what Restero had said about her in the *Wall Street Journal,* it was likely that potential investors and venture capitalists would regard her as high risk. She couldn't self-fund anything. She was without assets or collateral.

She'd blown all her assets to retain the law firm of Astor, Roswell, and Cade—a firm with a track record for defending people in her situation. The US False Claims Act was supposed to protect corporate whistle-blowers from harassment and job retaliation, but those provisions meant nothing until Willow got a court date. Until she proved that Restero and its CEO, Corbin Martinson, had committed Medicare fraud by knowingly selling defective hip replacements, she would always be a disgruntled troublemaker out for revenge.

She was mulling over this depressing reality when a thirtysomething woman with straight black hair and sky-blue eyes sidled up to the bar and ordered a margarita, a manhattan, and a lemon-drop martini. There was something vaguely familiar about the woman, but Willow couldn't quite place her.

The woman turned, her forehead rumpling. "Willow? Oh my God, is that you? It's me, Courtney Wallace, remember, from tenth grade?"

Willow blinked a few times, trying to jibe this beautiful woman with the Courtney Wallace she'd known in high school. That Courtney had zits and braces and was the undisputed geek girl in their graduating class.

"Hi," Willow said, suddenly awkward.

"It's been years, Willow. Are you visiting for a while?" Courtney asked.

"No. I've moved back. I'm living with Mom at the farm." Her face heated with the humiliation of being thirty-four years old and suddenly living at home with her mother.

"That's wonderful,"

No, it wasn't wonderful, but Willow refrained from saying that out loud.

"Here you go," Juni said as she finished mixing Courtney's drink order. "You want to put this on a tab?"

"Yeah," Courtney said, picking up the margarita and the lemon-drop martini. "Come on, Willow. Grab your beer and the manhattan and come on back to say hey to the girls."

Willow didn't want to socialize with high school acquaintances. Not with her life in shambles. It would be embarrassing. But Juni had other ideas. "Go," she said, giving a little wave from behind the bar. "You need to re-connect, you know? I'll send your burger over when it's ready."

And that was that. Willow had been hung out to dry by her little sister, who was so obviously trying to get her to move on with her life. Willow gave her sister the stink eye, then picked up her beer and the manhattan and followed Courtney off to a table in the back corner where two women were sitting.

"Hey, guys, look who I found at the bar," Courtney said as she placed the margarita in front of a woman with long dark hair and smart-girl glasses and the lemon drop in front of a thin woman with brown hair carefully styled in a smooth pageboy.

The women at the table blinked up at Willow, the confusion on their faces proving that they hadn't recognized Willow any more than Willow had recognized them.

"The manhattan's mine," Courtney said as she plopped down on one of the empty chairs. "Sit down, Willow."

Willow sat and then immediately started thinking of ways to excuse herself. She didn't know or remember any of these people, and she didn't want to endure the awkwardness that always came when people realized who she was.

By the same token, she didn't want to be rude either. She had to live in this town, and she knew how things worked. Being pleasant was the best way to get along with people—especially those who were ready to judge her for whatever reason.

Lemon-Drop Girl cocked her head and stared. "Do we know you?" she asked.

"Oh, for goodness' sake," Courtney said, gesturing

with her manhattan. "This is Juni's big sister, Willow. She was my lab partner in tenth grade and one of the very few people at Braddock High who never once said a single word about my braces or my zits." She turned toward Willow with a sheen in her eyes. "I'll never forget that day when you punched Dusty McNeil for calling me a pizza face and told him he was lewd, rude, and socially unacceptable."

Willow had no recollection of this specific incident, although she had frequently called Dusty all kinds of names. The two of them had spent high school endlessly dissing each other. And when they weren't hurling insults, they were bass-hole buddies with fishing rods, whiling away the hours on Liberty Run. Willow had worked hard to rise above that younger version of herself.

"I'm Arwen Jacobs," Lemon-Drop Girl said. "Juni and I were in the same graduating class, which probably explains why I don't remember you."

"Hi, Willow. I also graduated in Juni's class," Margarita Girl said. "I'm Melissa Portman. My grandmother owned the bookstore in town, and I remember you coming into Secondhand Prose with Shelly Marchand all the time."

The memory warmed Willow. "You were the skinny kid with big glasses who always had her nose in a book."

Melissa nodded. "Yup, that's me. I remember that you never bought many books, but Shelly was addicted to paperback romances."

Which Shelly had consumed like candy until David Lyndon had come down from the hill to fish on Dusty McNeil's land. And then Shelly had found her own real-life romance.

"It's so sad the way she died," Arwen said as she lifted her lemon-drop martini. "Here's to Shelly, the local girl who landed her prince."

"Yeah," Courtney said, lifting her manhattan. "To Shelly."

Willow raised her beer but said nothing. Having spent all afternoon at the inn and the old chapel, she didn't trust her voice. Shelly's death had left a hollow, achy place in Willow's heart.

"As a technical point, I don't think David Lyndon is a prince," Melissa said, "but I'll drink to Shelly."

"You know," Courtney said, giving Melissa a direct, blue-eyed stare, "you need to give up this thing you have about the Lyndons. David Lyndon *is* a prince. And you are about to marry another prince of the same family."

"His last name isn't Lyndon. It's Talbert."

"What's all this about?" Willow asked, suddenly curious.

"Melissa just got engaged to Jefferson Talbert-Lyndon, the journalist. She's never been a big fan of the Lyndons, which is why it's so funny that she's marrying one of them," Arwen said.

Melissa's cheeks pinked. "Don't listen to them. They tease me all the time about this. But the thing is, Jeff, my fiancé, legally changed his name. He's Jeff Talbert now. The Lyndons need to get that into their thick skulls."

Willow recognized Jefferson Talbert-Lyndon's name. He'd made news last spring with an article that put an end to the president's first choice for the Supreme Court. He was also Nina Talbert's son, and Nina was one of America's richest heiresses.

"We were just discussing the wedding," Arwen said. "In fact, that's the main reason we're here drinking."

"You've got that right," Melissa said, picking up her margarita and draining it.

"Go easy on that, girl. Remember what happened the last time you overdid it with the margaritas? It was crying-jag city, and we don't want that to happen again, right?" Courtney said, then turned toward Willow. "You see, the problem is that Melissa wants a small wedding, but Jeff's mother and father have invited the world. Which is awkward because his father is Thomas Lyndon and his mother is Nina Talbert. So when I say 'the world,' I mean a lot of people. Like four hundred of them."

"Also," Arwen added, "since Jeff's mother and father are divorced and his father is the ambassador to Japan, he's deputized his sister-in-law, Pamela Lyndon, to make sure that the wedding is up to the usual Lyndon standards. And even worse, Pam Lyndon and Nina Talbert are old friends from college. So they've planned this big Christmas wedding in New York City. At the Plaza Hotel. And they have, more or less, completely ignored Melissa's opinions about virtually everything."

Melissa *thunk*ed her head on the table a couple of times. "I hate this wedding. I need another margarita."

"Aw, c'mon, sweetie. You don't have to get married in New York. You know that." Courtney gave Melissa's back a little rub.

Melissa looked up. "You're right. Jeff and I are going to elope."

"You'll do no such thing. That's what this intervention is all about tonight," Courtney said.

"We're here to convince you to plan your own alternate wedding," Arwen said.

"How can I do that? There's no time to plan a wedding.

Not to mention the fact that Jeff's mother and aunt will be furious with me."

"They'll be furious if you elope, and so will Arwen and I. No woman really wants to elope," Courtney said, then turned toward Willow. "Don't you think that's true, Willow?"

Willow had never given this question any thought. After Corbin Martinson's betrayal, marriage wasn't on her short-range to-do list. It wasn't even on her long-range bucket list. "I don't know much about weddings," she said. "But I do know that if anyone can drive a girl to Vegas for a quickie wedding, it's Pam Lyndon."

"Boy, you sure have that right," Melissa said on a deep breath.

Willow continued. "Shelly wanted a small wedding with a reception at Eagle Hill Manor, which was her *home*, for goodness' sake. But Pam wanted something else altogether. And Shelly was bullied into this big, extravagant thing in DC. There were three hundred guests at her wedding, not to mention Secret Service at every door because the vice president was there. It was awful."

Melissa's eyes brightened behind her glasses with a sheen of tears. "Pam Lyndon is a royal pain in the ass."

A fierce need to protect Melissa settled in Willow's gut. "Don't you let Pam Lyndon make you cry," she said. "Shelly made one concession after another. Nothing was the way she wanted it—not even her wedding dress. And then, on the night before the wedding, she ended up bawling her eyes out. I had to sit there and hold her hand. It was awful."

Willow took a big sip of her beer, trying to push away the sudden burning memory of that night. David and

Shelly had loved each other, and their wedding could have rivaled a royal wedding. Unfortunately, it wasn't the wedding Shelly had wanted.

"Thank you, Willow," Melissa said, taking off her glasses and wiping her eyes. She sat up straight and looked at her friends. "Okay, girls, I admit it. You're right. I shouldn't have to elope and I shouldn't have to go to New York to get married in some hotel with a zillion strangers as wedding guests. Shenandoah Falls is my home. It's where Jeff and I will live after we're married. We should get married here, with our friends and family present."

"Now you're talking," Courtney said.

"And I'd want my ceremony at Grace Presbyterian, where Grammy was a member all her life. At Christmastime."

"Check," Courtney said. "To be totally honest, honey, I called Reverend Gladwin the day before yesterday and scheduled him for December nineteenth. So the church and the pastor are already taken care of. We just need to talk about the reception."

Melissa's face registered her surprise and delight. "You're kidding me. Really? You did that for me?"

Courtney took her time finishing her manhattan. "I'm not kidding. You have a minister and a church all scheduled, so there's no need for you to go traipsing off to Vegas."

"But we still have a huge issue with the bridesmaid dresses. I, for one, am not wearing that hideous thing Pam Lyndon chose for me," Arwen said, fishing the olive out of her empty martini glass and popping it in her mouth.

"I admit the dresses are a big problem," Courtney said,

"but we can always make dresses, if all else fails. The bigger issue is the reception. The fellowship hall at Grace Presbyterian is taken on December nineteenth. They're holding their annual Christmas pageant there."

"If it's a small enough wedding, we could probably hire out the main taproom at the Red Fern Inn," Arwen suggested.

"That won't work. You could get, like, three people in there. Melissa needs a bigger wedding than that," Courtney said, pulling a day planner from her purse and flipping through the calendar section. "Unfortunately, the tasting room at Bella Vista Vineyards is also booked on December nineteenth, so finding a venue in Shenandoah Falls is going to be next to impossible. We might have to consider Winchester or, failing that, there's always Berkeley Springs. Maybe the Castle is available."

The conversation went back and forth between Courtney and Arwen for a solid fifteen minutes while Juni delivered Willow's burger and another round of drinks. Melissa said little as she watched her friends bounce ideas around like Ping-Pong balls. And then, just as Willow had consumed her last French fry, Melissa held up her hands and spoke. "Stop, you guys. I know what I want, and I'm sure the space is available."

"Where?" Arwen and Courtney asked in unison.

"Eagle Hill Manor."

"But it's closed," Courtney said.

"I know, and that's why it's sure to be available."

"But—"

Melissa held up her hand again. "Don't you guys remember how beautifully decorated the inn used to be at Christmastime? Grammy took me there for high tea every December. She loved that place. And besides, Eagle Hill Manor is a part of our town, whether it's closed for business or not. It would be perfect for a wedding reception."

"You're right," Willow said in a cautious tone, the depression that clouded her heart lifting a little. "But I don't see how you'll ever get David Lyndon to allow it. I spoke with him earlier today, and he's putting the place up for sale. And even if he puts off selling the inn, I'm afraid it's gotten a little shabby over the years."

"We could help David fix it up before he puts it on the market," Melissa said. "Jeff is fabulous at fixing things up. You should see what he's doing to Secondhand Prose."

"It's more complicated than that," Willow said. "He'd have to defy Pam to allow it. I know it would be a wonderful place for a wedding, but I—"

"We should do it for Shelly."

Melissa's words were almost like a slap to the face—the kind that clears a cloudy mind. Shelly would have been overjoyed to host this wedding.

Unfortunately, Shelly's husband would never agree. Not in a million years.

"Melissa, it's just not that simple," Willow said in her kindest tone. "Based on something David said to me this afternoon, I think he blames the inn for Shelly's death. So all he wants is to be rid of it. I think you guys need to look at reception places in Winchester or Leesburg or even Berkeley Springs, because you'll never convince David Lyndon to host the wedding."

"Three-no-trump," Walter Braden said, giving Poppy Marchand one of his I'm-in-charge-of-this-bridge-hand looks. Unlike her late husband, Walter was an aggressive bridge partner. She personally hated playing no-trump hands, but Walter seemed to relish them. Well, he'd get his way with this hand. She laid down her cards and sat back to watch him in action.

It was delicious fun. He was movie-star handsome with his silver hair, cleft chin, and brown eyes. He was also a consummate player who had participated in several bridge tournaments with his late wife.

"He's at it again," Faye Appleby said with a wink at Poppy. Faye was so transparent. She was always throwing Poppy and Walter together because they were the two "single" members of the bridge club. If Poppy were ten years younger, she might have appreciated Faye's match-making efforts. But she was too old for romance, and besides, Walter was a baby. He hadn't even reached the six-decade mark.

"Well, that's it for tonight," Harlan Appleby said, once Walter had played the hand and won the game. Across the room, Budd and Viola Ingram and Scott and Dakota Fowler were finishing up. It was a small bridge club, but they'd been playing together on Tuesday evenings for years.

"Poppy, dear," Faye said as Harlan packed up the cards, "is it true, what I heard today from Gracie Teague? Is Eagle Hill Manor really up for sale?"

"It's true," Walter said before Poppy could respond. "I'm the listing agent. David wants to put it on the market next week. I've told him he should take a little time and at least give the place a coat of paint, but he seems to be in a hurry to move on."

Poppy lowered her gaze and focused on her hands, folded on the card table. Why was she so surprised by this news? She'd known for years that David planned to sell the old place, but it still hurt to hear that her son-in-law had met with Walter and hadn't even bothered to mention it.

Faye reached over and gave Poppy's hand a squeeze. "I'm so sorry. I know how much the manor means to you."

"Well, it was inevitable," she said, looking up right into the kindness in Walter's eyes. "Clement Spurling has announced his retirement, and David is going to run for his congressional seat. He doesn't need an inn if he's a member of Congress. And to be honest, he never ran the inn. He left all that to Shelly. And me, after Shelly died. Y'all, I'm too old to be an innkeeper anymore."

Harlan frowned in her direction. "Since when are you too old?"

"Harlan, I'm sixty-three, and I'm ready to retire. It's hard work running an inn, especially without David's help."

"Well, if you ask me," Viola Ingram said, as she stood up and stretched her back, "we ought to put our heads together and figure out a way to make David reconsider."

"That's not going to happen. David Lyndon was born to run," Poppy said.

Bud Ingram immediately dropped into a not-very-good impression of Bruce Springsteen and sang a few bars of "Born to Run" while he played air guitar.

Faye ignored Bud's antics. "We need to do something about this. I mean, it's sad that Eagle Hill Manor has closed its doors, especially at Christmastime. Everyone loved your teas, Poppy. It's like Shenandoah Falls has lost some of its luster. And it's David's fault."

"No, it isn't David's fault," Poppy said. "It's just the way it is. Craig and I were ready to give up being innkeepers a long time ago. Shelly wanted to continue on, but she's gone now, and that's not anyone's fault except maybe Amtrak's."

"Well, I don't like it," Fay grumbled. "Where will you go when the inn is sold?"

Before Poppy could respond, Walter spoke again. "David is looking for a new house with a separate apartment for Poppy. She'll be fine."

"Be quiet," Faye said, giving Walter her evil eye. "You're a traitor, you know that? I can't believe you agreed to help David sell the inn."

"I'm a Realtor. It's what I do."

Faye turned her back on Walter. "Poppy, sweetie, it's nice that David is looking for a house with a separate apartment. But what happens when David remarries?"

"Do you know something I don't?" Poppy asked. Her heart lurched in her chest.

"No, I don't. Not really. Except that my niece Arwen works at LL&K, you know, and she told me that there's something going on between David and Roxanne Kopp, the managing partner's daughter."

This was news. It could be gossip, or it could be something important. "I don't know anything about David's love life," she said.

"Well, you ought to," Faye said. "You have a vested interest in who he sleeps with. I mean, he's probably going to remarry, and that woman is going to be Natalie's stepmother. Have you ever met Roxanne Kopp?"

"No. And near as I can see, David is living the life of a monk. So hearing that he has a love life is surprising."

"That won't always be true," Bud said. "He's a young guy. He's going to get horny."

"Oh, for goodness' sake, Bud," Viola said, punching her husband in the arm, "that's such an immature thing to say."

"I don't know. It has the ring of truth to me," Harlan said. "Sooner or later he's going to shack up with someone."

Faye almost exploded from her chair. "Harlan Appleby, that's the most insensitive thing I've ever heard you say."

"Okay, but you know it's true. And if he marries someone his mother picks out for him, that won't be good for Poppy." Harlan leaned back in his folding chair and continued. "If it's inevitable that David's going to get horny one day, shouldn't we make sure that whoever he has a love life with is someone Poppy likes?"

"Oh," Viola said, "that's a good idea. Maybe we should make a list of eligible women and vet them."

Poppy stood up, putting an end to this ridiculous conversation. "Look, y'all, I'm glad you're concerned about me, but I'll be fine. And under no circumstances are any of you to even think about developing a list and vetting it. David needs to stop grieving before he can move on."

She picked up the half-full bowl of bridge mix and carried it into Faye's kitchen. Behind her, she heard an ominous murmur that sounded like her friends had chosen to ignore her request. Courtney Wallace's name was definitely mentioned before Poppy even made it to the kitchen door. This was likely to end in complete disaster if she didn't stop them.

Walter followed her into the kitchen and dropped another half-full bowl of bridge mix on the counter. "You didn't know that David had met with me about the inn, did you?" he asked.

"Well, I…"

"Don't lie. You're so bad at it."

"No," she said on a long sigh. "I knew he was going to sell it. I just didn't know that he'd spoken to you about it."

He took her by the shoulders, and something carnal crept through her body. How adolescent, although it was strangely reaffirming, as if her body were saying that she wasn't all that old after all.

"I'm sorry," Walter said in that deep voice of his. He'd come from someplace in Tennessee, and he'd never quite lost the sexy Southern lilt. "I'd assumed David told you about the inn and the house hunting. And I meant what I said. He told me that a separate apartment for you was a requirement. He's going to look after you, Poppy."

Walter gave her a dazzling smile, and for some reason she wanted to slap his face. She didn't want to be beholden to David Lyndon. She wanted…

Well, she didn't know quite what she wanted. More. Of something. Something that she'd lost these last few years.

She shrugged off Walter's hands. There was no sense in being silly about the man, and besides, it was slightly embarrassing that he thought she was one step away from being homeless.

"I have only two things to say to you, Walter Braden.

First of all, don't ever assume anything. And second of all, I am not helpless. I don't need anyone to 'look after' me. Until just recently, I was managing an inn all by myself."

She turned her back on him and stalked out of the kitchen.

Chapter 3 ——————————

On Wednesday morning, David's younger sister, Heather, dropped by his office for a postmortem on last night's barbeque party, which had been so much more than a social event. A lot of business had been conducted, and David now had a long to-do list.

Heather was there to help.

She sat in the Queen Anne chair beside David's desk looking every inch the political professional she had become. She wore a dark business suit with a slim skirt, a white blouse, and a round pearl pin in her lapel. Her dark eyes gleamed with excitement as she spoke. "So, I'm thinking we can count on support from Douglas Miller, Henry Blumstein, and Barbara Dahl. All three of them would make excellent members of your steering committee."

Heather wanted and expected to become David's campaign manager, and he couldn't think of anyone better. She was two years younger than David, but she had always out-excelled him. She'd graduated top of her class from William & Mary and then had taken top honors at the John F. Kennedy School of Government at Harvard. After that, she'd volunteered on several political campaigns, turning that experience and Dad's connections into a position at OnTarget, the political consulting firm owned by Hale Chandler, one of the A-list political consultants on Mother's invitation list last night.

The Election Day barbeque had been a complete success. David had gotten a few commitments of support from key county and party officials, and Hale Chandler himself had attended. Heather, Dad, Hale, and David had spent long hours talking into the night about virtually all aspects of the upcoming race.

The plan was to announce his candidacy on January 18, giving him a scant two months to form an advisory committee, develop a written plan, put together a fundraising committee, find a treasurer, and fill several positions, such as volunteer coordinator and scheduler.

It was almost overwhelming, but Heather seemed to have it all under control. She was the picture of calm as she made herself comfortable in the chair, crossed her legs, and started twirling a lock of hair around her fingers. "We need to sketch out our issue platform right away," she said. "I can do that in the next couple of days. I'm sure your views are more or less identical to Dad's."

She didn't wait for his assent before she spoke again. "Oh, and Hale called me early this morning. He told me he was impressed with you. He thinks you're totally salable, especially being a single father. He did mention one concern about Natalie. She was a little sullen last night. We'll need to get her to smile more. And she needs to get over being shy around grown-ups."

Guilt prickled through David. "Sullen" wasn't precisely the word he'd use to describe Natalie's behavior. She'd been quiet and painfully shy last night. But this morning she'd been rebellious, giving him the silent treatment over their morning Cheerios.

Heather dropped her hair and leaned forward. "Davie, are you listening to me? You had one of your faraway looks on your face."

"I was listening. And I was thinking that next time Mother holds a party like that, I'm going to leave Natalie at home. Remember how we were brought up, going to all of those dull parties? I hated it."

"Speak for yourself. I loved campaigning with Dad. You're the one who always wanted to go fishing."

"I guess. But it just seems wrong to put Natalie on display like that. Sorry, but if you're going to be my campaign manager, and if Hale is going to be my consultant, then you both need to know that Natalie is off-limits, starting right now."

Heather grinned. "You want me to be your campaign manager? Really?" She sounded like a kid who'd just been told she's going to Disney World.

Affection tugged at his heart. He loved his little sister. "It's sort of been assumed all these years."

"Yeah, but you know, Dad wanted Eric Flannigan. That's all he talked about last night. I thought you were going to do what he said."

"Eric is Dad's guy. You're mine."

Just then David's office door burst open, and Gillian, David's assistant, said, "No, stop, Mr. Talbert. You can't go in there. He has someone with him."

Jefferson Talbert, David's first cousin, ignored Gillian and strolled into the office anyway. "Hi, guys," he said in an accent that betrayed his upbringing in New York City. He dropped into the second Queen Anne chair and crossed one jeans-clad leg over the other. He was wearing a red T-shirt with a portrait of Jack Kerouac, captioned with the words, "I have nothing to offer anyone except my own confusion."

"I need to talk to you," Jeff said, aiming his intense gaze at David.

"Okay, but I'm talking to Heather right now. Maybe—"

"No, it's fine. I'm dying to know what Jeff has on his mind. And also I'm thinking we should hit him up for the advisory committee." Heather gave Jeff a big grin.

"When I hear the words 'advisory committee,' I know my checkbook's going to be involved somehow. I guess it's official. You're running for Congress, huh?"

David nodded. "Yeah, I am. But I'm sure you didn't swing by this morning just to tell me you wanted to be on my advisory committee."

"Well, if you want to know, I'm here about the wedding. I need your help with it."

"What?"

Jeff dropped his leg so he could lean forward in an aggressive posture. "Neither Melissa nor I like the idea of turning our wedding into some kind of big, political gala. I'm not running for Congress, and I don't see why we have to accommodate your career at our wedding."

"Oh boy," Heather muttered. "You really don't know how it works, do you?"

"How what works?" Jeff turned toward Heather.

"How the family works. Every event is an opportunity for political maneuvering. Sometimes it's a campaign. Sometimes it's Dad trying to work a compromise on a piece of legislation. Don't underestimate how much of what happens in Washington occurs at weddings, bar mitzvahs, and intimate dinner parties. In fact, if more legislators socialized at events like that, there'd be a whole lot less gridlock in Washington."

"Well, this is not Washington, and none of that is going to happen at my wedding. I'd like to do this the nice way, by talking things through and coming together with a compromise."

"What do you want?" David asked.

"I want you to tell your mother to back off and let Melissa plan her own wedding."

"Mother isn't the only one planning this wedding," Heather said in a sharp, angry tone. "Your mother is also involved."

"I'll deal with my mother. She'll see reason. Aunt Pam is the problem. I need to make her understand that we are not ever going to agree to a guest list with three hundred people, half of whom are there because you guys want to hit them up for campaign contributions."

"The invitations are going out tomorrow or the next day," Heather said. "The venue has been booked. The dresses have been bought. Everything has been planned down to the smallest detail. If this was a problem, you should have raised your concerns way earlier."

"Melissa did raise her concerns, and Aunt Pam

brushed them aside the way she always does when she gets on a roll." Jeff's voice rose in volume. "So I would be obliged if you would tell your mother not to send those invitations. If she does, it will be a huge embarrassment. Melissa and I are now working on alternate wedding plans."

"Oh my God, please don't say you're going to elope," Heather said. "That could cause a major family meltdown."

"Eloping is not out of the question at this point, especially if Melissa can't have the wedding she wants."

"What on earth does she want that she's not getting?" David asked, stepping in before Heather and Jeff came to blows. "I gather the reception is going to be at the Plaza Hotel, and no expense has been spared on anything. If she wants something more, then she's spoiled."

"Spoiled? Melissa?" Jeff's face turned red. "I don't think so. She's no more spoiled than your wife was. Last night—"

"Keep Shelly out of it. She's not relevant—"

"I'm sorry, David, but Shelly is actually very relevant to the conversation. Melissa went out with her girlfriends last night and evidently met up with a woman who was a bridesmaid at your wedding. Someone named Willow, who told Melissa a bunch of horror stories all about how Shelly—"

"Horror stories? About *my* wedding? What are you talking about? My wedding was a lovely affair. Shelly looked beautiful in her dress. I'll never forget the moment I saw her coming down the aisle. There wasn't anything horrible about my wedding." David touched his wedding ring. He would remember that day forever, especially when she slipped his wedding ring on his finger after he made his vows. That vow meant everything to him, even now after her death. He missed her, body and soul.

"I'm sorry, David, that was unartfully said," Jeff said. "I'm not saying that you and Shelly had a bad marriage. I'm saying that there were issues with the wedding. And I'm not surprised that you are unaware of them. Let's face it; we're guys. We don't care about weddings. But Melissa cares a lot. When she heard how Shelly cried the night before her wedding, it had a huge impact. Melissa came back from her night out with the girls determined to either elope or plan a small wedding here in Shenandoah Falls."

"My wife did not cry over our wedding. That's a lie." David's chest tightened, and it was all he could do not to jump up and punch Jeff in the face. Shelly had been beautiful and radiant and happy on her wedding day. That was a memory he held sacred.

"Um," Heather said, "she sort of did cry, David."

"What? Impossible. She was so happy that day."

"I think she was happy on the day of the wedding. But the night before, she and Willow Petersen got sloppy drunk, and both of them ended up bawling. Shelly kept saying that she was homesick and how much she regretted the fact that you weren't having your wedding at her parents' inn."

David stared at his sister while anger and regret churned in his stomach. How dare Willow Petersen tell stories like this around town. *How dare she.*

"Look, David," Jeff said, "I didn't come here to pick a fight or to upset you. I came here for help. And you know darn well it's not easy for me to ask help from the Lyndon side of the family. I need Aunt Pam to back off. And I need one other favor."

"What?" David spat the word.

"Melissa is planning a wedding here in town. We'd have the ceremony at Grace Presbyterian on December nineteenth, but there isn't any place in town to have the reception. All the acceptable places have been booked, even the tasting room at Bella Vista Vineyards. So Melissa thought that it would be nice to have the reception at Eagle Hill Manor."

"What? No. The inn is closed for business."

"You don't have to reopen the inn to host our reception. You could just host the reception there. It would solve a big problem. Otherwise we'd have to have the reception in Winchester or in some hotel in Tysons Corner, and Melissa doesn't want to do that."

"Sorry. The inn is going on the market this week or next. And quite honestly, it needs repairs. It's not an acceptable place for a wedding reception."

"I'd be happy to pay for the repairs," Jeff said. "And that might even improve the selling price. Come on, David, work with me here."

"You're asking the impossible. If you want my advice, I suggest you save yourself a lot of trouble and elope."

Heather almost gasped. "David, you don't mean that."

"I do." He stood up, the anger still churning in his gut, his throat so constricted he could hardly breathe. "Now, if you don't mind, Heather and I have work to do."

Jeff stood too. "Okay, I'll tell Melissa precisely what your views are on this subject."

David met his cousin's stare. "You do that."

Serenity Farm, where Willow had grown up, sat on twenty acres of land west of the Shenandoah River. The one-hundred-year-old farmhouse had plenty of character, if you called scraped, creaky floors, an avocado-green kitchen, and a wraparound porch with a few missing balusters charming.

It was a far cry from the sleek, modern apartment on Manhattan's Upper East Side where Willow had been living up until a week ago. Moving back to the second-story dormer bedroom had seriously maimed Willow's self-confidence.

Even though her current situation was the direct result of doing the right thing, her fall from grace would have been easier to take if she hadn't been so blindly in love with Corbin. He'd been her lover and her friend and her mentor. She'd even believed that one day she might become his wife.

But once she'd discovered the cover-up, the only way to keep Corbin would have been to shut her mouth and pretend nothing had happened. She couldn't do that.

So here she was earning her keep by shoveling alpaca poop in the old barn.

Thankfully there were only two alpacas—Bogey and Bacall—the breeding pair that in five years' time had yet to conceive any babies.

When she finished her early-morning chores, she headed back to the farmhouse, where she found Mom in the dining room that served as her office. Willow couldn't remember a time when the dining table hadn't been piled high with papers relating to Linda's various business interests. In addition to owning the Jaybird Café, Mom also provided wool to several spinners in the area and produced herbal soaps that were sold at gift shops from Alexandria to Winchester.

Linda Petersen looked as if she'd stepped right out of the 1960s. She was wearing a blue tie-dye T-shirt and a pair of jeans with holes in both knees. Her gray hair spilled out of the ponytail holder at the top of her head in a mess of unruly curls, while a pair of long feather earrings brushed her shoulders.

"Hey, Will," she said as Willow poked her head into the dining room after pouring herself a mug of coffee from the big urn in the kitchen. "You got some free time? I could use some help."

"What are you doing?" Willow asked after taking a big gulp of the strong brew her mother made. Thank God coffee was on the approved list for vegans.

"I'm painting signs," Mom said.

Of course she was. Painting protest signs was what Mom did when she wasn't tending livestock or making soap or booking musical acts for the Jaybird.

"What corporation are you protesting today?" Willow asked.

"They want to open up a Holy Cow restaurant downtown."

"Mom, I know you're a militant vegan, but the rest of the human race likes hamburgers. And Holy Cow's burgers are made with one-hundred-percent kosher beef. They only use animals that are humanely treated."

"Humanely? They still slaughter them." Mom put the finishing touches on her sign. It read, KEEP THE COW OUT OF OUR TOWN.

Mom scrunched up her face before speaking again. "What do you think about 'There's nothing holy about Cow'?" She paused, then shook her head. "No, I don't think so. That one will offend people who are Hindus. How about, 'Stop the unholy Cow alliance' instead?"

Willow refrained from pointing out that the population of Hindus in Jefferson County was likely to be minuscule. Instead she said, "What's the beef?"

Mom chuckled. "This has nothing to do with my choice to go meat-free. This is about zoning."

"Zoning?"

"Yup. We need to convince the Town Council to approve a zoning change that will keep chain stores from opening on Liberty Avenue. They're having a meeting today at two o'clock, and I've organized a protest. I need four or five signs for my volunteers to wave around."

"What's wrong with chain stores?"

Mom shook her head and glanced heavenward before she gave Willow one of her you're-hopeless looks. "I know you never saw a huge corporation you didn't love, but seriously, we have a problem here. Developers are slapping up tract houses everywhere, and we're becoming a bedroom suburb of both Winchester and DC. The local merchants are being priced out of their Liberty Avenue storefronts, and the big chain stores are moving in. How would you feel if Gracie's Diner had to move out and some fast-food joint like Holy Cow moved in?"

Willow hated to admit it, but Mom had a pretty good argument this time. She loved Gracie's place almost as much as she loved the Jaybird, which was immune to the escalating rents because Mom had wisely purchased the building thirty-two years ago. Mom might be a throwback to the counterculture, but when it came to business, she was no pushover.

"So you want to help?" Mom asked again.

"Okay." It wasn't as if Willow had anything else on her agenda for the day, except finding a notary public for some legal papers her attorney needed her to sign.

Mom looked up with a startled expression. "Really?"

Willow shrugged. "Sure."

"You want to help us picket the zoning board meeting?"

Mom's tone was so hopeful that Willow hated to disappoint. But painting signs was one thing; showing up at a protest was quite another. Restero's PR machine was working overtime, creating the impression that Willow was a perpetual troublemaker. It would be better to stay far, far away from any of Mom's various causes.

"I'm the last person you want on the picket line," Willow said as she picked up a paintbrush.

"Why? Because you've gotten a reputation for standing up to big corporations? Baby girl, I've never been prouder of you than I am right now. You're my hero."

Willow didn't feel like a hero. Restero had yet to admit any wrongdoing. And discovering that she'd been taken in by Corbin had left her unsure about herself. How could she have given her heart to a man with no conscience at all, and why had she stayed with him for so long, refusing to see the truth?

"Yeah, well, I'll be a hero when the government decides to bring Restero to justice for Medicare fraud.

Until then, I'm exactly what the Restero PR department says I am—a money-grubbing troublemaker with anger-management issues, which is only to be expected because I'm the bastard child of the notorious Lucas Kuhn, the late, great lead singer for Twisted Fusion."

Mom put her paintbrush on the can of paint. "Are we going to have that argument again?"

"It's not an argument. It's the truth. And even though my parentage is irrelevant to the fraud Restero committed, Corbin and his hatchet men have decided that their best defense is to challenge my credibility. And what better way to suggest I'm nuts than by telling the world that my mother was a groupie without morals and my dad was a druggie rocker who killed himself? God, Mom, I'm so sorry I ever told Corbin about Dad."

Tears gathered in Mom's eyes. "Baby girl, none of this is your fault. If Lucas were alive today, he would be just as proud of you as I am."

Through the years, Mom had insisted that the legendary Lucas Kuhn had intended to marry her. And given the fact that Kuhn's heirs had reached a monetary settlement with her, maybe it was true. But it could just as easily have been a payoff for Mom keeping her mouth shut about Willow.

Either way, the money from Kuhn's estate had allowed Mom to buy the Jaybird and Serenity Farm. So in a way Willow's father had provided for her, which was more than Juni's father had ever done. Of course, no one knew who had fathered Juni, and Mom had never volunteered that information. It was entirely possible that she didn't know the answer to that question. Mom had always been a big fan of free love.

"Let's change the subject, okay?" Willow said. "I understand your point of view about Holy Cow, but I'm not going to help you protest. I need to get some papers notarized, and then I need to start my job search." Willow kneeled in front of a piece of poster board and dipped her brush in the bright red paint.

"Why do you want to work for the man?" Mom asked as she went back to painting.

"What do you mean? I need a job."

"No, you don't need a job. You need an income. There's a big difference. I've supported myself most of my life, and I never did it working for anyone but myself."

Willow turned to stare at her mother. Why had Willow never seen this truth? Mom may not have gone to Wharton, but she'd been an entrepreneur all her life.

"You think I should start a business?"

"Yeah, I do. Isn't that why you went to grad school? To learn how to do that sort of stuff?"

"You and Juni have been talking, haven't you?"

"Maybe." Mom stepped back to admire her handiwork. The letters on her sign were kind of crooked, but they made their point. Mom spoke again without making eye contact. "Don't let Corbin defeat you, baby girl. You're stronger than he is. And besides, I taught both of my girls how to stand up for themselves. Neither of you needs a man in your life."

Willow agreed with that. The one man she'd allowed herself to love had destroyed her. She wasn't going there again.

"What do you think about 'Down with the Cow'?" Willow asked, her paintbrush poised.

"Go for it, babe."

Willow started painting the slogan all the while thinking that what she really wanted was a huge sign that said DOWN WITH RESTERO AND ITS DICK OF A CEO, CORBIN MARTINSON.

Chapter 4

Right after lunch, Mom went off to protest at the zoning hearing, and Willow drove herself to town intent on finding a notary public for her legal papers. She parked in the lot near the courthouse square, which was ringed with an assortment of county government offices and law firms. The biggest of these was a historic brick building in the Georgian style that sat back from South Third Street in a vest-pocket park dominated by a couple of hundred-year-old oaks. The trees were bare now, but in the summer they would provide a lot of shade for government workers who wanted to spend their lunch hour picnicking on the lawn.

A group of workers was busy decorating the building's facade. Pine roping had been wrapped around the two columns that held up the old-fashioned portico, and mixed-green wreaths with red bows were being hung on the oak doors. The decorations weren't particularly splashy or glittery like the ones that graced the lobby of Restero's New York headquarters building every year.

But they were pretty. And the contrast between this beautiful greenery and the tinsel that was annually draped all over New York startled Willow. She'd lived for so many years in the hustle and bustle of New York City that she'd come to expect glitz and glitter. And yet now that she was back in Shenandoah Falls, she didn't miss any of that shiny Christmas hype. She found herself smiling, the holiday spirit infusing her mood.

She was almost to the building's front doors when David Lyndon came hurtling through them, almost knocking one of the workmen off his ladder. He didn't stop to say he was sorry. He just marched up to Willow with a frown on his forehead that looked like a thundercloud ready to storm. He wasn't wearing a suit jacket or an overcoat, just a pale blue dress shirt and a red-and-blue-striped tie. He managed to look both formal and formidable in spite of their absence. "What are you doing here?" he demanded.

His question annoyed the hell out of Willow. Who had put David Lyndon in charge of the world? He wasn't royalty, no matter what Courtney and her pals had said about him last night at the Jaybird.

She straightened her shoulders. "I'm exercising my rights as a citizen of the United States. I'm here on legal business related to my suit against Restero."

"You weren't coming to make more trouble?"

Damn it all to hell and back. For an instant he reminded her of Corbin, standing there all poised and cold and in charge. Corbin always got his way too, and it was so irritating. Her emotions spilled over, and she poked

David right in the middle of his chest. "I. Am. Not. A. Troublemaker. All I did was point out a case of Medicare fraud that affected hundreds of patients. People should be grateful to me for what I did. So just get the hell out of my way."

"I'm not talking about all that. I'm talking about your little plot to get me to reopen the inn."

What plot? *Oh, crap.* David must have gotten wind of Melissa Portman's alternate wedding plans. No wonder he was ticked off.

"Look, David, I have nothing to do with Melissa Portman and her wedding plans. I'm not here to bother you. I just need a notary public. Now, if you'll excuse me, I'll—"

She tried to walk around him, but he grabbed her by the arm. A hot-cold shiver ran through her synapses. Corbin had grabbed her like this. Once. His violence had shaken her both emotionally and physically. She wanted to pull away from David, and yet that touch locked her in place.

She braced herself for his violence, but it didn't come. "I need to talk to you," he said on a long, deep puff of air that turned into steam as he spoke.

She pulled her arm from his grasp, mildly surprised that he let her go so easily. "About Melissa Portman's wedding? I know nothing about that topic."

He shoved his hands into his pants pockets. Was that because of the cold, or was he ashamed about the way he'd tried to manhandle her?

"Please." His jaw flexed, and the tension along his neck and shoulders and the bruised-looking skin beneath his eyes told her a lot about his state of mind. A deep pang of sympathy wrenched her chest. He was still mourning Shelly. Deeply.

"All right, David. But let's get out of the cold." She stepped around him, but he caught up with her in time to open the front door for her—something of a surprise after the way he'd just grabbed her.

"Come on," he said, striding down the marble-floored hallway to the ground-floor offices of Lyndon, Lyndon & Kopp. "We can talk privately in my office, and then Arwen can notarize your papers."

"Arwen Jacobs works here?"

"She's one of the paralegals," he said as he ushered her through the reception area and into his office, which commanded a view of the county courthouse and city hall through gigantic double-hung windows. Someone had spent a lot of time and money decorating the room with authentic-looking antiques. Probably Shelly. The office bore her unmistakable attention to every historical detail.

He gestured to a pair of leather-covered wing chairs that stood beside a gorgeous antique partner's desk. "Sit down." It was a command.

She didn't like being commanded by anyone, but she needed to clear up this misunderstanding. So she took off her ski jacket and settled into the chair. He unconsciously straightened his tie and took the seat behind his desk. Then he leaned forward with a take-no-prisoners stare.

Game on.

She straightened her spine and concentrated on sitting square in her chair. That would make her look bigger than she was. In her career, she'd had to deal with plenty of powerful men who thought they were entitled. The key to success was to command a presence of her own. She wished to hell she was wearing her black Dior suit with a red silk shell and her Louboutin heels. She'd feel well armored in those clothes.

But she'd dressed for barn chores today in worn jeans and her ancient UVA sweatshirt. The informal clothes left her vulnerable, so she didn't wait for David to initiate the conversation. "I think you've jumped to an incorrect conclusion. I never—"

"I want to make it absolutely clear that you are not ever to talk about Shelly in public again."

"What? David, Shelly was my best friend."

"Did you tell Melissa that my wedding was a disaster?" He sat back in the chair. Was that a retreat? Or was he getting ready to pounce on her? It was right then that she noticed the wedding band on his left hand. He hadn't taken it off, and right now his thumb was touching it.

Wow. She'd stepped into a big pile of it, hadn't she? She'd told the truth, but without regard to how it might hurt him. Obviously, Shelly had never told David about her breakdown the night before the wedding. And if he'd learned about it from someone else who hadn't even been there, that would have been a big blow. "David, I'm sorry. I assumed you knew all about what happened that night."

"My wedding was not a disaster. Is that clear?" He stopped playing with his ring and stood up. He leaned over his desk, his face a study in misplaced fury. "And you will tell Melissa the truth about it."

Willow took a couple of deep breaths, trying to slow her pulse. She had never seen David so angry before. "David, I never said your wedding was a disaster. Not to anyone. What I told Melissa was that Shelly didn't have the wedding she wanted because she allowed your mother to bully her. And I advised Melissa not to let that happen to her."

"Jeff came in here this morning and practically demanded that I host his wedding. He said you put this idea into Melissa's head."

"I didn't do anything of the kind. Melissa came to that conclusion on her own. In fact, if you want to know the truth, I told Melissa you would never agree to having the wedding at Eagle Hill Manor."

"Of course I won't. I told them to elope."

Willow stood up and reached for her ski jacket. "David, do you really think having Jeff and Melissa run off to Vegas is a better idea than letting them use the inn for their reception?"

"Mother has already planned a beautiful wedding for Jeff and Melissa. It's too late to change plans now. They're being difficult, and I don't like being dragged into the middle of it."

"It's not too late. And while I'm sure the wedding that your mother has planned will be extravagant and expensive, it's not the wedding Melissa wants. Melissa was near tears last night, David, just like Shelly all those years ago."

"And I'm sure you took advantage of those tears. Really, Willow, you've created a huge mess. Everything would have been fine if you'd just kept your mouth shut."

Just keep your mouth shut? Really? How many times had she heard that from Corbin and his minions at Restero? Don't say anything. Just cover things up. Just be a good girl and go with the flow.

Willow finally found her anger. David might be grieving, but he was also behaving like a self-absorbed jerk. She pulled on her ski jacket, trying without success to control her pulse rate. A wise woman would have turned around and walked out.

But there were so many words trapped inside her, begging for release.

She leaned on David's desk, coming eye to eye with her best friend's husband.

"First of all, Melissa was upset about the wedding before I said one word. Second of all, you don't get to tell me who I can speak with or what I can speak about. And third, I think if Shelly were alive, she would be thrilled to host Melissa's wedding at the inn. And what's more, if there's a heaven and she's looking down at you right now, she'd be so disappointed."

Willow stormed out of the legal building without getting her papers notarized. She needed to walk off her fury, so she headed down Church Street into downtown Shenandoah Falls. The wind chafed her cheeks and raised tears, which weren't entirely wind-induced.

Still, she couldn't pinpoint the reason for her out-of-control emotions. Was it anger? Sadness? Grief? Or maybe some mix of all three. She'd come back to Shenandoah Falls, but her friends Shelly and David were lost to her now.

The irony crashed down on her. When she'd been young, she'd counted the days, hours, and minutes until she could leave this small backwater and get on with the rest of her life. But now that her life had turned into a bowl of sour cherries, she resented and mourned every change that time and absence had brought to her hometown.

She walked all the way to Liberty Avenue, her head down, wiping the tears from her cheeks as she went. But when she reached the corner of Liberty and Church, she stopped and raised her head, wiping away a final tear. She squared her shoulders and took a good long look at Shenandoah Falls's main street.

Things *had* changed here, but maybe for the good.

The traffic on Liberty Avenue was heavy. The storefronts were occupied. New, wrought-iron lightposts edged the street, and storefronts had been restored and updated. There was even a new, high-end coffee shop right there on the corner.

Juni's words from the night before came back to Willow. Eagle Hill Manor wasn't the only business opportunity in Jefferson County. Shenandoah Falls itself looked like one big, fat business opportunity waiting for the right person to recognize it. People with jobs in DC and Winchester were buying houses nearby. The population was growing and the pressure on downtown commercial rents suggested a healthy real estate market.

Oh yes, a person could do a lot of business in this town. And Mom had made a valid point this morning about Willow's future. Maybe she ought to quit trying to fit in and work for other people. Maybe it was time to work for herself.

A glimmer of an idea began to sprout. What if Willow bought Eagle Hill Manor? What if she could swing that deal right now, in time for Melissa and Jeff to have their wedding there?

She hurried into Bean There Done That, got herself a chai latte, and settled into one of the coffee shop's easy chairs. She spent the rest of the afternoon reading the online lifestyle section of the *Washington Post* and the society page of the *New York Times,* followed by *Brides* magazine and half a dozen wedding-planning sites.

Holy crap, people were spending ridiculous amounts of money on weddings—and not merely rich and well-connected people like Pam Lyndon. Middle-class people blew huge amounts of money just to get married.

Willow opened up the word-processing program on her tablet and started outlining what she knew about the demographics of Northern Virginia and what she'd need to research further. She also made notes on the size of the wedding industry and a few back-of-the-envelope guesses about the cost of renovating Eagle Hill Manor and the old chapel—basically the plans that Shelly had talked about the last time she and Willow had lunched together in New York.

Maybe she could make Shelly's plans for the inn a reality. Maybe she could dig herself out of the hole Corbin Martinson had thrown her into.

The beginnings of a business plan began to emerge. All she needed was an investor—someone who would overlook the things Restero was saying about her.

Ordinarily that might be a problem, but Willow had an ace up her sleeve named Jefferson Talbert-Lyndon, who happened to be number thirty-seven on the *Forbes* list of billionaires.

Chapter 5————————————

David's uncle Jamie, the CEO of the Lyndon family's vineyard and agricultural business, believed in putting up Christmas decorations before Thanksgiving. There were good marketing reasons for this, but the real reason was that Uncle Jamie was a Christmas junkie whose birthday fell the first week of November, and he just liked having tinsel around when he blew out the candles on his cake.

As a result, Jamie's birthday party—a big bash held at the winery every year—marked the unofficial start of the holiday season for the Lyndon family.

He'd outdone himself this year. White lights twinkled in the naked wisteria vines that wove through the patio's pergola. Two gigantic wreaths hung on the barn doors that led to the tasting room. Yards of pine roping wrapped every post, beam, and window frame.

"Bah humbug," David mumbled as he and Natalie

walked down the path that led from the parking lot to the winery's tasting room.

"What does that mean, Daddy?" Natalie asked.

Busted. "It's just an expression."

"An expression of what?"

His face burned. How do you tell a kid that you hate Christmas? "When you're older, you'll understand," he said. Boy, he was a master at using that line.

It worked this time because Natalie was more excited about Uncle Jamie's birthday party than she was curious about his foul mood. She skipped ahead, drawn to the shiny tinsel the way moths are drawn to candlelight. Her enthusiasm for the holiday was enough to drive any respectable Scrooge right into a bottle of bourbon.

But maybe it was okay. Natalie certainly didn't understand how the holidays coincided with the bleak advent calendar in David's heart, which counted down the days until the anniversary of her mother's death.

They entered the brightly lit tasting room, and Natalie shed her coat in one lightning-fast move and then shot forward, disappearing into the crowd of party guests without even a backward glance. David deserved that. His Christmas spirit had been killed two years ago.

He picked up Natalie's jacket from where she'd dropped it, shed his overcoat, and headed in the direction of the cloakroom. He hadn't gotten far when Roxanne Kopp, the long-legged, dark-haired daughter of his law firm's managing partner, intercepted him. He'd known Roxy since they'd both been children, and he knew his mother, father, and boss wanted something to blossom between them.

"David," she said in a voice like silk over warm skin.

She plucked the coats from his fingers. "Let me help you with that."

Roxy was all grown up now and had a Siren somewhere in her distant heritage, or maybe a Rhinemaiden, given her family's German ancestry. Either way, she possessed the ability to whisper unsuspecting men to their doom. Her low, sultry voice wasn't her only weapon. She was slim, tanned, and had a nice rack, which she was expert at displaying.

Tonight she wore a tight skirt, a pair of screw-me heels, and a white, sheer blouse with half the buttons undone. Lace and cleavage peeked out from the V of her neckline. It was hard not to notice.

"Roxy," he responded as he stomped on the urge to snatch his coat from her manicured hands. He didn't want to deal with her tonight. He didn't want to look at her cleavage, even though she was shoving it in his face.

But he was a man. A lonely man whose sex life had been cut off two years ago. So he did look. The view was impressive but uninspiring.

Roxy took care of the coats and then sidled up to him, deftly taking him by the arm. His whole body reacted to her touch. But he didn't want her. He had to stop himself from pulling away from her.

"David," she whispered, leaning her breasts into his arm, "you don't have to be frightened of me." Her breath feathered across his cheek. "I could show you a good time. And, baby, you look like you need something like that. Besides, we've been friends forever. You can trust me."

He wasn't frightened. But he didn't want a mindless hookup with Roxy either. They each deserved more than that. He let his thumb wander over to touch the gold band he still wore on his left hand. Being attracted made him feel guilty. He still took his vows seriously. He wasn't ready to let them go.

He wanted to get away from Roxy, but there was no graceful way to escape. So he let her hang on his arm as he snagged a glass of Bordeaux from one of the circulating waiters. And then he followed her lead as she headed toward the fireplace, which was roaring away in full holiday blaze, its mantel festooned with greenery and colorful quilted Christmas stockings.

His mother was waiting there, sipping a glass of red.

"Hello, dear," Mother said, giving him a warm and somewhat intense hug. She pushed him back at arm's length. "I heard that you and Heather had a visitor this morning."

Here it came. He braced for her displeasure.

"Did you really tell Jeff he should elope?"

"What?" Roxy pulled away a fraction of an inch. "David, you didn't. Really?"

"I wasn't the one who put the idea in his head. Jeff made it quite clear that Melissa didn't like your plans for her wedding. He asked me to host the wedding at Eagle Hill Manor and then threatened to elope. I called his bluff. It seemed the simplest solution to his problem."

Mother and Roxy rolled their eyes in unison. He sipped his wine, fortifying himself for the battle to come.

"They can't elope," Mother said in her take-no-prisoners tone. "It would be a disaster. We need that wedding, David. You of all people should realize that. We're inviting all the A-list New York donors, most of whom are Nina's good friends."

Mother hadn't said anything he didn't already know. But for some reason the truth, spoken out loud in that tone of voice, raised a deep shame that spilled through him like a poison.

Shelly would be so disappointed in you.

Willow's parting words, meant to hurt, had done their job. She'd left him scored and bloody on the inside.

"Did Shelly cry the night before our wedding?" he asked.

Mother's gaze narrowed. "David, what on earth...?"

"Did she? Willow Petersen says she did."

"I have no idea. David, your wedding was beautiful. My goodness, we had the vice president there. And your father managed to work out that deal on—"

"She did cry. And she never said one word about it."

"David, really, we're not talking about Shelly. I know this is hard for you, but—"

"Yes, Mother, I know. We're talking about my political career and Dad's political career and how my wedding was mostly about that deal Dad worked out with the vice president. And, you know, I can suddenly see Jeff's point."

"David, really, listen to—"

"No, you listen." He pulled away from Roxy and pointed rudely at his mother's chest. "I don't want this wedding to be about my election. And I sure as hell don't want to play host to anyone at Eagle Hill Manor. So if neither of those options is going to work for Jeff and Melissa, then the best thing they could do for themselves and the rest of us is to elope."

He turned away and strode through the crowd looking for Natalie. He found her sitting on Uncle Jamie's lap, having a fabulous time being the center of attention.

Damn. He didn't want to stay here a minute longer. He wasn't in any kind of holly-jolly mood. He just wanted to be alone. Didn't people understand that? The second anniversary of Shelly's death was coming up. This time of year would never, ever be happy for him again.

What he wanted was to drown himself in the bottle of bourbon waiting for him at home.

"Natalie. We're going," he said.

His daughter looked up. He wasn't immune to the disappointment in her dark chocolate eyes.

Damn.

That look clawed at him, and he had to suppress the urge to drop to his knees and give his child an endless hug and promise that he'd find some way not to disappoint her all the time.

But he didn't know how to make his knees bend or his arms open. Besides, if he stopped and gave Natalie a hug right here in front of everyone, he might hold on to her forever. He might not be able to let go. He might weep.

And Lyndons weren't supposed to cry. Not in public. Not even in private. And certainly not in the presence of their children.

If there hadn't been some urgency, Willow might have taken as long as a week to put the finishing touches on her business plan. But there wasn't any time. If she was going to buy the inn in time for Melissa's wedding, she needed to get her act together.

So she spent all of Thursday closeted in her tiny bedroom under the eaves at Serenity Farm doing quick and dirty market research via the Internet. By Friday morning she had a written plan. It had holes and gaps, particularly in her estimates of the costs of fixing up the inn. But it would have to do. She had an eleven o'clock appointment with Jefferson Talbert-Lyndon.

She pulled out her Christian Dior suit and a pair of no-name basic heels. Black might be a boring color, but no woman ever went wrong wearing it to a business meeting. Let Hillary Clinton wear jewel tones. Willow believed that black was the new black.

For the past decade, most of her sales meetings had been in giant skyscrapers located in New York or London or Hong Kong. But today she parked her POS Honda in the town lot on North Second Street and walked to Secondhand Prose, where Jefferson Talbert-Lyndon spent his days.

She had to walk under the scaffolding to find the bookshop's entrance and was pleasantly surprised to find a cat tree in the front window. A big, gray cat slept there like a sentry, with one amber eye trained on the sidewalk. There had always been a cat tree in Secondhand Prose's front window, although the cat Willow remembered from her childhood had been a tabby.

Aside from the cat in the window, almost everything else about the bookshop had changed. Gone were the dusty bookshelves and the disorganized mess of used books stacked every which way. Now the place smelled like old books and had a vibe to it, like one of those bohemian indie bookstores in the Village or Brooklyn. Recessed lighting had banished the gloom, the wide plank wood floors had been refinished, and the building's interior brick walls had been exposed. Comfy chairs now occupied several nooks where customers could sit and read to their heart's content, and the merchandise included literary gift items and some new titles in addition to the fabulous collection of old books.

She headed toward the checkout counter, where a hipster dude wearing a literary T-shirt manned the cash register. "Hi. I'm here for a meeting with Mr. Talbert-Lyndon," she said.

The clerk looked like a refugee from Brooklyn with his slightly shaggy hair, five-o'clock shadow, and the blue T-shirt that said *Be silly. Be honest. Be kind.* Willow had never heard that quote, but the T-shirt claimed it had been penned by Ralph Waldo Emerson. Who knew someone that old and dusty could be so fun?

The clerk gave her the once-over. Something about those dark eyes seemed familiar. "You must be Willow Petersen," he said.

"Mr. Talbert-Lyndon is expecting me."

That got a laugh. "The last name's not Talbert-Lyndon. It's just plain Talbert now." He held out his hand. "It's nice to meet you, Willow. You didn't have to dress up for me."

Uh-oh. Her confidence plummeted about as fast as the heat raced over her face. She'd done a lot of research on Jefferson Talbert's net worth and not once had she bothered to look at a photo of the guy. She'd assumed that he'd dress in the Lyndon uniform of choice—a gray or blue suit. "Uh, oh, um, hi," she said, shaking his hand.

"So, you said you had something you wanted to talk about. Something about Eagle Hill Manor?"

Great. This was not going as planned. She'd anticipated making this pitch in an office, across a desk. Not standing here in the middle of a store. But there didn't seem to be an office in sight. She was going to have to do an elevator pitch.

She took a big breath to slow her pulse and pulled her plan out of her briefcase. "I met Melissa at the Jaybird a few days ago, and she was telling me how much she wanted to have her wedding reception at Eagle Hill Manor. I know you talked to David Lyndon about that. And I know he wasn't very cooperative.

"And all of that got me to thinking, especially since your cousin is putting the inn up for sale. It's a great opportunity." She handed him her business plan.

"An opportunity for what?"

"For investment. That's a plan," she said, nodding at the papers she'd put into his hands, "for renovating the inn and turning it into a wedding destination." She continued on, gaining confidence as she gave him her three-minute summary of the opportunity, the equity position, and the expected ROI. Then she stared him right in the face and asked for a boatload of money. It was just as hard to ask for gigantic sums of money as it was to ask for smaller amounts. So she went big.

Jefferson Talbert-Lyndon smiled at the figure and said, "Your reputation precedes you."

This was not what she'd expected to hear. She counted to five and made a show of reading the words on his shirt. If only she could be silly about this. Honesty had not worked for her. And she'd always been kind.

The smile faded from his face. "You know, this is tempting, but my situation is complicated."

"Complicated how?"

"I wasn't talking about the business. The truth is, I'm not interested in investing in an inn. The failure rate for businesses like that is high. And the rate of return isn't all that stellar either. To be honest, I would prefer to convince David to host the wedding. I shouldn't have to buy him out to make that happen."

"I see. But David is unlikely to do that."

"I know. And that's why Melissa and I have more or less decided to get married in Vegas. It's easier all the way around."

"But that's not what she wants, is it?"

"She's the one who suggested it. So, while I thank you for trying to help us solve this problem, the bottom line is that it's cheaper and easier for us to elope than for me to buy an inn just to have a wedding reception. I'm sorry, Willow." He handed the plan back to her.

"No, keep the plan. Read it. You might change your mind."

She turned away, certain that Jefferson Talbert would never read her plan. She'd have to come up with some other idea for her future.

Since Shelly's death, David negotiated his life by routine. Routine kept him from thinking too much and feeling too much. And not feeling was the best way to keep him away from that bottle of bourbon that lived in his bottom desk drawer at home. That bottle had taken a hit on Wednesday night, after Uncle Jamie's party.

But it was Friday now, and David was back in control of himself. And when noon arrived, he left his desk and took the five-block walk to Gracie's Diner. Lunch was the anchor of his day.

He was such a regular at the diner that Gracie unofficially reserved his favorite booth—the third from the door—and she always had his tuna sandwich on whole wheat toast with lettuce and tomato ready for him the moment he sat down.

But today the routine changed. Instead of putting his sandwich in front of him with her usual bright smile, Gracie Teague hovered. And when Gracie hovered, it usually meant she had information to share. Gracie was the chair of the Liberty Avenue Chamber of Commerce and had her finger on the pulse of the community. She was like a living and breathing focus group, which made her enormously useful to anyone in local politics.

"What's up?" he asked.

He expected Gracie to lean over and impart some important news, but instead she continued to hover with an uncertain look in her eye.

"What's the matter?" A heavy sense of dread settled into his gut.

Gracie slipped into the booth's facing bench and leaned in before she spoke. "Mr. Lyndon, you have no reason to do me any kind of favor. But here's the thing. Melissa is like my own baby girl. Her momma was my best friend, and, well, I would go to the ends of the earth to make her happy."

Gracie paused while David waited for the punch line that was surely coming. When her silence became more than he could bear, he said, "Gracie, just spit it out. I don't have all day. I have a brief to write this afternoon, and I just want to eat my lunch."

"Oh, well, I don't want to keep you from your lunch." She got up.

"Gracie, wait. What the hell is it you want to say?"

She folded her arms across her blue waitress uniform. "Melissa told me this morning that even though the Presbyterian church is available on the date they want, she and Jeff are still planning to run off to Vegas to get married because they can't find an acceptable place for their reception. And I gather you're the one who told them it would be best if they eloped." Gracie's voice turned watery, and unshed tears filled her eyes.

"I didn't put the idea in their heads, Gracie. They're the ones who didn't like the wedding Mother was planning for them in New York. Don't make this out to be more than it is or blame me for what they decide is right for them."

Gracie's spine snapped. "Really? Is that what you think? You could have helped them. You could have let them have their wedding party at the inn. And now, instead, they're going to elope, and I won't get to see my girl in a wedding dress. And it's your fault, Mr. Lyndon."

"Now, Gracie, that's not—"

"It is your fault. You showed that you're not a kind or caring man. And make no mistake, if Jeff and Melissa elope, I will have no compunction about telling folks exactly how that came to happen." Gracie turned her back on him for the first time ever.

Damn.

This was a big problem. He didn't want Gracie Teague supporting Bill Cummins in the primary election. But even more than that, he liked and admired Gracie. She was a decent person, and he hated the idea of disappointing her.

Sort of like he hated the idea of disappointing Natalie. And Shelly.

But what else was new? For days now, Willow's angry words had been worming their way through him.

But he couldn't please everyone. If he helped Melissa and Jeff, his mother wouldn't be happy. Mother was already annoyed at him for telling Jeff to elope.

And Heather and Dad wanted that big wedding in New York because dozens of rich donors would be there.

How on earth had a wedding gotten so tangled up in politics?

He was screwed no matter what he did.

Willow picked up a copy of the *Winchester Daily* at the drugstore and headed down to Gracie's Diner. So much for her plan to work for herself. Maybe she needed to lower her sights and check the want ads after all. Because if Jeff Talbert wasn't going to invest in her plan, it was unlikely anyone else would.

She needed some real food to bolster her flagging confidence. Two days of eating lentils and oatmeal had left her ravenous. The appetite-enhancing aroma of fried bacon and coffee made her stomach growl as she came through the diner's front door.

And saw David Lyndon at one of the window booths.

Crap. He was the last person on the face of the planet that she wanted to see today. Especially after Jeff's rejection.

But Shenandoah Falls was a small town, so avoiding David would be impossible if she ended up staying here. Still, the sight of him froze her to the gray linoleum and made her heart turn in her chest. She owed him an apology for what she'd said on Wednesday. She ought to suck it up and go say something nice right now, something that would smooth over the controversy.

He looked up from his lunch out of dark, brooding eyes, haunted by Shelly's ghost. His gaze caught and paralyzed her as he got up from his spot and approached.

He grabbed her by the upper arm before she could think about running. On Wednesday his touch had frightened her. Today it sparked a current of something surprising, and maybe even forbidden, that flowed up her arm and into her core.

"I need to talk to you," he said.

"And I need to—"

Just then Gracie popped up and said, "Let her go, Mr. Lyndon. I don't want any trouble in my diner. And besides, she hasn't done anything to you except tell the truth. And if you can't handle the truth, well, that's your problem, not hers."

"Um, Gracie, it's all right."

David dropped Willow's arm, but the buzz he'd ignited remained. "Can we talk?" he asked.

"Sure."

Gracie followed them back to David's booth. "It's nice to see you back in town again, Willow. What will you be having today, hon?"

Willow ordered a tuna sandwich on whole wheat toast with lettuce, tomato, and mayonnaise and a diet Coke. Gracie bustled off, but not before glaring at David.

"David, I'm so sorry for the way I mouthed off the other day. Really. I shouldn't have said what I did. I was angry, and I regret it. Deeply."

"Apology accepted," he said, his gaze warming, "but

I think maybe Gracie is right. You spoke the truth, and I didn't want to hear it."

She nodded and the conversation stalled for a moment, until David spoke again. "Look, I want to talk to you about Jeff and Melissa. Did you know that Gracie has blamed me for their decision to elope?"

"Well, that's ridiculous. Melissa was ready to elope on Tuesday when her friends took her to the Jaybird to try to talk her out of it. And I understand why you don't want to host their wedding. That would put you between Melissa and Jeff and your mom. I told Melissa you would never go for the idea. I thought maybe I could find a way to make it all work out, but Jeff has put the nail in that coffin." She shrugged and looked away, out the windows at the traffic on Liberty Avenue.

"What did he do?"

She returned her gaze to David. "Oh, well, I got this harebrained idea that I could buy the inn, renovate it the way Shelly wanted to, and turn it into a wedding destination. I wrote a business plan and asked Jeff to invest in it. I figured if he invested in my plan, we could buy the inn, do a quick fix-up, and have the wedding there without putting you in the middle of it."

"Really?"

She nodded. "But he refused. He's already made up his mind about eloping and doesn't really want to invest in an inn. Or me, probably."

"Do you really want to buy the inn, or were you just suggesting this to help Melissa?"

"Helping Melissa was part of it. But bottom line, I think I really do want to buy the inn."

"Why?"

"I need a job, David. No, scratch that. Mom would say I need an income, and the inn is as good a business opportunity as any in town. Plus I'd like to fix the place up the way Shelly wanted it."

His lips thinned, and Willow understood how he might not want to be reminded of Shelly's plans. But she was being honest with him. And honesty was often painful.

Gracie interrupted their conversation with Willow's sandwich and diet Coke. "Here you go, hon." She nodded in David's direction. "Is he bothering you?"

Willow shook her head. "No. We're okay. And you shouldn't blame him for Jeff and Melissa wanting to elope. It's not his fault, Gracie. It's his mother's fault."

"You think it's not? He could host their wedding at the inn if he wanted to." Gracie turned her back and bustled away.

"See? She's furious with me. Can I see your business plan?"

Their gazes locked again. "Why? You want to sell the inn, not invest in it. And I have the feeling that you blame the inn for Shelly's death."

It was his turn to study the traffic on the other side of the window. "Yeah. I do. And I even know that blaming the inn is stupid," he said in a low voice. "But when you lose someone in such a senseless, random way, you just need to blame someone or something. Otherwise it doesn't make any sense. There was only one fatality in that derailment. Why did it have to be her?"

He turned back toward Willow, his face haggard. Her heart lurched. David was struggling, and she hadn't helped him much the other day by getting all up in his face and making him feel guilty.

"I can't answer your question, David," she said. "Bad stuff happens to good people all the time." She reached into her briefcase and pulled out a manila folder containing a second printout of her business plan. "Here's my plan if you want to look at it. It's still kind of rough. I rushed it because I know Melissa wants to get married on December nineteenth. That doesn't leave much time, you know?"

She laid the printout on the table and pushed it in his direction.

He didn't pick it up. "You're probably right about that. Even if you bought the inn today, it might take weeks before we could go to closing. So buying the inn wouldn't really solve Melissa's problem, would it? Not without my help, anyway."

"David, do you want to help Melissa?"

Did he want to help?

David looked away from Willow to the busy street as he toted up the pros and cons of his situation. He couldn't make everyone happy, that was for damn sure. But maybe he could negotiate a compromise. Isn't that what good politicians did?

And maybe hosting the wedding at Eagle Hill Manor was a better solution than allowing Jeff and Melissa to elope. Not only would he win Jeff's goodwill, which might come in handy since Jeff knew a lot of wealthy potential donors, but it would solve his Gracie Teague problem. And, who knew, maybe Heather could sneak a few politicos onto the much-reduced guest list.

He touched his wedding band, feeling that tug of emotion that never left him.

He turned back toward Willow, sitting there with her backbone perpetually straight and all that blond hair tucked up tight. She was wearing her power suit today, but even in jeans and a T-shirt, Willow wasn't any kind of pushover. He'd known that from the moment he'd first met her when they were both sixteen. She could outfish him, outthink him, and outargue him.

And she'd never lied to him. Ever. If she said Shelly cried the night before their wedding, then it was the truth. And what she'd said on Wednesday was true too. Shelly would have wanted him to host this wedding.

"Okay," he said, his voice steady, as he worried his wedding band with his thumb. "Here's what we're going to do. First, I'm going to hire you to manage Jeff and Melissa's wedding. We're going to hold the wedding reception at Eagle Hill Manor on December nineteenth. I'll give you a reasonable budget to spruce up the inn—just enough to make the reception possible, as well as for anything that Walter Braden says is required before I list the place. You can talk with him and Poppy about what's needed and give me an estimate that includes your time to manage the renovations and staging of the inn and to deal with whatever Melissa wants and needs. I want to make this clear—Melissa gets anything she wants. Your job is to make her wedding day everything she has ever dreamed about. If any crying happens the night before her big day, I want those tears to be tears of joy."

He paused, catching his breath. "I want to make it clear, right up front, that I'm not changing my mind about selling the inn. Walter will continue to show it to prospective buyers, but I promise you it will not be sold until after December nineteenth, so if you want to raise the money to buy it, then go for it. I won't stand in your way."

Once he finished laying out his plan, he halfway expected Willow to jump up and down and squeal and throw her arms around his neck. That would have been nice. And also inappropriate.

Thank God Willow wasn't that kind of woman. She didn't squeal or hug him, but she did give him a killer smile that drew his attention to her mouth. And her lips. Which were...kind of kissable. He'd never noticed that before.

Whoa, wait a second. That wasn't something he was supposed to notice. It wasn't something he wanted to notice. But right then a jolt of sexual attraction swept through him, shocking him to his core.

No. He didn't want that. Willow was Shelly's best friend. She was off-limits.

Chapter 6————————————

The skies opened up Monday morning as Willow was making the walk from her car to the grand portico at Eagle Hill Manor. The rain was a cold reminder that she had barely six weeks to spruce up the inn, make all the arrangements for a society wedding, and find investors who would help her buy the place outright.

Christmas would be here before she knew it.

She turned up the collar of her coat and rang the bell. David Lyndon was the last person she expected to open the door.

Nor did she expect him to stand there, staring at her with an intense gaze that left her oddly breathless. Wait, what was up with that? David was Shelly's husband. Her libido needed to take a cold shower.

And besides, Willow had sworn off guys like David. Her next boyfriend was going to be a regular guy with a regular job, not a CEO or a congressman or any other person in the limelight. She'd had her fifteen minutes of infamy, thank you very much.

Willow gulped down a calming breath and met his stare again, and noticed for the first time that Prince David was carrying a pink polka-dotted Hello Kitty backpack in his right hand.

"Good morning," she said. "Hi. I'm sure you want to know why I'm here so early. I made an appointment to talk with Mrs. M. You know, about sprucing up the inn for Jeff and Melissa?" Why did she suddenly feel as awkward as a teenager with a crush on the big man on campus? She was actually babbling. In David's presence, no less.

"Oh, great. We were just on our way out. We have a meeting this morning with Natalie's teacher."

Thank God he turned toward Natalie, who was standing in the middle of the lobby dressed in a pink North Face fleece jacket that brought out the pink in her cheeks and the fire in her hair.

"C'mon, Natalie, we're going to be late," David said in a parental tone.

Willow didn't know a thing about kids or parenting, but the look on Natalie's face opened up a whole can of familiar fears and memories. Nothing was worse than having to go to school with a parent for the dreaded parent-teacher meeting.

Willow had been through dozens of them. Mostly because Mom had "views" about public education and was not at all shy about expressing them…especially to people in authority.

The poor kid.

Willow dropped down to be on Natalie's level. "Hey,"

she said as she stuck out her hand, "I don't think we were properly introduced last week. My name is Willow. I was one of your mother's friends." She ought to have told Natalie that she was her godmother, but it seemed presumptuous since she'd never taken the responsibility seriously. She decided, right on the spot, to make amends for her neglect.

Natalie cocked her head to one side but didn't shake Willow's hand. This child was far more reserved than Shelly had been. "Grammy says I'm not supposed to call grown-ups by their first names."

So polite. But then her last name was Lyndon.

"You're right about that," Willow said, painful memories of Mom's "call me Linda" phase riffling through her mind. "Why don't you call me Miss Willow, then?"

"Okay." The little girl nodded her head vigorously, her long, red ponytail bouncing. A pair of adorable pink and green polka-dotted leggings and green cowboy boots completed her outfit. She looked cute enough to warm the heart of any mean old teacher.

Or even a negligent godmother.

Willow was about to give Natalie a big pep talk about the whole parent-teacher thing when Mrs. M arrived on the scene and said, "For goodness' sake, David, you're going to be late if you don't get going soon. Given what I know of Mrs. Welch, being late won't help matters."

"Mrs. Welch?" Willow asked. "I hope it's not the same Mrs. Welch who used to teach third grade back in 1990? That Mrs. Welch would be like a hundred years old by now."

"Not quite a hundred, dear," Mrs. M said. "More like her late fifties."

"Don't tell me this is the teacher your mother picketed that time," David said.

Willow didn't answer David's question. Instead she gave Natalie a pat on the shoulder. "Don't let the spelling tests get you down," she said.

Natalie's face lit up. "You know about those?"

"Yeah, I'm afraid I do. But, you know, it's okay. I learned a lot from Mrs. Welch too."

"What's a picket?" Natalie asked.

"Don't answer that," David said.

She looked up at him, expecting to find a grumpy frown on his face. Instead he looked down at her with just a tiny humorous twist to his lips.

She stood up, feeling suddenly light-headed. She'd forgotten how winning his smile could be.

"Yes, well, I don't think David is going to picket the school, are you?" Mrs. M said. There was an edge to her voice, and the smile at the corner of David's eyes vanished.

"No. I don't think that's quite the appropriate response." He turned toward his daughter, who had been watching this exchange with undisguised interest. "Come on, let's go. We don't want to keep your teacher waiting," he said, taking his daughter's tiny hand in his much, much larger one.

The sight of his big hand enveloping Natalie's little one did something goofy to Willow's insides. The warmth pooling inside her wasn't precisely sexual, although it awakened every cell in her body. It tingled over her skin and made her aware of him in ways she'd never been before.

Inside that princely, entitled exterior was a sensitive core. She saw it in the way he held his daughter's hand, in the way he touched his wedding band, and in the way he still grieved for Shelly.

He wasn't at all like Corbin, was he?

Poppy watched David's encounter with Willow with growing interest. Had her son-in-law smiled at Willow? Almost. And that was practically a miracle given that David had been behaving like a caricature of a brooding hero from out of the pages of those idiotic Gothic novels Shelly had loved so much.

No, she hadn't imagined it. He had smiled. He'd also given Willow the look a man gives a woman when he's interested. Something was happening here, which explained a lot of things, not the least of which was David's sudden change of heart about his cousin's wedding.

Poppy flashed back to the discussion last Monday at bridge club. Bud Ingram was right. David's libido was reawakening.

This could be good or bad news, depending on the personality of the next woman in David's life. If he chose Willow, that would be very good indeed.

For Poppy, at least.

But would it be good for Willow?

What to do? She didn't know. She'd need to talk this out with someone like Faye. Faye was much better at trying to run other people's lives.

She gave Willow a hug. "Come along. I've set up some breakfast in the library. It consists of coffee and some scones from Grateful Bread, I'm afraid. I do miss Antonin's blueberry muffins."

"I do, too, but the scones from Grateful Bread aren't half bad," Willow said.

They crossed the inn's lobby and walked into the library, where Poppy had set up a table with a faded chintz tablecloth and her favorite Royal Albert rosebud cups, saucers, and bread and butter plates. She'd once had enough of this pattern to serve tea to twenty. The years had taken their toll on the china, and at almost sixty dollars a place setting, she'd never be able to replace the broken pieces. But then, she was unlikely to ever serve tea to twenty again either.

"So," Poppy said after she poured coffee, and they'd buttered their scones, "you've managed to convince David to host a wedding. How remarkable."

Willow sat in her chair like a queen, with her back tall and inflexible, her shoulders straight and even. She'd never slouched, not even as a teen. And that rigid back telegraphed every single one of Willow's insecurities. Willow had often been the adult in Linda Petersen's household. And the little girl had learned early how to make herself look bigger. She'd also been the one who smoothed over Linda's most outrageous acts of nonconformity, which explained why Willow always wore black, or beige, or gray. Her dress today was black with a high neckline. Her hair was pulled back neatly. And aside from that small moment by the front door, she appeared to be the very picture of calm control as she sipped her coffee.

"Willow, darling girl, I've heard all about your business plan, and I have only one question. What on earth made you decide to do this? Restoring the inn was Shelly's dream, not yours," Poppy said.

"I know. But maybe I need to borrow Shelly's dream

for a little while because my dream turned into a night-mare."

If Poppy wanted to encourage romance between David and Willow, this new development would certainly throw them together. But the situation was far more compli-cated. What if they actually stuck? What then? Willow's plans to buy the inn and restore it would become a major bone of contention, wouldn't they?

And that was the very best reason for Poppy to stay out of any matchmaking attempts. They were likely to blow up in her face.

"All right," Poppy said, "tell me about your plan, then."

Willow started talking fast, jabbering the way she al-ways had. She spoke about marketing plans, and high-end weddings, and demographics, and a whole raft of things that Poppy knew nothing about. Poppy knew how to wel-come people into her home as if they were family. Poppy knew how to feed them and take care of them. Poppy knew how to order groceries and manage maid service.

"Mrs. M," Willow said, as her spiel came to an end, "you're absolutely right. I don't know a thing about wed-dings or running an inn, except, of course, the stuff I learned by hanging around with Shelly as a kid. I know you want to retire, but I need your help. I need your ad-vice. I need you as a consultant."

Poppy laughed. "I'm happy to help you with Melissa's wedding, Willow. It will be fun."

"Fun?"

"Yes, Willow, fun. Trust me. Weddings are always fun. They are my favorite thing to host here at the inn. So let's get started. I've already phoned Walter Braden, and he'll be here around ten o'clock to go through his to-do list for getting the property ready to show. But, of course, there is much more that needs to be done if we're going to host a Christmas-themed wedding reception. For starters, we need to think about holiday decorations. I'm afraid the old ones are kind of tired, and last year they weren't stored in the barn correctly. The mice got to the lights, so we'll need to replace all of them.

"And we'll need to figure something out about the catering. I wonder if I could induce Antonin to come back to cater the reception. He always did such a wonderful job, especially with Christmas weddings. His shepherd's pie is to die for.

"And we'll need to think about flowers and repainting the lobby and the dining room. Oh my, we have a lot of work to do."

Was it her imagination, or did Willow's face pale a little bit as she dug in her briefcase for a legal pad? "Slow down, Mrs. M," Willow said. "I need to take detailed notes."

Chapter 7———————————————

David guided Natalie through the doors of Daniel Morgan Elementary School. It was a good half hour before the children would arrive for the day, and Natalie clung to his hand as if it were a lifeline.

The hallways brought back reminders of childhood. Children's art projects hung on every wall, and the place smelled of chalk, poster paint, and textbooks. He guided his child into the principal's office, where Mrs. Geary was waiting for them.

The slight tightening of Natalie's grip told him she was scared of this woman, and rightly so. Mrs. Geary was almost six feet tall, with thinning dark hair and a mouth that turned down at the corners in a perpetual scowl. She wore a charm bracelet on her thin wrist, which jangled as he shook her hand.

Boy, the woman was a little bit scary, but he was determined not to let this woman or Natalie's teacher, Mrs. Welch, punish his daughter for nothing.

The principal guided them into a small room with a conference table that took up almost all the space. A fifty-ish woman with short gray hair and round nervous eyes was waiting for them.

"Mr. Lyndon," the woman said, standing up, "I'm Mrs. Welch, Natalie's teacher. I'm sorry we didn't get to meet on back-to-school night."

Oh, low blow. He'd missed back-to-school night and the first-quarter teacher-parent conference because he'd been staying at Mother and Dad's DC apartment, working on a major case at trial before the US Court of Appeals for the Federal Circuit. Poppy had covered for him on both occasions and had given him a full report. Natalie had always been a good and diligent student.

"Please, sit," Mrs. Geary said.

They all sat. Natalie's posture said it all. His little girl was scared out of her mind. But she wouldn't be for long.

"Mr. Lyndon," Mrs. Geary said, "you asked for this meeting. What seems to be the problem?"

David pulled Natalie's spelling tests from his inside jacket pocket. The papers were badly creased and crin-kled because Natalie had been hiding them in the bottom of her backpack, ashamed to show them to him, even though there wasn't a blessed thing wrong with them.

He smoothed them out and passed them across the ta-ble to the principal. "This," he said in his bulldog County Council voice.

Mrs. Welch picked up the spelling tests before the principal could reach them and then gave Natalie a glare that made David want to strangle her.

"You know you're supposed to have your father sign these and return them, don't you, Natalie?" she said. "I would never have had to call your father if you'd—"

"No, Mrs. Welch," David said, interrupting the teacher. "I'm not talking about your rules here. I'm talking about the grade."

"I realize that you and your family are used to getting your—"

"This has nothing to do with my family. It has everything to do with the grade on that paper."

"Now, Mr. Lyndon, you—" Mrs. Geary started to say in a conciliatory tone.

"What kind of school are you running here? Is it your practice to penalize certain children by flunking them on spelling tests even when any idiot can see that the words are spelled correctly?"

"They are not spelled correctly." Mrs. Welch sat up straight in her chair and glared at him.

"What on earth are you talking about? Just look at them."

"I'm sorry, Mr. Lyndon, but Natalie does not form her 'O's or 'E's properly. Therefore, the words are not correctly written."

"Oh my God, are you marking her down for penmanship? Really? That's your excuse?"

"Mr. Lyndon, please," Mrs. Geary said, "keep your voice—"

"Mrs. Welch," David interrupted again, "the senior partner in my law firm, who is admitted to the Supreme Court Bar and has argued some of the seminal cases of our time, has worse handwriting than Natalie's. I had less trouble reading Natalie's spelling test than I do notes from him. I had no trouble distinguishing her 'O's from her 'E's."

"Her handwriting does not meet our standards for—"

"Oh, for crying out loud. I'm fed up with stupid teachers who spend all their time trying to teach to some stupid standard while they miss the most obvious thing."

"Mr. Lyndon, keep your voice down, please," Mrs. Geary said. "I understand your concerns about handwriting, but you yourself were among the school board members who supported a back-to-basics curriculum a few years back. And that curriculum included the teaching of cursive writing."

"What?"

"You can look it up. We are required by Jefferson County to teach cursive writing in third grade. We have always interpreted that to mean that we should mark down spelling tests when the writing doesn't meet acceptable standards."

David stood up and leaned over the table. "I don't give a damn what your interpretation of the back-to-basics program is. Can't you see that you've petrified my daughter? You've convinced her that she can't spell and that she's failing in school. She was so ashamed she hid these papers from me and—"

"Mr. Lyndon, as a parent it's your duty to make sure your child doesn't hide papers from you. You should be checking her backpack regularly." Mrs. Geary got up and matched his aggressive stance.

Well, that was that. He was done, finished. He loved his daughter. It might be that he left a lot of the day-to-day to Poppy, but he certainly wasn't going to stand there and let two old biddies suggest that all of Natalie's problems were his fault. And he certainly wasn't keeping his child in this kind of toxic situation.

He turned toward his daughter, who was looking up at him with wide, dark eyes. "Come on, we're leaving now. You'll be coming to the office with me today."

He took Natalie by the hand as she hopped down from the chair.

"Mr. Lyndon, are you withdrawing your child from the school?"

"Yes," he said.

"You know that's against the law. She is required to attend school, and if she doesn't attend school, I will have to report her as truant. And if you, as a parent, encourage truancy, it's considered a misdemeanor in the Commonwealth of Virginia."

"Mrs. Geary, I intend to enroll my daughter at St. Luke's, where I went to school as a boy."

He stepped around the principal and walked right out the front door just as school buses began to unload kids. David and Natalie were a lot like salmon swimming upstream as they headed toward the parking lot.

It was raining pretty hard, and he hadn't brought an umbrella. Cold water pelted him, cooling him down. It suddenly occurred to him that Bill Cummins might have a field day with what had just happened.

"Am I not going to school today?" Natalie asked.

"No, you're not."

"I don't mind going to school, really," she said. "I mean I kind of like it, especially recess and lunchtime with Ilene and Olivia."

He stopped and turned to face his child. He was so much taller that she had to crane her neck to look up at him. That didn't strike him as fair, especially since the rain had started to fall in earnest. So he squatted down and took her by the shoulders.

"You listen to me, okay?" he said, blinking as the rain hit his face. "What happened today is not because you did something wrong. For one thing, you didn't fail any spelling tests. You spelled all your words correctly, and I'm proud of you. And I don't think your handwriting is all that bad, although it's a little bit sloppy, but then, you're left-handed and that makes it hard. We can work on that, okay? It's not a big deal. But it's a big deal when people try to make you feel like you're stupid. I don't like that. Not one bit."

His words stuck in his throat and his chest constricted. Damnit. He loved her more than anything on the face of the planet. He opened his arms and she stepped into them. He pulled her close and pressed his nose to her beautiful red hair, breathing her in.

After spending the morning with Mrs. M and Walter Braden, Willow had a long list of repairs and upgrades that needed to be taken care of before the wedding reception, not to mention the gigantic list of things Poppy said were necessary in order to plan a wedding properly.

That list was daunting. It left her feeling oddly unprepared for her luncheon meeting with Melissa and her two bridesmaids at Gracie's Diner. Willow found Melissa, Courtney, and Arwen waiting for her at one of the big booths near the diner's front door.

"Hi, everyone," she said, plastering a bright, businesslike smile on her face. "Sorry I'm a little late. I was out at the inn taking stock. There's a lot to get done. Including new holiday decorations."

"What's wrong with the decorations?" Courtney asked.

"They need replacing."

"Oh. That's bad, you know, because part of why Melissa wants to have her reception at the inn is because it's always decorated to the nines. I mean, it's like a tradition to go there for high tea in December just to see all the lights and wreaths and greenery."

"I know. We're working on it." In fact, she and Mrs. M had spent quite a bit of time talking about the Christmas decorations. The mice had destroyed so much.

"I'm sure you and Mrs. Marchand will have the inn looking as beautiful as ever. I'm not worried," Melissa said.

Just then Gracie came over carrying four plates in her arms. She put a patty melt in front of Arwen, a ham and Swiss on rye in front of Melissa, a cobb salad in front of Courtney, and a tuna sandwich on whole wheat toast with lettuce, tomato, and mayo in front of Willow.

Willow frowned up at her. "How did you know I—"

Gracie waved her hand. "It's not magic. The thing is, most folks come in here and order the same thing every day. This is what you had yesterday, so I figured I'd take a chance and make you another one." Gracie gave her a wide grin. "Did you know that you and David Lyndon like the same lunch? Isn't that nice?"

No, it was kind of creepy or something, but she smiled back at Gracie. "Uh, thanks. For lunch and for helping me land this job."

Gracie gave another carefree wave. "Don't even think

about it, hon. You're the one who put the wheels in motion." She gave Melissa a sappy look. "I just want to make sure Melissa gets exactly what she wants on her wedding day." Gracie leaned down and got right up into Willow's face. "I'll tell you a secret," Gracie whispered. "I've seen Melissa pining over a picture in *Brides* of a wedding dress with a big, white fur-lined cape, like something right out of a fairy tale. I want her to have that."

After delivering this bomb, Gracie straightened up and headed off toward the kitchen.

A fur-lined cape? Really? Oh boy, Willow was in deep, deep trouble. So many questions entered her mind that her head almost exploded. She knew nothing about wedding dresses. Was she supposed to be responsible for that too? Where the heck did you go for a fur-lined cloak, and how much would that cost, and did Melissa want real fur or would faux-fur do? Not knowing what else to do, she picked up her sandwich and took a bite.

Melissa came to her rescue. She pushed her big, black glasses up her nose and said, "I don't really need that cloak. Gracie just saw me admiring it, and you know how she can be."

"Of course you need the cloak." Courtney put down her fork and pulled an iPad from her satchel purse. "I knew we were having this meeting so I thought I'd pull together some ideas on Pinterest." She booted up her tablet. A moment later, she turned the screen so everyone at the table could see.

Courtney had pinned at least a hundred images to a board she'd named "Melissa's Fairytale Christmas Wedding." The images ran the gamut from white fur-lined cloaks to dozens of photos of red bridesmaid dresses. It didn't end there. Courtney had place settings (heavy on the pine boughs and red roses), candles wrapped in beech bark, and at least a dozen images of cinnamon sticks being used creatively in one way or another, either as food or decoration. She also had more than twenty images of Christmas decor wrapped around banisters and on mantels and gracing front doors. It was clear Courtney wanted Melissa to have a wedding that was all wrapped up in pine roping and tied with a tinsel bow... with a bunch of cinnamon sticks.

Willow continued to eat her sandwich while Courtney, Melissa, and Arwen dived right into a discussion of the merits of every blessed photo on Courtney's Pinterest page. Willow eventually took out a notebook and tried to keep up, but she soon came to the conclusion that she should let Courtney plan the whole thing. Wow. Who knew Courtney would grow out of her braces and her aptitude for math and science to become a wedding planner in the making?

A fiendish thought crossed Willow's mind. Maybe if she could come up with the money to buy the inn, she could hire Courtney and put her in charge of planning all the weddings. Would she give up being a nurse? Doubtful, but it was worth considering.

Willow was beginning to relax about the whole wedding-planner thing when the bell above the diner's door jingled and David strolled into the diner, holding his daughter by the hand. The moment his highly polished wing tips crossed the threshold, the atmosphere in the place changed. It got hot. And hard to breathe.

Gracie apparently had no problems with the atmosphere. She greeted Natalie with a gigantic smile and said, "Hey, honey, you sure are pretty today in your polka dots. You want a grilled cheese sandwich?"

Natalie said nothing. She continued to stand there with a death grip on David's hand. In the few hours since Willow had last seen her, the little girl had lost her hair ribbon and ponytail elastic. Now her hair tumbled around her shoulders in a fiery tangle that looked as if she'd gone running outside in the rain and then let her hair dry on its own.

Gracie looked from the child to her father, her smile fading a little. "You're late," she said. "I had to give your usual table to Rick Sharp." She nodded toward the third table from the door, where a rotund man in a three-piece suit was eating the fried chicken special. "And to be honest," Gracie continued, "I gave your sandwich to Willow. Did you know that you and she like the same lunch?"

David followed Gracie's glance, which was how Willow found herself caught in his stare again, just like earlier in the morning. Only this time it seemed to last forever before David broke it by glancing down at the crusts of bread on her plate.

Willow decided right then and there that she was giving up tuna sandwiches. From now on she'd be a turkey-on-rye kind of girl.

Melissa took that moment to jump up from her seat and tackle David with a big, joyful hug that knocked her glasses a little sideways. "Thank you, thank you, thank you, thank you," she said, and then let him go.

His ears got red in the most adorable way. Then he gave Melissa the tiniest of smiles—one that barely brought his dimple out. "I haven't done anything," he said in a gruff voice.

"Yes, you have. And thank you so much for hiring Willow to make it all happen. She's already been so helpful." Melissa straightened her glasses and glanced back at the table where Courtney and Arwen waved at David like a couple of goofs.

Willow sat on her hands. She wasn't going to wave at him.

Or do anything else that came immediately to mind, because most of those thoughts were inappropriate. She was not supposed to notice how sexy he looked in his suit or the way his slightly too-long hair curled over the collar of his shirt. She wasn't supposed to notice the aura of power and competence that surrounded him, even when he was in parental mode.

It was wrong to feel this tingling in her belly. It was wrong to imagine him without the shirt and tie. To imagine what it might be like to touch his skin, feel the rasp of his beard against her face.

So wrong.

Last Friday Willow had worn a black business suit with a skinny skirt that showed her long, amazing legs. Today it was a black dress that hugged all her curves. Funny how that high neckline was way sexier than the open buttons down Roxanne's blouse the other night. David didn't need to go looking down Willow's blouse to admire her shape. That dress displayed her like it was painted on. And when he looked at her, it didn't disturb or disgust him. He enjoyed the view. He enjoyed it so much that he forced himself to look away and focus on finding a place to sit, since Rick Sharp had ensconced himself in David's favorite booth.

Unfortunately, the only booth available was the one right next to Willow's. He made sure to put Natalie in the bench seat that backed up to the bride and her bridesmaids. That way his daughter and the booth blocked his view of his wife's best friend. Equally important, he wouldn't have to worry about feeling the heat against his back. It seemed like a good idea until Natalie got antsy, hopped up on her knees, and leaned over the top of the bench seat.

"Hi, Miss Willow," she said in a loud voice that everyone in the diner could hear, and then followed it up with, "Daddy told Mrs. Welch that she was stupid."

"Natalie, sit down. Now. And don't use that word," David said.

"But, Daddy, you—"

"Sit down and stop bothering Miss Willow."

Natalie complied but not without a defiant pout that he found annoying as hell.

Willow peeked around the edge of her booth. "You have a moment?" she asked.

Well, crap. He didn't want to talk to her. He totally regretted having hired her. And he was embarrassed by Melissa's recent show of affection. He just wanted to be left alone.

But that wasn't about to happen, was it? "Sure," he said, then took a bite of the tuna sandwich Gracie had just delivered.

Willow turned back to Melissa and her friends. "Courtney, you and Melissa make a list of everything you want, okay?"

"Everything?" David heard one of the women say.

"Yup, everything. Including the fur-lined cloak. We'll need to figure out if it's possible to get something like that on short notice. So I'll need that list, with specific suppliers and manufacturers, as soon as possible."

Squeals followed, and David had the sinking feeling that this wedding wasn't going to be a small, inexpensive affair after all. Good thing Jeff had called this morning and insisted on paying for the reception, including the food, beverages, flowers, cake, and dresses. David was paying for the repairs to the inn. And Willow's salary, of course, but that was negligible.

Willow slid into the facing bench, next to Natalie. "So I guess your dad took you out of school for the day, huh?"

Natalie nodded. "Yeah, and I got to go to the office with him, and Miss Gillian let me play with a computer and I did some math and then we came here for lunch." Natalie picked up her grilled cheese and started munching.

Willow turned toward David. "Mrs. Welch got the better of you, huh?"

"I guess."

"Well, don't feel bad. My mother had the same reaction."

"I remember the story. She kept you out of school. For how long?"

"About a week."

"You got to stay home from school for a whole week?" Natalie asked, clearly impressed.

"Well, it wasn't as fun as it sounds. Because I was home, I had to help my mom clean goat poop in the barn in the morning, and then we staged a sit-in at the school in the afternoon. That was kind of embarrassing, to tell you the truth."

"Don't worry, Natalie. We're not going to stage a sit-in," David said. "And you're not staying out of school for a week."

"I'm going back tomorrow?"

"No. We have an appointment with St. Luke's Episcopalian School."

"What's an ipopsickle?"

"Never mind. It's a new school."

Natalie blinked at him, her eyes suddenly bright. "But...I don't want to go to a new school."

Crap. He'd disappointed her again, apparently. But before he could come up with something reassuring to say, Willow put her arm around her. "Oh, sweetie, don't cry. You're a lucky girl to be able to go to the Episcopal school. It's the best school in Jefferson County. You should thank your daddy. He's not going to make you stay home for a week or shovel goat poop."

Natalie giggled at that. "We don't have a goat."

"Lucky thing. Goats are smelly and noisy."

"Do you still have a goat?"

Willow shook her head. "Nope. We have two alpacas named Bogey and Bacall. Want to see a picture of them?"

Natalie nodded, and Willow whipped out her cell phone and started showing Natalie pictures.

After a few minutes, Natalie asked, "Can I come over to your house and pet them?"

"Sure, if your dad says it's okay."

Natalie looked at him expectantly.

"We'll see," he said, and gave Natalie his I'm-in-charge look. He didn't like the idea of her visiting Linda

Petersen's farm. God only knew what that woman was growing out there in her greenhouses. The stories continued to circulate that she was cultivating marijuana in between the herbs she used for her handmade soaps.

Natalie leaned back against the seat and gave Willow her I'm-a-poor-little-girl pout. She'd learned that look from Shelly, and it was both cute and annoying. "Daddy doesn't like animals much," she said. "He won't let me get a dog or a cat or even a fish. And I want a dog for Christmas." She folded her arms across her chest.

Enough. He didn't need Natalie airing the family business for everyone to hear. "Finish your lunch," he directed, and then turned toward Willow. "You wanted to talk to me about something?"

"Uh, yeah, it's about the budget for the inn. I walked through the place with Walter this morning. We made a list, and I'll be calling contractors today. I should have an idea of the budget by Monday or Tuesday, but there's one additional item we need to discuss."

"What?" He barked the word, but Willow didn't even blink. She stared at him in that forthright way that had his gonads in a sudden uproar. What the hell?

"I made an inventory of the inn's holiday decorations," she said. "They have to be replaced. Melissa is expecting the inn to look the way it did back in the day, when visiting Eagle Hill Manor for holiday tea was a highlight of the Christmas season."

"I never visited the inn for tea."

She sat up ramrod straight, the way she sometimes did when someone challenged her. "Really?" she said.

"My parents hosted their own teas."

That got him a long, unreadable stare. What the hell

was going on in that beautiful mind of hers? The wheels and cogs were obviously turning.

"Melissa wants the place to be transformed into a Christmas wonderland. And you told me to make Melissa happy."

What was it about Christmas? Ordinarily sane people started spending ridiculous amounts of money on ribbons and evergreen and cutesy ornaments made in China by people who didn't even believe in Jesus. He hated it. He hated the excess. The consumerism. The way people went about *Merry Christmas*ing people right and left. There was nothing merry about this particular season. Not for him.

"Use the old decorations," he said. "Clean them. Repaint them. Repair them. I don't care what you do with them," he said. "But I'm not spending money on new Christmas crap that I will have no future use for."

Chapter 8

Hale Chandler was a big man. Big in gesture. Big in voice. Big in body. He barely fit in the wing chair beside David's desk. His shoulders seemed too broad, his legs too long. He wore a rumpled blue suit and an equally wrinkled shirt. His tie was undone, his shoes needed resoling, and his hair was a little too long and graying at the temples.

It might be easy to dismiss the man with the red face and the extra fifteen pounds around his middle, but that would be a mistake. The spark in his brilliant blue eyes conveyed more than mere intelligence. The man played to win.

David's sister sat in the chair beside him. Compared to Hale, Heather looked dainty—a word David had never used to describe his sister before.

Both Hale and Heather were justifiably furious with him.

"It was the height of stupidity to pick a fight with the local elementary school," Hale said. "Yelling at teachers and pulling your kid out of public school isn't going to go over too well with voters."

"Not to mention the fact that Chief LaRue called Dad this morning. Apparently the principal was so ticked off by your out-of-control behavior that she was ready to send the chief of police to pick up Natalie as a truant. The chief wasn't about to do that without talking to Dad first, but still, David, really?" Heather gave him her you're-such-an-idiot look.

And he was an idiot. He knew better than to call any teacher stupid, especially when he'd supported the idiotic back-to-basics curriculum. He'd lost his temper and his perspective and mismanaged the situation. He knew better. But he couldn't shake the feeling that he'd done the right thing by stepping in and protecting Natalie.

"Look, I lost my cool, okay? But it's water over the dam. Let's move on. I have an appointment with St. Luke's at eleven. And until Natalie is enrolled there, I'm homeschooling her. The principal has no grounds for this power play." He glanced at the grandfather clock in the corner of his office. It was only nine. It felt as if this meeting had been going on for hours.

"You're putting your daughter in private school?" Hale asked, his bushy eyebrows lowering.

"It's the best school in Jefferson County. Both Heather and I attended school there through the eighth grade. I'm sure Mother will be overjoyed."

"Maybe so. But you yelled at those teachers, and now the whole town is buzzing about it."

"David," Hale said, leaning forward in his chair, "this

fracas you've had with Natalie's teachers has undoubtedly emboldened Bill Cummins, and that's unfortunate. If you face a primary challenge, we're going to have to raise more money. A lot more money."

"I suppose the good news is that you've gotten yourself on Jeff's good side by agreeing to host his wedding," Heather said in a breezy tone. "Given that the big New York party is off, we'll definitely need to hit him up for a major contribution. Maybe he'll make some calls to his rich New York friends for you. He ought to. I mean, he owes you a huge favor."

Having his sister give voice to his own thoughts did nothing to cheer David. He suddenly wished he'd agreed to host the wedding because it was the right thing to do, instead of justifying it by thinking about Jeff's money or Gracie Teague's influence with the business community. The deeper he got into the planning of this campaign, the more he had to sacrifice himself.

"Maybe we should get Jeff to endow a super PAC," Hale said, turning toward Heather. "Make a note and follow up on that, okay?"

Heather nodded.

David's heart sank.

"Now, David," Hale said, turning back toward David, "you need to apologize to the teachers at Natalie's school. And it wouldn't hurt if you sent a letter of apology to the Jefferson County Education Association and cc the Virginia Education Association. You don't want the major public school teachers' association endorsing Cummins, do you?"

The grandfather clock chimed the quarter hour, and David stomped on the sudden and irrational desire to scream at his campaign manager and chief political consultant. He also wanted to get up, walk across the room, and break the clock. Who needed a grandfather clock? It was big and noisy and required daily winding.

But Shelly had insisted that he needed one, and he'd allowed it. Now, every fifteen minutes the damn clock reminded him that his wife was dead.

He leaned back in his chair and counted to twenty while he took deep breaths. When he had calmed himself sufficiently, he said, "Do either of you even care why I was so upset with that school?"

"No," they answered in unison.

That answer was depressing. It reminded him of those summers when Dad had insisted that David campaign instead of going fishing. He'd hated every minute of Dad's state-wide senatorial campaigns. And that had been way before the Supreme Court had opened the door to vast quantities of super-PAC money.

The more Hale and Heather talked, the more David realized that being a congressman had more to do with endlessly begging people for money and appeasing interest groups like the Virginia Educational Association than it did actually representing the people of the twelfth district.

"I have a lot of respect for teachers," David said. "But Mrs. Welch was destroying Natalie's self-esteem. And it might come as a surprise to both of you, but I'm a parent first and a candidate second."

Heather leaned forward and put her hand on his desk. "Natalie will survive a few failed spelling tests. It's not the end of the world. You overreacted."

"She didn't misspell a single word. That woman gave

her Fs because she has trouble with cursive writing. Cursive? Why are we teaching that in Jefferson County?"

"Because the school board passed—"

"I know, I know. I remember. And I was an idiot to support that back-to-basics idea. It's no fun being hoist by my own petard," David said. "It's damn annoying."

Heather smiled. "Davie, Natalie is going to be okay. We can work on improving her handwriting."

Heather was right, and he'd totally lost his temper on Monday. If Shelly were still alive, she would have talked him down. She was so good at that.

He touched his wedding band, but it didn't make him feel any less annoyed or worried.

"Let's move on," Hale said. "Heather has the issue platform ready for your review, and we've got a list of people we think would be great for volunteer coordinator. We'll need to schedule interviews for later this week. We want to get our ground game up and running fast, just to discourage Cummins from thinking about a run."

Hale continued to speak, outlining an endless list of chores for David, while the clock ticked and chimed its way through two hours.

Willow spent Wednesday at Eagle Hill Manor interviewing potential contractors, none of whom could guarantee that they'd be able to finish Walter Braden's list of must-do repairs by December nineteenth.

Short of engaging in bribery—something Willow would not do—Walter was going to have to pare down his list, which was already the bare minimum needed to make the lobby and the dining room presentable for a wedding reception. The rest of the inn—the bedrooms, bathrooms, and kitchen—were not slated to be renovated in any way. Those would have to wait until a buyer came along.

Willow still aimed to be that buyer, but to truly find investors she needed to work out a detailed budget for renovations, marketing expenses, and first-year operating costs.

Shelly had kept copious notes on her plans for the inn. The last time Willow had seen her, she'd been lugging the notebook around with her. Willow had hoped the notebook had survived the train accident, but unfortunately Shelly's Louis Vuitton tote bag had been lost in the wreck. The NTSB or Amtrak had the bag, but that was like saying it had fallen down a big, black hole.

So in addition to asking the contractors for bids for the short-term work, she'd asked them all to come back with estimates on a much larger list of renovations, including the bathrooms, the kitchen, and restoring the Laurel Chapel.

With all of that going on, she was pretty stressed out when she walked into the Jaybird Café ready to beg another bacon cheeseburger from her sister. Wednesday was the slowest night of the week, so it wasn't too surprising to find Juni sitting at the nearly empty bar.

"Hey," Juni said as Willow snagged the empty seat beside her, "your aura is off."

"I'm not surprised. I've had a rough day." She flagged down Rory, the adorable Irish bartender, and ordered a Blue Moon and a burger.

"No, I'm not kidding. It's really off," Juni said.

Rory put a frosty pilsner glass in front of Willow,

garnished with an orange slice. She hoisted her glass. "Here's to having off-color auras. Who wants to be a conformist anyway?"

Juni smiled her toothy smile and threw her long, curly hair over her shoulder. Willow's sister was wearing an embroidered peasant shirt and a pair of jeans that hugged her curvy figure. The feather earrings were Mom's.

"I see you've been diving in Mom's jewelry box again," Willow said as she put her glass down on the bar.

"And you, dear sister, have an alarming note of red in your aura, and I'm thinking those Jimmy Choo boots you're wearing today probably explain that on several different levels."

Willow studied her ankle boots. "These aren't Jimmy Choos. They're replicas I bought online for half the price."

"Uh-huh, and that would be what? Three hundred dollars?"

"Yeah, I guess, but that's better than six hundred, right?"

Juni shook her head. "I could buy ten pairs of shoes at Payless for three hundred dollars."

"I know. And when I bought them, I had money to burn. But I have to be honest, Juni. I never thought that my shoe addiction would show up in my aura."

"Well, among other things, red is an indication of materialism."

Willow lifted her glass again. "That's me, the quintessential material girl."

"I don't think so." Juni shook her head. "I see a lot of turquoise in your aura. And blues are pretty rare, you know? But the red is something new."

"So are you trying to tell me that I should give my shoes to Goodwill and go help Mom shovel alpaca poop?"

"Well, I suppose a little alpaca poop might do you some good," Juni said, "but I don't think it would eliminate the red in your aura." She paused a moment, then changed the subject. "You certainly dressed to impress today."

Willow looked down at her white man-tailored shirt, jeans, and high-heeled boots. "This is not my dress-for-success outfit."

"I didn't say you had dressed for success. I said you'd dressed to impress. Someone has piqued your interest, my dear, sweet sister. The red notes in your aura are very strong. In addition to materialism, the red indicates that someone has sparked your sex drive."

Crap. Willow hated the way Juni and Mom pretended to be all tuned in to the greater wavelengths of the universe. It was all a load of BS. The two of them were off on a fishing expedition, trying to figure out if Willow had lost her perspective when it came to David Lyndon. Mom seemed especially worried about that turn of events.

But Willow had not lost her perspective. Just because the guy suddenly revved her engines didn't mean she was destined to go the distance with him. For goodness' sake, he was her best friend's husband. He still wore his wedding ring. He was grieving for his wife. He was her boss for the moment. How many reasons were there for keeping David at a distance?

The delivery of her cheeseburger garnished with a big pile of sweet potato fries put an end to the irksome conversation. She picked up the burger and took a big bite—a process that almost required her to unhinge her jaw.

So her mouth was completely full when David Lyndon

walked through the door with a savage look in his eyes. He gave the café a once-over, spotted Willow, and made a beeline in her direction. He took the empty stool on her right.

Willow snatched up her napkin and wiped the excess ketchup and mayonnaise from her mouth. As she continued to chew, Juni hopped down from the seat on her left. But before Willow's sister drifted away, she rested her hand on Willow's shoulder and leaned in to whisper, "Yup, you've definitely got red in your aura, and so does he."

There was a bottle of Maker's Mark in the bottom bureau drawer in David's bedroom. If he wanted to, he could drink alone. But tonight he wanted company. That's why he'd come here to the Jaybird Café—a place he'd never visited before because he wasn't a big fan of country music or sensitive singer-songwriters, which was what passed for entertainment here.

But he hadn't come looking for entertainment. He'd come looking for Willow.

Hell, he'd spent the afternoon watching Willow from his home office as she walked the grounds with one contractor after another. He should never have come home early today. But Natalie's boredom at the office had become disruptive. And then, when he'd gotten home, he'd discovered that Poppy had a lunch meeting scheduled with Faye and then a doctor's appointment, followed by a visit to the beauty shop. Poppy was used to Natalie being in school during the day. So he'd been stuck. At home.

With not much to do, since he sucked at playing dolls with his daughter.

Poppy had eventually returned from her errands and taken over the babysitting. But now David definitely needed a drink.

Willow gave him the cold shoulder as he took his seat, making a big show of eating a gigantic cheeseburger. He ordered a bourbon and then leaned toward her and murmured in the vicinity of her ear, "Turning your shoulder toward me won't make me go away."

She whipped her head around. "Why are you here?"

"I like to drink at tinsel-free bars. Every other watering hole in Shenandoah Falls has Christmas crap draped all over it. It's not even Thanksgiving yet."

"Maybe I should call you Ebenezer."

The bartender returned with his bourbon. David took a long, slow sip and put the glass gently down on the bar. "Bah humbug," he said.

"Careful. You know what happened to Scrooge."

"What's that supposed to mean?"

"He was reformed. If you keep going around town being grumpy about Christmas, you're likely to be visited by three waves of busybodies determined to redeem you, or at least make you their holiday project."

He took another sip of his drink and tried hard not to smile. "There are already people who want to make me their project."

"Really? Like who? I'd like their names, please, because I'm thinking about organizing a picket line to change your mind about the decorations for the inn."

The laugh couldn't be contained, as much as he wanted to continue scowling at her. God, he'd forgotten about her snarky sense of humor. He looked up from his drink right into her eyes. "Picket lines, huh? Well, I guess the apple didn't fall far from the tree, did it?" He said it to annoy her. He settled on his barstool and waited for the predictable outburst.

But it didn't come. What was up with that? Maturity? Self-knowledge? What the hell? This grown-up Willow was a lot more interesting than the teenager he'd once known.

"You're right," Willow said as she plucked a sweet potato fry from the pile on her plate, dredged it in ketchup, and ate it with a lot of lip puckering and a little flash of tongue. Watching her put that fry into her mouth drove him slightly crazy, and not because he was hungry. For food, at least.

When she finished chewing, she said, "I guess it is true. Mom and I are both troublemakers. And I've just decided to make trouble for you."

"Like you haven't already?"

Her green eyes widened with disingenuous innocence. "I haven't done any such thing. Near as I can see, I'm helping you. And I'm going to help you change your mind about the Christmas decorations."

"I'm going to lose this argument, aren't I?"

"Absolutely. I'm like the spirit of Christmas present. And it's my job to make you examine certain inconvenient truths." She pulled her iPhone out of her pocket and punched up the camera roll. "I took photos of the Christmas decorations that Mrs. M stored in the barn. Here, take a look," she said, passing the smartphone over. "See those little black dots everywhere? I wouldn't expect a refined senator's son like yourself to know what you're looking at, but I'm a farm girl and I know mouse poop when I see it. Rodents are a common problem in barns, which is why you should have a barn cat. Mom's got a few to spare if you're interested.

"But in the meantime, the pine roping is covered in rodent crap. And the mice have chewed most of the light strings. I guess Mrs. M was too tired last year to pack the stuff away in plastic containers like it should have been."

"We hired someone to do that stuff."

"Well, knowing you, Mr. Scrooge, you probably hired the lowest bidder, and that's always a mistake. Mice carry all kinds of nasty diseases, and I don't think we want to be responsible for starting a hantavirus epidemic right here in Shenandoah Falls. Oh, and by the way, mouse poop is not exactly a good way to attract prospective buyers."

"How did we get on this topic?"

"You said 'bah humbug,' and it pissed me off. Plus I spent all day at the inn walking around in various forms of rodent manure."

He made a great show of glancing down at the boots she was wearing. "And I see you dressed for it."

She didn't even glance at her high-heeled boots. Instead she bit her lower lip, just a little bit, as if maybe she was holding back another snarky comment.

After a long, uncomfortable moment, she tilted her head a little. "David, don't BS me. You didn't come here to escape Christmas. Did you come here to find me?"

He tore his gaze away and studied the ice in his now-empty glass. "I don't know why I came here." He took a long breath. "No, scratch that. I came here because I didn't want to drink alone." He looked up at her. She had her elbow on the bar and her chin in her hand.

"Why are you drinking?" she asked.

"It seemed like a better idea than screaming at my mother."

"Oh, well, join the club, then."

"What club is that?"

"It's the I-love-my-mother-but-I-want-to-kill-her-so-I'm-drinking-at-the-Jaybird club." Her smile widened, and he had the overwhelming desire to kiss away the dab of ketchup at the corner of her mouth and taste the woman at the same time.

"How many members are in this club?" he asked instead.

"Right now just you and me, but on a busy night, I could find a few more recruits, I'm sure."

"Probably got that right." He waggled his glass at the bartender for another drink. "So what does this club do, precisely?"

"We're like group therapy or AA. You can't be a member without spilling the beans on what brought you here. In my case, Mom is cooking fried tofu tonight. And I'm not a fan. That, plus she'll spend the entire evening asking my opinion about her campaign against Holy Cow, which is a franchise I actually like. She might even spend a few minutes telling me why it's a bad idea for me to work for you. That's been very high on her list recently. So that's my story. What's yours?"

"Your mother disapproves of me?" He found that notion more than merely interesting. His parents disapproved of Linda Petersen. How democratic to discover that the feeling was mutual.

"See?" Willow said, as she picked up another French fry. "It's not any fun to discover that you're disapproved of, is it?"

"No, I guess not. What particular thing is Linda upset about?"

"You'd have to ask her. And besides, all these questions are just a ploy on your part to avoid the topic at hand. I told you why I'm avoiding my mother. Now it's your turn."

"Because my mother is making me take Natalie back to Daniel Morgan Elementary tomorrow morning bright and early."

"She's making you?"

The bartender arrived with another round of drinks, and David took a long sip before he spoke again. "Well, not really, but Mother has helpfully reminded me that I didn't listen to her advice all those years ago when she told me it was a political mistake to run for the school board. Unfortunately, I was elected, and I made a pledge to send my kids to public school."

"Let me guess. You made this pledge before you had kids?"

He nodded.

"Ah, so your mother rubbed your nose in your own stupidity. Moms are so good at doing that."

"She wasn't alone. My campaign manager and political consultant pointed out the same thing. And they are making me issue a public apology not only to Mrs. Welch but to the Virginia Education Association."

"What did Mrs. Welch do? In my case, she failed me on every spelling test for a solid year because I have crappy handwriting. Thank God no one teaches cursive writing anymore."

He laughed, and something deep in his gut eased. When was the last time he'd laughed like this? "You are misinformed, Willow. It turns out that we teach cursive right here in Jefferson County."

"No, you don't. Really?"

"It's part of a back-to-basics movement that I stupidly supported when I was on the school board. Just about everyone has reminded me of that."

"Oops."

"Yeah, oops. And furthermore, Mother has pointed out that there are other children in that school who are also left-handed or otherwise cursive-challenged who don't have the option of taking their kid out of school over a dumb thing like a spelling test."

"That's true."

He sipped his drink, feeling a weight lifting from his shoulder. Not because of the booze, but because Willow was good at listening. He'd forgotten about that. She'd always been a good listener. For him. For Dusty. For Shelly.

"So I'm more or less screwed," he said, feeling oddly unconcerned.

"Only if you care what people think about you. You could escalate things further, like my mother did, by picketing the school and making a nuisance of yourself until the principal moves Natalie to the other third-grade class."

"You mean your mother actually won the fight?"

She nodded. "To be honest, while Mom's tactics were *eventually* effective, I sometimes think the principal stepped in because she was worried about me. So, for Natalie's sake, I wouldn't recommend that approach."

"What would you recommend?"

"Well, you could probably get Mrs. Welch fired, or at least force her to take early retirement. She's the only teacher who has this thing about handwriting. Everyone else grades spelling and handwriting separately."

"My political consultant already pointed out that I would become an enemy of public school teachers everywhere if I did that. I want to get the endorsement of the VEA."

"Okay, so maybe you could find out if there are other children who are having the same problem. And maybe you could organize the parents and schedule a group meeting with the teacher. Maybe you could suggest that the teacher grade spelling as spelling and handwriting as handwriting. You know, it's not a bad thing to teach kids cursive writing, even in this day and age. But Mrs. Welch always paid way too much attention to that subject."

He didn't know whether to laugh or say a prayer to the Almighty who had guided him here to this place and this woman in his hour of need. A part of him—not just the parent and the candidate—wanted to stand up and give Willow Petersen a hug. But he didn't dare do that. A friendly hug would turn carnal in a nanosecond.

He'd stopped thinking about her as Shelly's friend.

"That's a brilliant suggestion. Why didn't your mother think of it?" he asked.

"Because my mother never compromises. It's her way or the highway."

"Mine too."

"But it doesn't have to be that way. I mean, in business school we learned all about the power of collaborative thinking and mediation and all that stuff. We put that kind of thinking in place at Restero—" She stopped speaking and looked away, her jawline tensing.

"But when the shit hit the fan, you didn't compromise, did you?"

"You can't compromise when it comes to people's health." She snapped the words, sounding a lot like her uncompromising mother. She got down from her barstool. "I've had more beer than I should have. I think I need to go now." She turned away and headed toward the door.

"No, wait," he said, getting up and grabbing her by the arm, exactly as he'd done the other day at the diner. And just like then, desire flowed up his fingers and right into his core like a stream rushing uphill. He let go before he did something stupid.

"Let's not talk about Restero, okay? Come on, you don't have to run."

She turned, her shoulders tense. "Even if we don't talk about it, it's like the three-hundred-pound gorilla in the room. And it always will be."

"Okay. But thanks for the suggestion on how to deal with Mrs. Welch."

She nodded. "It's just a compromise, David. I know that's become a dirty word back there in Washington these days. But compromise is always the way to solve problems. You could solve Natalie's problem. And even better, you could help other kids who have trouble with their handwriting too." She turned and started toward the door.

"Hey, Willow," he said to her back. She stopped and looked over her shoulder.

"About the Christmas decorations," he said, "get whatever you, Poppy, and Melissa want. I have issues with the holiday, but I guess it's a waste of time to try to impose them on the rest of the world. Maybe I need to compromise with Christmas, too, huh?"

She turned back toward him, her eyes going kind of liquid. But she smiled through the unshed tears and said, "David, I'm so sorry for your loss. I know the anniversary of the accident is coming up—the day before Melissa's wedding. I haven't forgotten. Shelly was my best friend. I was closer to her than I am to my sister. So if you ever need a drinking buddy or want to convene a meeting of the club, you know where to find me."

Then Willow Petersen did the unthinkable. Instead of turning her back on him, she took a step forward and kissed his cheek. It wasn't intended as a come-on, but the touch of her lips seared his skin and left him struggling to breathe. It took all of his willpower not to grab her by the shoulders and turn that little, friendly kiss into so much more.

With so much to do before December nineteenth, including finding and managing contractors, ordering holiday decorations, and arranging the catering, flowers, invitations, and dresses, Willow decided that it would be best if she spent her working hours at Eagle Hill Manor instead of trying to manage things from Serenity Farm. So on Thursday morning she arrived at nine o'clock and set up a card table in the library to serve as her desk.

Her plan to rely on Courtney Wallace for a lot of the wedding details was starting to backfire. Courtney had sent her no less than fifty e-mails over the last week, each of them containing more than one idea for Melissa's wedding. Courtney now had no fewer than forty-eight pictures of Christmas centerpieces on her Pinterest board, and she wanted to discuss the merits of every damn one of them. The woman would. Not. Stop.

If she allowed Courtney to distract her, she'd get nothing done. And there were two big priorities for today: finding a painting contractor who could take care of the peeling paint on the front facade and nailing down the bridesmaid and flower girl dresses.

She spent hours on her cell phone trying to accomplish these tasks, and by early afternoon, she'd made little or no progress. Every painter in Jefferson, Clarke, Frederick, and Loudon Counties was booked through the holidays.

And who knew that bridesmaid dresses took up to eight weeks to order? Courtney and Melissa were going to have to pare down their choices to nondesigner, ready-to-wear dresses. She was deep in conversation with a wedding dress consultant from Kleinfeld of New York when Natalie arrived home from school and came bounding into the room.

The little girl had come to play with her American Girl doll, which sat in a doll-size rocking chair in the corner, surrounded by her clothes and accessories. The moment Natalie arrived, Willow lost interest in her conversation with arguably the best-known wedding dress retailer in America.

And in any case, Kleinfeld didn't have what Willow was looking for, even though they had tried to do backflips for her the minute she'd dropped Jefferson Talbert-Lyndon's name.

She ended her call, turned off her phone, and stretched

her back. She had an obscene amount of work to do, but she wasn't going to pass up this opportunity to get to know Natalie better.

"Hi," Willow said. "I really like your doll. Does she have a name?"

"Angelina."

"She looks like you."

Natalie didn't reply. Instead she looked away, conveying her shyness and making Willow feel like a dolt. Where should she start? She didn't know anything about kids or their interests. Maybe it didn't matter as long as she made an effort, which was more than she'd done in the past.

"So, did Mrs. M tell you that you're going to be a flower girl in your cousin's wedding?" Willow asked.

"Mrs. M?"

Willow cringed. Of course Natalie didn't know Poppy by that name. "Grammy," Willow corrected herself.

Natalie nodded but didn't make eye contact.

"I've been searching for bridesmaid and flower girl dresses all day. Yours is the only one I've managed to buy. You want to see it?"

"Not really." Natalie picked up her doll and had started to stuff various accessories into a pink tote.

"Going somewhere?" Willow asked.

Natalie continued to look away.

"I guess I've disturbed you, huh? I'm sorry. Mrs. M— Grammy—told me to set up my table here. I could move to the lobby if you want."

"No, it's okay." Natalie stood up, carrying the pink bag that was almost as big as she was. She didn't look in Willow's direction, choosing instead to stare down at her shoes. Willow wanted to give the kid a hug, but Natalie wasn't ready for that.

"You sure you don't want to see your dress? It's pretty."

"I hate red dresses." Natalie finally met Willow's gaze, and the fire in her dark brown eyes was impressive.

"Oh, honey, of course you do. I wouldn't put you in a red dress. What made you think I would?"

"You were just talking to someone about red dresses. Grandmother is always putting me in red dresses, and I hate them."

Willow opened her arms. "Come here just for a minute and I'll show you the dress I got for you. It's green. And I think we'll put baby's breath and green plaid ribbons in your beautiful hair. You'll look like a little ginger princess."

"You think my hair is pretty?"

"Of course I do. It's just like your mom's and just like Angelina's." Willow's heart swelled. "Did your mommy help you name your doll?"

Natalie nodded. "How did you know?"

"Because she had a doll with that name once a long time ago. We played with her Barbie dolls all the time. Your mom and me. You sure you don't want to see your dress?"

Natalie stood there for a long moment while she evidently weighed her choices. After almost thirty seconds, she finally moved to Willow's side and inclined her head toward the computer screen, where Willow had brought up an image of the dress.

Natalie's eyes grew wide. "It looks like Little Red Riding Hood only green."

"I know. Melissa loves fairytales. And all her friends thought it would be fabulous to dress you like Little Red Riding Hood, only in green because of your red hair. I'm trying to find a hooded cloak just like yours in white for Melissa. It hasn't been easy, though."

"I really like that dress."

"I'm really glad you do, sweetheart. So, I know you're planning to go someplace else to play, but I was just about to take a break. I'm going for a walk. Want to come with me?"

Finally a smile. "You know about the secret place, don't you? You helped Daddy find it."

Willow nodded. "I used to go out to Laurel Chapel with your mom all the time. We used to play a game called Pretend Princess. Do you know that game?"

Natalie shook her head.

"No? Well, one of us gets to be the princess and the other gets to be the prince. The prince has to slay a dragon, rescue the princess from the stony tower, and awaken her with true love's kiss."

"That sounds fun. Can I be the prince?"

"Of course you can." Willow was surprised. And then it occurred to her that in all her years playing that game with Shelly, Willow had never, ever gotten the chance to be the princess.

"C'mon, let's go." Natalie put down her doll and grabbed Willow's hand. The next thing Willow knew, an eight-year-old was dragging her from the library and her Herculean task.

And she wasn't in the least concerned.

Chapter 9————————————————

David hadn't been to church in a long time. He sent Natalie off to Grace Presbyterian Sunday school with Poppy, but he was too angry to visit God's house. Instead, on Sundays when the weather was good, he rose at dawn and headed off to Liberty Forge—the derelict foundry located on Morgan Avenue on the south side of town.

A hundred and fifty years ago, Liberty Forge had been the manufacturer of cast-iron "Liberty Stoves," making the McNeil family, who had owned the ironworks, one of the wealthiest families in Jefferson County. But cast-iron stoves had gone out of style, and the forge had closed more than eighty years ago. Now the crumbling brick building with its chain-link fence, no-trespassing signs, and heavily padlocked gate was the biggest eyesore in town.

On this particular Sunday, David parked his car on Morgan Avenue, grabbed his fishing gear from the trunk, and unlocked the padlock. Once through the gate, he strolled around the building to a set of concrete steps that led down to a weedy open area behind the forge. He took the dirt path that cut across this field, passing the ruins of a much older blacksmith's forge that dated back to the 1700s. The path eventually led through a stand of oaks and into a large expanse of meadowland that provided access to the spring-fed stream called Liberty Run.

This land was owned by David's friend and fishing buddy Dusty McNeil, the sole heir of the family who had built both the eighteenth- and nineteenth-century forges. Dusty let his friends fish this section of stream, and David was honored to be one of them, with a key to the padlock on the front gate.

It was a sunny, seasonally cool day, perfect for worshipping nature by casting a line. David strolled along the run's banks to his favorite spot, put on his waders, and settled into the snapping motion of his casts and the graceful fall of the leader as it laid his fly on the run's riffled surface. The bubble and rush of the creek crowded out conscious thought, along with his sorrows, worries, and all his disappointments.

David enjoyed this solitude for more than half an hour before Dusty disturbed it. "Hey," Dusty called from the stream's bank.

The real world returned with an unpleasant rush as David looked over his shoulder. Dusty stood with his hands thrust into the pockets of his gray fishing pants, a frown on his normally happy face. Dusty had a day job as a nursery foreman, but he was also one of the best fishing guides in Jefferson County. He knew the location of every good fishing spot on the Potomac and Shenandoah Rivers and could tell you what kind of fly to use in any possible situation.

David fished with him often, and it was a known fact that you could spend a whole day with Dusty and not have to worry about any conversations lasting more than two minutes. But not today, apparently. Today Dusty squinted at David from underneath the wide brim of his fishing hat and said, "I was hoping to find you out here. I need to talk to you about something important."

"What's up?" David asked.

"I need the advice of a lawyer."

Crap.

David reeled in his line and waded to shore. "What's the matter?"

Dusty unzipped one of his pants pockets and pulled out an envelope marked with a certified mail sticker. His hands trembled as he passed the letter to David. "I got this letter on Friday. Can the County Council do this to me?"

David pulled a sheet of Jefferson County Council stationery from the envelope and several other documents that appeared to be real estate plats. The main document was a notice from the Jefferson County Council of its intention to hold a hearing on December eighth to accept public comment on a plan to develop the historic site known as Liberty Forge into a county park. The plan, according to the document, included demolishing the old foundry building and restoring the eighteenth-century forge in order to turn it into a historic interpretative site that would be managed by the Jefferson County Historical Society. The county also wanted to take all the land surrounding the forge in order to turn it into a day-use park with picnic tables, athletic fields, and public fishing access.

"Can they?" Dusty's voice cracked with emotion. "I'm not opposed to a new park, David, but you know I've had plans for this land for years. They can't take my land, can they?"

The breadth of the county's intentions was nothing short of stunning. They wanted Dusty's fishing access, his land, and his personal heritage all in one fell swoop. It was akin to the county deciding to make Charlotte's Grove one of those publicly open plantation houses like Mount Vernon or Montpelier or Monticello.

When had the county hatched this plan, and why hadn't David or Dusty heard anything about it before this? Something wasn't right. Was Bill Cummins pushing this thing now because he knew Dusty was David's friend?

It wasn't all that far-fetched a notion. People would flock to this idea like cats to catnip. And any local politician lining up against a park was likely to be unpopular. "I'm afraid the county has the authority to take anyone's land if they plan to use it for the public good," he said.

"You're kidding me."

"No, I'm afraid not."

Dusty turned, took a few steps, then slapped his hat against his thigh. A long stream of linked-together expletives followed.

When Dusty had finished venting, David spoke again. "Look, this is far from a done deal. There are a bunch of hoops the county has to jump through. For a start, they have to hold this public hearing. Unfortunately, a lot of people are probably going to say that tearing down the warehouse is a great idea. But—"

"You know I plan to take that building down. I just need to build a little more capital."

"I know, Dusty. But the county's got the jump on you now. Of course they'll have to appropriate funds, and God knows where they're going to get the money. When I was on the council, we didn't have enough money to manage the parks that were already in the system."

"Yeah, but with this hanging over my head, no one will invest in my plan. I'm dead. The county has destroyed me."

"Dusty, calm down. It might be nothing. And besides, the Fifth Amendment of the Constitution protects you. The county will have to pay you for the land."

Dusty pivoted and gave David an angry glance. "Really? I always thought the Fifth Amendment was the one that crooked politicians hid behind."

"Well, that too. But it's also there to protect private landowners from the government unjustly taking their property."

"You call that protection?" He pointed at the letter.

"Well, it's public notice, which is more than a lot of people get."

"Can you help me stop this?"

David didn't want to answer that question. Heather and Hale would tell him to stay the hell away from this controversy. But how could he?

Before he could say another word, a familiar female voice called out, "Dusty McNeil, your momma is so old her birth certificate says expired."

He and Dusty turned toward the wooded area to the

southwest where Willow Petersen, wearing an ancient floppy hat and carrying an even older bamboo rod and fishing creel, waved.

Willow had obviously come up from the Appalachian Trail, where there were no fences, just a bunch of faded no-trespassing signs that she had obviously ignored. From Serenity Farm, the walk was close to five miles. If she picked up the trail on Route 7, it was about a mile and a half. David knew part of that route well. As a boy, he'd walked two miles down the trail from Charlotte's Grove every time he came here to fish with his friends.

Dusty let out a hoot. "Willow Petersen," he hollered, "I heard you were back in town." The worried expression left Dusty's face. He jogged through the meadow grass toward Willow. When they met, Dusty picked her up, swung her around, and gave her a kiss.

It wasn't a super-erotic kiss or anything like that, just a friendly peck on the lips—not much more than the kiss she'd given David on Wednesday. The kiss that he'd revisited many times over the last several days.

There had been nothing but friendship in Willow's kiss. They had been talking about Shelly. They'd been sharing their grief.

So why couldn't he get that kiss out of his head?

And why did he suddenly resent the fact that she'd kissed Dusty?

Dusty and Willow had always been tight—so tight that David had often wondered if Dusty's inability to settle down with one woman had something to do with Willow. Well, she was back in town now. So maybe the two of them would finally hook up.

He hated the idea. A slow resentment boiled in his gut as he watched Dusty and Willow walk with arms linked and heads together.

"You beat me to the stream," Willow said with a grin as she and Dusty approached. "Don't you go to church anymore?"

"Not so much," David said.

"Guess I'll have to get up earlier, then. I never let you beat me to the stream when we were kids."

"No, you didn't."

"It's a glorious day, especially for November." She tilted her head back, closed her eyes, and faced the sun. Her old hat fell to the ground, and the sun lit up her hair with gold. The tomboy had grown into a graceful, poised woman. She wasn't the same girl he'd once known. There were so many new and interesting facets to her.

She retrieved her hat and plopped the old thing on her head. In that instant, the girl she'd been melded with the woman she'd become. And something deep in David's chest hitched.

She winked at Dusty. "I hope I can still fish here. I ignored your no-trespassing signs. Those are new."

He shrugged. "Yeah. Probably a dumb idea. I was trying to discourage some of the kids who've decided it's easier to splash around in the run down here than to take the hike up to the falls. They leave beer cans and crap all over the place. I'll bet some fisherman got their panties in a wad, and that explains the trouble I'm in."

"What trouble?" Willow asked.

Dusty took the letter from David's hands and showed it to Willow. She read it, a frown folding her forehead. She looked up, her green eyes bright with ire. "Oh my

God," she said in a tone laced with outrage. "We can't let this happen. We need to organize a protest or something."

The fire in Willow's eyes and voice ignited the dry, dead debris that was David's libido. It flamed to life. And like one of those Liberty Stoves that Dusty's ancestors had once built, it warmed him down to his toes.

He wanted her naked right there on the grass. He wanted to run his fingers through her incredible hair. He wanted to cup her breasts.

He wanted her. And wanting her was completely unacceptable.

"What do you think?" Dusty asked David. "You know the council. If we organized some kind of big protest, could we change their minds?"

David took a deep breath and tried to jettison all of the forbidden ideas and images that had just sprung to life in his mind. "Look, I don't know," he said. "Let me call some of the county councilors and see where this is really heading. If the county doesn't have the money for this plan, then it's not going to happen."

Willow gave him an appraising look that almost turned him inside out. She didn't say one word. Instead she turned back toward Dusty and gave him a warm smile that David didn't like. Not one bit. The idea of Willow and Dusty hooking up seriously upset him.

Wow. Not good.

He touched his wedding band, and it reminded him that he'd loved Shelly with all his heart.

"I don't know if a protest will change their minds," Willow said, pulling David back from the brink. "You know how people can be in this town. But Mom would tell you that silence is your worst enemy. God knows I've heard her say that about every issue she's ever protested. Even Holy Cow."

Dusty laughed. "I never, ever thought I'd hear you quote your mom. Isn't she the one who's so old she rode dinosaurs to school?"

"Yeah, and your momma was so dumb she thought a quarterback was a refund."

Dusty laughed and gave her another irritatingly warm hug. "I'm sure glad you're home," Dusty said with that wide smile that the single women of Jefferson County found so irresistible. And apparently Willow wasn't at all immune.

Dusty McNeil had always been easy—easy on the eye, easy to like, easy to be with. Not that Willow had ever entertained any sexual fantasies about him, because Dusty was a buddy—a stand-in for the brother she'd always wanted but never had, sort of like Shelly had been her sister from another mother.

Dusty was as much an orphan child as Willow, so they understood each other. Growing up, they had constantly swapped "your mother" jokes, but the truth of it was that Dusty had never known his mother, and his old man had been a mean, nasty drunk.

With Willow's father MIA and her mother the subject of endless local gossip, it was natural for them to form a bond. They were the outcast kids who'd created their own special place together in each other's company. They had been fishing buddies for years before David Lyndon strolled down from the hill the summer they'd all turned sixteen.

And now here they were again, the three of them, all grown up, fishing three separate pools along the run. For Willow, the day might have turned peaceful and even spiritual were it not for the fact that every time she looked up to admire the scenery or the beauty of Dusty's cast, she found David watching her.

Willow didn't for one minute believe any of the crap Juni dished out about auras, but there was no mistaking the fact that something had changed in the way David looked at her.

And something had changed in the way she reacted to those looks.

There hadn't been one thing remotely carnal about the kiss she'd given David at the Jaybird the other day. And yet her lips remembered the texture of his stubble. Her tongue remembered the taste of his skin. That one, innocent kiss had been enough to turn Willow slightly adolescent when it came to David Lyndon.

But she wasn't an adolescent. She was a grown-up. And she was smart enough to know that his attention and her reaction were something to avoid.

He was a Lyndon; she was a Petersen. That pretty much summed up the problem.

There was also the fact that she'd come off a relationship with a well-known CEO who had shattered her trust on so many levels. She needed time to process that. Jumping into bed with a man who was equally well-known and equally entitled would be just plain stupid.

Finally, of course, was the fact that David was Shelly's husband. Shelly might be gone, but that didn't mean a thing. David was still grieving for her, still wearing the ring she'd put on his finger. He almost never stopped touching it with his thumb.

There was no place for Willow in that duet, and she wasn't interested in being part of a love triangle that included a ghost.

A few days later, Willow found herself sitting at the small butcher-block table in the kitchen at Serenity Farm. It was the third night in a row that Willow had dined with Mom so, naturally, Linda had jumped to the conclusion that Willow was trying to cleanse her body of all those toxins she'd been consuming along with her red meat.

In reality, Willow was eating at home every night so as not to run into David at the diner or the Jaybird or any other place. In fact, although she worked daily at Eagle Hill Manor, she'd taken to carefully timing her arrivals and departures in order to avoid him. After fishing with him on Sunday, she no longer trusted herself around him.

Mom plunked down a plate filled with baked squash with apples and quinoa, seated herself across the table, and said, "So I heard David Lyndon staged a protest at Daniel Morgan Elementary yesterday."

And, right on cue, the minute Mom said David's name, Willow's body sparked in a totally adolescent manner. She needed to nip this silly thing in the bud. Right now.

She looked up from her plate of quinoa. "What kind of protest?"

"Well, from what Pippa Custis told me this morning, he called every single parent in Natalie's class to find out if that old witch Mrs. Welch been giving their kids a hard time about penmanship."

Warmth pooled in Willow's midsection. "Really?"

"That's what I heard. Pippa knows because her granddaughter, Ilene, is in that class. Ilene has beautiful handwriting, but I gather there are other kids who don't—mostly the lefties, and I guess Natalie is one of them. Pippa said David organized a meeting with the principal, and every one of those parents came down to demand a change."

Good God. David had taken her suggestion.

Right then Willow knew that something fundamental had changed in the way she thought about David. Something that had the potential not only to ruin her relationship with Shelly's husband, but also her growing attachment to Shelly's daughter.

A couple days of playing princess and American Girl with Natalie, and Willow was completely and utterly smitten. Why had she stayed away so long? She'd missed so much of Natalie's childhood. But she was here now. And she had no intention of ever straying again. She had a responsibility to Natalie, and she couldn't allow something stupid, like her libido, to mess it up.

"Eat," Mom commanded, giving her a sharp look.

Willow picked up a forkful of the unappetizing meal and managed to choke it down. The texture was disgusting, and the whole sweet-and-sour thing didn't excite her taste buds.

"I gather the new principal is way smarter than that old bat I tussled with for years," Mom continued. "Pippa told me that Mrs. Welch was told—not asked—to start grading spelling and handwriting separately."

"Good for David Lyndon."

"Well, the way I see it, the principal had to make a change. I mean, it was a Lyndon asking for it, you know?"

Yeah, she knew. Willow let go of a long sigh.

"That sigh sounded mournful. What's on your mind, baby girl?"

Time to change the subject. "Nothing much," Willow said, "except finding a painting contractor for Eagle Hill. I've got everything else figured out. I hired Dusty's landscaping company to do the outside cleanup. And Dusty has a few friends who are plumbing and electrical contractors who were willing to squeeze our work in before the wedding. I'm sure he bribed them with access to his fishing hole, but I'm looking the other way on that. To tell you the truth, I'm ready to bribe one of the half dozen painting contractors I've interviewed who've told me they are scheduled right through Christmas. Who paints their house in December, anyway?"

"Why do you need a painter?"

"Because the paint on the front facade is all cracked and peeling, and the inside really needs a sprucing up."

"Okay, so? You don't need to hire a painter for that."

"Well, I'm not going to paint it myself. It's a huge building, and I'm afraid of ladders," Willow said.

"I wasn't suggesting that you paint it yourself. I was suggesting that you round up a bunch of volunteers—like Jeff and Melissa's friends. You could have a paint-in."

Willow nearly choked on the second bite of baked squash.

"It would be fun," Mom continued. "You know, like one of those HGTV shows where they redo someone's house in two days with the help of their friends and family."

"Okay, maybe. I'll think about it." Willow chugged down several swallows of water.

"So," Mom said, "has Dusty learned anything more about this historical park idea?"

"Not much. He told me that David made a few phone calls for him and discovered that the county doesn't have the funds to buy Dusty out or convert the land to parkland. But if they ever do get the money, they could force him off his land."

"We should organize a protest."

"I told David and Dusty the same thing last Sunday, but David said protesting wouldn't help."

Mom gave Willow one of her sharp, political looks. "Of course he said that. He's running for Congress, and I'll bet Commissioner Cummins is going to come out with flags flying in support of the park proposal. David probably doesn't want to hurt Dusty's feelings, you know? But he's going to have to support it too."

"You think?"

"Of course he is. And it stands to reason he doesn't want us kicking up any kind of fuss. But, you know, a fuss would sure make it harder for the county to move forward. Nobody ever got justice by staying quiet."

"But making noise doesn't guarantee justice either. I mean, look at me. I haven't gotten justice for all those patients who got defective hip replacements."

Mom reached across the table and captured one of Willow's hands. "But you will get them justice. One day. And as far as this park proposal goes, baby doll, Dusty is your friend, and while a park is nice, we need to give him some support."

Willow nodded. "Okay, Mom. Let me talk to Dusty

and see what he thinks. In the meantime, I've thought about your idea of a paint-in. I think we should do it, before it gets too cold. Would you help me organize it?"

Mom grinned. "I happen to be killer with a bucket of paint."

"I know. That's why I asked."

The Red Fern Inn was two hundred years old and boasted a room where George Washington had supposedly once slept. As far as Poppy Marchand was concerned, the historical evidence for this claim was slim at best.

On the other hand, Poppy had many photographs of Winston Churchill hunting with William Archer McAllister, the original owner and builder of Eagle Hill Manor. There was no doubt that Churchill had slept at Poppy's inn. So had dozens of congressmen, senators, a governor or two, and numerous statesmen. The photographic evidence lined the upstairs hallways.

So it was a trifle annoying to find herself sitting in the Red Fern's dining room with Faye and Viola. When Craig had been alive, she'd been forbidden to set foot in the tiny inn owned and operated by Bryce Summerville. She still felt like a traitor every time Faye Appleby invited her to lunch here.

Poppy would rather have eaten at the Olive Garden down at the highway interchange, but Faye would never stand for that. Neither would Viola.

"So I have news," Faye said, hoisting her wineglass. "Arwen has confirmed that Roxanne Kopp was at Jamie Lyndon's birthday party. She got the news from one of her friends who works up at the winery. Apparently she was all over David like a cheap suit."

"Not cheap," Viola said, "more like a designer suit. I've done some research on her, and her father is loaded. He's the Kopp in Lyndon, Lyndon, and Kopp, and runs the firm from his DC office. Here, I found a photo of her on social media." Viola fired up her iPhone and angled it so both Faye and Poppy could see.

Poppy studied the photo and concluded that Roxanne Kopp was precisely the sort of woman one might expect a man like David to marry. Beautiful and with an impressive pedigree. Shelly would have hated this woman on sight.

"She's quite beautiful," Poppy said.

"Well, if she has Pam Lyndon's approval, that immediately disqualifies her," Viola said. "Pam is a terrible matchmaker. Everyone knows this. She's the one who matched Nina up with Jeff's father. And that marriage lasted less than two years."

"You're absolutely right." Faye nodded. "So, let's not get discouraged by this Roxy woman. Instead I think we should focus on the qualities we'd like to see in David's next wife, besides the fact that she has to like Poppy, of course."

"Good idea," Viola said, looking Poppy in the eye. "What kind of woman do you think we should be looking for?"

"I have no clue," Poppy said.

"Oh, come on, you must have some idea. I know this is hard, but it's important for you and for Natalie. And for David, of course." Faye reached across the table and gave Poppy's hand a squeeze. "We all miss Shelly."

Poppy nodded. "And as near as I can tell, that's the main problem. Pam may be trying to push this Roxanne woman at David, but I'm not entirely sure he's ready to have anyone pushed at him. He still wears his wedding ring, and he's become a hermit. He doesn't go to church. He doesn't go out. He just works and goes fishing whenever he can, and sometimes he drinks alone in his room. I'm quite worried about him. I don't think he's sleeping well."

"Not the epitome of husband material, is he?" Faye said.

"No, I'm afraid not. Ladies, I think this is going to be much harder than we think. And I'm still worried about the morality of what we're planning. I don't really believe in manipulating people."

"We're not manipulating anyone. We're matchmaking. There's a big difference," Viola said with a grin.

"Hmmm, same thing in my book," Poppy replied as she pushed her lettuce around her plate. The salad dressing had too much vinegar. The food at the Red Fern had never matched the quality of the food Antonin had prepared at Eagle Hill.

"Well, since we aren't sure what kind of woman David might be interested in, maybe we should think about women with strong maternal qualities. After all, this is as much about Natalie as it is David," Viola said, pulling a small notebook from her purse and handing it to Poppy. "Now, I've made a list of women who have a reputation for being kind and generous and connected to the community. You tell me which of these women we should focus our attentions on."

Poppy scanned the list of names. "Don't you think

Joanne Ackerman is a little old for him? She must be forty if she's a day."

"I know," Viola said on a sigh. "But she's a stalwart member of the St. Luke's Ladies Auxiliary, and she has such impeccable taste. I think she'd make an excellent congressman's wife and a wonderful mother. Plus she would decorate David's new house to the nines. I've always wanted to hire her to redo my living room."

Poppy shook her head. "No. Scratch her off the list. And Alicia Mulloy is way too young for him. She couldn't be more than twenty-five."

"So?" her friends asked in unison.

She supposed they had a point. Men like David were always marrying much younger second wives, and Alicia was active in the Girl Scouts.

Poppy stared at the list. Courtney Wallace's name was there, which made sense since she was a nurse practitioner at Dr. Page's office and a really sweet woman of David's age. Faye's niece, Arwen, was on the list, too, but that was probably because Viola didn't want to hurt Faye's feelings.

The list was comprehensive, but still, one name was absent.

"I don't like this list," Poppy said, handing it back to Viola. She laid her fork across her salad plate.

"Poppy," Faye said, "we thought you had come around to thinking this was a good idea, but if you don't—"

"No, it's not that. It's just that I have a candidate, but it's a complicated situation."

"Who?" they asked in unison.

"Willow Petersen." Poppy said the name and watched as both of her friends displayed the expected disapproving facial reactions.

"Now, ladies, before you object, let me explain my reasons."

"I'm dying to hear them," Faye said.

"Well, for starters she was Shelly's best friend, and I can't help but feel that Shelly would approve of her. After all, Shelly named Willow as Natalie's godmother. Even more important, over the last few days, Willow and Natalie have spent a lot of time together. Last Friday I walked into the library, and the two of them were down on the floor playing dolls together. Natalie was giggling.

"Have you any idea how long it's been since that child giggled about something?" Poppy's voice wavered, and she had to blot her eyes with her napkin.

"We didn't know," Faye said.

"I know. That's why I just told you. Look, ladies, I watched Willow grow up. She was always underfoot, hanging around with Shelly. To be honest, I mothered her some because I always felt she needed it. It can't have been easy being Linda Petersen's daughter. And now, here she is, lavishing attention on Natalie. I agree that she stayed away too long, but it seems to me she's making up for that."

"Well," said Faye, "it's a bold move, I'll give you that. But are you sure they fit? I mean, Willow and David have Shelly in common. They've been friends a long time. Do you think they could become, you know, lovers?"

"I don't know," Poppy said, although she suspected that David and Willow had started to notice each other in that way.

"We need to throw them together and find out what happens. Maybe you could ask Willow to babysit Natalie. Maybe on bridge nights. That way David and Willow and

Natalie would all be together. Alone." Faye drew out the last word into something quite suggestive.

"That's not going to work. David watches Natalie on bridge nights. And if he's not available, I send her off to Charlotte's Grove for an overnight with her other grandmother."

"Hmm. Well, maybe you could spring it on him or something. Like a surprise," Viola said.

"No, wait, I have an idea. You're having that paint party on Saturday, aren't you?" Faye said.

Poppy nodded. "Yes, Willow and her mother organized it. God help us, I hate to think about all those amateurs dribbling paint all over my wood floors." Poppy picked up her wine and took a healthy swig.

"Well, paint can always be cleaned up, Poppy," Faye said. "But I'm thinking we need to make sure that David doesn't go off fishing on Saturday. Maybe you can tell him that you're worried about the mess or something and insist that he stay and oversee the madness. And then we can spend the entire day making sure that Willow and David spend time together."

"That's a good idea," Viola said. "We can reassess our plans after the painting party. Because if there aren't any sparks between them, then there aren't any sparks. We want Natalie to have a wonderful mother, but she has to be a mother her daddy loves and desires."

Poppy glanced from Faye to Viola and back again. "I don't know about this," she said. "It seems so, I don't know, dishonest or something."

"Maybe," Faye said, "but remember we're doing this in the name of love."

Chapter 10————————————

The weather gods cooperated on the Saturday before Thanksgiving by providing a perfect, sixty-degree, Indian-summer day for the Eagle Hill Manor paint-in. Thirty-two volunteer painters—friends of the bride and groom, members of Mrs. M's bridge club and church group, and a few of Mom's protester friends—were expected.

Willow had stocked two dozen paint rollers, an equal number of trim brushes, and gallons of paint in fabulous colors: Flirt Alert red for the lobby, French Parsley green for the dining room, Smooth Silk ivory for the first-floor restrooms, and Cotton Blossom white for the front facade and all the inside trim.

Over the last two days, thanks in large measure to the members of Mrs. M's bridge club, the floors had been covered with plastic drop cloths, the walls had been prepped and spackled, and the worst of the peeling paint from the inn's grand portico had been scraped away. Walter Braden himself had promised to get up the tallest ladder and scrape and paint the dental trim around the portico's eaves.

Willow arrived at Eagle Hill Manor at oh dark thirty and let herself in using the key Poppy had given her two weeks ago, right after David hired her to manage Melissa's wedding and reception.

All was in quiet readiness as she headed toward the kitchen carrying two sacks filled with donuts and bagels. She wasn't at all surprised to find Mrs. M in the kitchen with Faye and Harlan Appleby. Natalie was there, too, looking sleepy in her pj's as she ate a bowl of cereal, her hair a big red tangle. One glance at the little girl put a smile on Willow's lips. She was adorable. Shelly would be so proud of her.

The inn's giant coffee urns were already hot, and the aroma of fresh coffee filled the air. "Bless you," Willow said as she dropped the grocery sacks on the stainless-steel countertop. "I could use a cup of that. What can I do to help before the volunteers arrive? I figure we've got about half an hour."

Poppy filled two large, polystyrene coffee cups and pressed them into Willow's hands. "First things first. Would you do me a favor and take this out to David? He's out on the patio being his usual grumpy morning self. Faye and I will take care of putting out the donuts and bagels. We're also making iced tea, and Walter should be here with the ice and the keg of beer shortly."

"David's here?" Willow asked.

"Where else would he be?"

"Uh, well, I just thought he'd be off fishing or working or something."

"Well, he's not. He told me this morning he wanted to keep an eye on things."

"What does that mean?"

"I have no idea. Perhaps you should ask him."

Willow stood there for a moment trying to figure out a way to avoid this chore. She'd been successful in avoiding David for the last week even if she had failed to rein in her red aura or forget the looks he'd given her last Sunday when they'd gone fishing together.

"Go on, he's waiting," Mrs. M said, a note of annoyance in her voice.

Willow straightened her shoulders and strode off toward the French doors to the library. She'd deliver the coffee and make a quick retreat back to the kitchen. Easypeasy, no need to spend any more time with him than was absolutely necessary.

She found him exactly where Mrs. M said he would be, on the terrace, sitting in one of the wrought-iron lounge chairs watching the sun rise. It was chilly out there, but he'd fired up a couple of the professional-grade propane heaters. As usual, he was dressed for the country club, not a paint-in, in a pair of crisply pressed khakis, a blue Ralph Lauren cable-knit sweater, and expensive-looking leather loafers.

She pushed through the French doors. "Good morning," she said in a falsely bright voice as she crossed the patio. "Mrs. M said you needed coffee. I'm the designated coffee bearer." She held out the cup.

He looked up at her, his dark eyes filled with a spark she didn't want to see. The damn propane heaters must have been turned up to blast furnace level. Either that or just looking at his handsome face gave her hot flashes.

He took the coffee from her, their fingers inadvertently touching, while her core melted down. Damn. She needed to find someplace else to be in a hurry. "So, you're good? I have things I need to do," she said as she pointed over her shoulder with her thumb.

"You have a minute?" he asked.

Crap. Would it be bad if she said no? "Sure." She remained standing.

"Poppy insisted that I hang around today," he said. "She seems to be worried."

"Worried? About what? Mrs. M gave me the impression you were the one who was worried."

"Me? I'm not worried about anything except the size of my credit-card bill after you feed everyone breakfast and lunch."

The man was frugal to a fault. "Feeding people breakfast and lunch will be cheaper than hiring professional painters. So don't get all Scroogy on me, okay?"

He cocked his head and gave her a sideways glance. "I think that's precisely Poppy's problem."

"What? That you're being cheap like Scrooge, or that I'm feeding everyone who volunteers?"

He gestured toward a chair, clearly annoyed by her snark. "Have a seat, Willow. It might be the only time you get to sit down all day."

"No, I really have things—"

"Sit down," he commanded.

She sat and took a sip of her coffee, scalding her tongue in the process.

"I think Poppy is worried that your volunteers are going to ruin the inn with their shoddy work."

How dare he? First of all, she was willing to bet her

life that Mrs. M wasn't at all concerned about shoddy work. She'd admired the efforts of Harlan and Walter over the last couple of days. They would be there watching, making sure the volunteers didn't do any damage, and Mrs. M knew it.

"Well, I guess we'll just have to trust in people, won't we? Especially since beggars can't be choosers." Her annoyance came through loud and clear in her tone.

"Whoa, back off," he said. "This isn't coming from me. I'm just saying that Poppy is worried. And I guess all of this is just a little upsetting for her, you know? I mean, she's lived in this house for decades."

"Yes, I know that. I'm very sensitive to the situation. Are you?"

He gave her the patented Lyndon frown. "Of course I am. I hope you will be too."

Had she somehow hurt Mrs. M's feelings? She only wished she knew what she'd done. As far as Willow could tell, she and Mrs. M were getting along just fine. She looked down at her coffee cup, suddenly worried that her enthusiasm for the inn had turned Mrs. M off or something. Maybe she'd been just a little too gung ho. Damn.

"I'm sorry, David. But I can assure you that I have been very sensitive to her situation." Willow stood. "I'll go talk to her now."

"No. Sit down. Don't talk to her. Just be..." His voice faded out.

"What?"

He shrugged. "I don't know." He took a big gulp of coffee. "I'm terrible at stuff like this."

They lapsed into silence for a moment before he spoke

again. "I like your sweatshirt," he said. It was a complete non sequitur.

"It's more than twenty years old. Perfect for painting."

"I have one just like it that I used to wear all the time. You know, it's funny, I never thought about this before, but we kind of missed each other at the University of Virginia. You did your undergrad there and I did law school, but we were never there at the same time, were we? We were like ships passing in the night."

He tried to smile. It reached his eyes but not really his lips. What was he trying to say? She didn't get it. But she was quite certain that if they'd been together at college they would have been friends. Period. Shelly and David were an established couple by the time he went off to Harvard undergrad. And Willow was focused on her future, not romance.

She ought to be focused on her future right now.

So she leaned forward. "You know, David, if you have an old UVA sweatshirt, you might want to put it on. Because that Ralph Lauren sweater and the Italian loafers aren't exactly what I'd call painting attire."

He glanced down at his clothing. "I wasn't planning on painting."

"That's obvious. You just planned to sit out here and criticize the rest of us, right?"

"Look, I was planning to go fishing, but Poppy asked me to stay and keep an eye on things, okay?"

"Fine, you do that." She stood up and put her hands on her hips. "But here's the thing, David—thirty people, give or take, are about to arrive here to help paint the inn in time for Melissa and Jeff's wedding. No one is paying these volunteers. No one is coercing them. They're show-

ing up because they care about their friends, and some
of them might even care about you and Mrs. M and this
place that used to mean so much to your wife. And not
just to your wife, to the entire town of Shenandoah Falls.

"People used to come up here every Christmas to see
the decorations and have holiday tea. They want to keep
that tradition alive. So that's why these people are
coming—to help friends and to recapture something
that's important to them. If you want to keep an eye on
things and be helpful and positive, then I suggest you stop
sitting there judging people and go change your clothes
and be ready to wield a paintbrush."

David sat in the chair after Willow left, sipping his coffee
and watching the sun creep up over the barren branches
of the big oak tree on the east lawn.

He'd deserved the tongue-lashing Willow had just
given him. He'd behaved like a total freaking jerk. Probably because he was inappropriately attracted to her, and
she knew it.

And that explained why she'd been avoiding him these
last few days.

It was enough to drive a man insane. And make him
completely inarticulate.

There were several things he wanted to say to Willow
Petersen, and none of them had anything to do with
Poppy or the paint party. He wanted to thank Willow
for her suggestions with respect to Mrs. Welch. And he
wanted to express his gratitude for the attention she'd
been giving to Natalie. Not to mention the fact that she

was managing Melissa and Jeff like she was a professional wedding planner.

Yeah, he was a jerk. A grumpy, Scrooge of a jerk. Maybe he needed a few ghosts to give him a visit. Or maybe the spirit of Christmas present had just visited him and told him exactly what he needed to do.

He drained his cup and headed back to the caretaker's cottage behind the inn, where he dug through his closet and found his UVA sweatshirt. Like Willow's, it had a little tear in the seam around the neck, which made it perfect for painting.

By the time he got back to the big house, the volunteers were arriving. He hung back, watching as Willow and her mother took charge. Harlan Appleby, Dusty McNeil, and Walter Braden were the designated crew chiefs, and each of them took a group of volunteers. They all seemed to know what they were doing.

"Hey, Daddy, are you going to paint?" Natalie came flying out of the kitchen wearing a pair of jeans that were short in the legs and an old Washington Nationals T-shirt.

"I guess I am," he said.

"Oh, goody, you can paint with me. Miss Willow told me to volunteer with Mr. Appleby." She took him by the hand and dragged him off to the dining room. "We're here," Natalie announced in her playground voice.

Harlan looked at his latest recruits. "Do either of you have any experience?" he asked.

"Nope." Natalie shook her head, her ponytail dancing.

"You?" Harlan asked, giving David a hard, assessing glance.

David's face heated. "Uh, well, no, actually."

Harlan's mouth twitched. "Not surprised, but don't

worry. I think you can master what's required." He handed David a full-size roller with a long handle, while Natalie got a pint-size trim roller. He pointed to a wall without windows. "You guys can start on that wall."

Painting turned out to be pretty easy, although Natalie was soon covered from head to toe in green paint, but she was having a wonderful time. Melissa and the bridesmaids were working in the dining room, too, and they soon stole her away from David. She was their little mascot, and she spent the morning giggling—a sound he hadn't heard in a long, long time.

Painting, he was discovering, was sort of like fly-fishing. He soon got into a Zen-like rhythm that would have carried him right into the afternoon if Poppy hadn't interrupted him about two hours later.

"Oh, David, there you are. I've been looking all over for you." She frowned, taking in his sweatshirt and jeans. "I didn't expect to find you painting."

"I was just making sure that you didn't have any worries."

"Worries? About what?"

"Poppy, didn't you tell me last night that you were worried about the quality of the work we were going to get today?"

"Oh, yes, I completely forgot about that. I guess I was wrong to worry. Walter and Harlan have been wonderful about quality control." Her face colored in a blush.

What the heck was going on with her? Was she going senile or something?

"Well, anyway, can you take a break? I need your help with the pizzas."

"What about the pizzas?"

"Someone has to pick them up, and there are so many.

Willow is going, and I think she needs help. Plus, your SUV is bigger."

"How many pizzas are we buying exactly that we need an SUV?"

"Don't be cheap, David. You know it used to annoy Shelly. We're buying a sufficient number to feed thirty-five people."

"I guess that's a lot of them, huh?" He tried to smile. "Sure, I can help Willow." Maybe that would give him a chance to apologize for the idiot things he'd said this morning.

He dropped his roller in the pan and followed Poppy out onto the portico, where Dusty McNeil and Walter Braden were up on tall ladders priming the eaves.

"Wait, Willow!" Poppy shouted as she hurried down the steps. Willow was standing by an ancient Honda, the late-morning sun glinting in her blond hair. She was beautiful, even dressed for painting in faded jeans and a sweatshirt. She took his breath away.

And that sensation was followed by a huge wave of guilt. What was happening here? He touched his wedding band as a reminder. Somehow the reminder didn't work this time.

"What?" Willow shaded her eyes.

"I thought it might be better for you to take David's car. It's bigger. And he volunteered to help."

Willow glanced his way, taking in his paint-smeared sweatshirt, old jeans, and sneakers. "You volunteered?"

"Well, actually, Poppy drafted me, but I can help with the pizzas." He tried to invest his voice with all the things he had wanted to say this morning but had been too dumb or caffeine-starved to get right.

She looked away and shouted up to Walter, "Hey, you guys still need a helper?"

"Yeah, that would be great," Walter said.

She turned and smiled. "Thanks, David. If you get the pizzas, I can help Walter and Dusty." She turned and strode away without so much as a backward glance.

Poppy heaved a big sigh. "If I didn't know better, I'd say she's trying to avoid you."

"That's exactly what she's doing." He turned toward Poppy. "Where are these pizzas?"

"At Marios, out by the interchange. We ordered twenty of them."

Hardly so many that they wouldn't fit in Willow's Honda. What the heck was Poppy up to?

Willow was helping Dusty and Walter prime some of the worst patches on the front facade and trying to come to terms with the fact that David had actually put on his old sweatshirt when, suddenly, out of nowhere, the iconic voice of Aretha Franklin boomed, telling the world that all she wanted was a little "Respect."

Willow turned toward the music. Out in the parking lot, Harlan Appleby had set up the beer keg and tables for the pizzas that would arrive shortly. On one of the tables sat an antique portable stereo system—the kind that ran on cassette tapes—its volume maxed out.

"In case you young'uns don't know what this is, it's called a boom box," Harlan yelled above Aretha's voice. "And I brought my party mix tapes."

"This should be fun," said Dusty, rolling his eyes.

Apparently Aretha Franklin was like some kind of pied piper for the baby-boom generation, because shortly after Harlan cranked the volume, the members of Mrs. M's bridge club came wandering out of the house, accompanied by Mom and her friends, Leslie, Alice, and Susan from the Colonial Acres adult community. In no time at all, the sixtysomethings were dancing.

"Come on, you guys, take a break," Mom yelled. "We'll teach you how to dance the Frug."

Just then David came rolling up the drive, and lunch was officially served. Everyone took a break. Pizza was consumed, and the older generation set about teaching the younger generation dances like the Swim, the Monkey, and the Stroll, a couple's line dance.

Harlan Appleby dragged Willow onto the blacktop as his dance partner, but somehow, when the moment came for strolling down the line of other dancers, she ended up paired with David. Harlan and David had switched places somehow.

What was David up to, anyway? Hadn't she sent enough signals to let him know that she seriously regretted the kiss she'd given him at the Jaybird and was put off by his sudden interest? Not to mention that dancing with him was not going to do anything positive about the red in her aura.

David snagged her hand, and the electricity flowed right up her arm. "We're supposed to be strolling down the line like this." He executed a flawless grapevine step. Who knew David Lyndon could dance? Apparently dancing was a required skill for the political set. Although she could think of several presidents who had embarrassed themselves on the dance floor.

If David ever reached that pinnacle of power, he'd be safe. He possessed a male grace that had always blown Willow away. Whether he was stepping on the dance floor or casting a fishing line, the man never looked awkward.

Oh, boy, this was bad. Worse than bad. She was enjoying the moment, the touch of his hand, the look in his eye. She wanted to kiss him again. But she couldn't do that. Not here in public.

So when they got to the end of the line and he let go of her hand, she turned her back on him and walked away, up onto the portico, into the lobby, and right into the ladies' restroom, where she hid out for ten minutes.

When she came back outside, David was standing on the edge of the parking lot watching the old folks get it on to the Rolling Stones' iconic hit "Satisfaction." Even Mrs. M was out there dancing—with Walter Braden of all people. Mrs. M looked like she had stars in her eyes.

The fun might have continued well into the afternoon if it hadn't been for Pam Lyndon, whose SUV turned into the driveway right as "Satisfaction" ended and the Beatles song "Yesterday" started up. A few couples hooked up—Bud and Viola, Faye and Harlan, and Walter and Mrs. M.

But everyone else turned to watch as Pam's white Land Rover, with its special United States Senate license plates, pulled into the parking lot.

"The Duchess of Charlotte's Grove has arrived," Melissa said as she came to stand beside Willow on the portico's top step. "Right in time to be a killjoy."

Willow put her arm around the bride-to-be. "It's going to be fine. Look around you. See how many friends came out to help today? And we've been having a great time. Pam's the one who missed out. You'll be talking about the paint party for years, you know?"

Melissa smiled. "Yeah, I will. Thanks."

Melissa and Willow watched as Pam unfolded herself from the driver's seat. Her black wool pants and matching cashmere cardigan were clearly not intended as painting attire. Pam wasn't alone. A tall, narrow woman with a sizable bust got out of the passenger's side. She wore a pair of skinny black pants with a man-tailored shirt over a tight-fitting tank top. A pair of three-inch black heels and a bunch of gold jewelry polished off the look.

Arwen came up beside Melissa and Willow and said, "Uh-oh."

"What?" Willow asked.

"It's Roxanne Kopp, August Kopp's daughter. David is eventually going to marry her."

Willow's insides dropped like they sometimes did when she'd ridden the penthouse elevator down from Restero's New York headquarters.

"He's engaged?" Willow asked.

"Nah," Arwen said. "Pam, August, and Roxy have to figure out a way to get him to take the wedding band off first. But, believe me, they are plotting and scheming. David and Roxy belong together."

"You think?" Melissa said.

"Yeah, sure. She's rich, smart, beautiful, and understands Washington. She'll help him become the politician he needs to be."

"What does that mean?" Willow asked.

Arwen shrugged. "I don't think David's heart is really in this congressional run. I think he's just doing what's expected of him, the way he always does. Now, his sister,

Heather? That's a whole different story. I think she'd jump at the chance to run for office if it weren't for her old man's misogynistic views. But then, she's just doing what's expected too. Loyal sister and all that. At least David has chosen her to be his campaign manager."

Pam strolled up the walkway in a pair of Kate Spade pumps. The duchess studied Eagle Hill Manor's scraped but as yet unpainted facade with an expression of disgust. Roxy followed behind like a long-legged puppy.

David came out of the house and brushed past Willow. He intercepted them before they reached the portico.

Pam gave him a kiss. So did Roxy, and the moment that woman's plump lips touched David's mouth, something ugly and intense burned a hole right through Willow's gut. She recognized the jealousy. She was such an idiot for letting herself fall into lust with David Lyndon.

With the pleasantries done, Pam cast her gaze over the volunteers, searching until she found Natalie, who was munching on a slice of pizza and hanging out with Alice and Leslie, two of Mom's friends.

"Natalie Marie Lyndon, what have you done to your hair? Oh, my God, David, she's got paint all over her head. I don't know what we're going to do about that child. She's always making such messes." Pam's reprimand was delivered in a loud enough voice for everyone to hear above the mellow tones of Paul McCartney's voice and acoustic guitar. She was so loud that Mrs. M and Walter stopped slow dancing, which was kind of a shame, because they seemed to be thoroughly enjoying each other.

Right then something snapped inside Willow, and a

pure, clean anger spilled through her like a river spilling over a dam. She stepped down onto the path and stalked right up to Pam. "You know," she said in a big voice intended for Natalie to hear, "there's a saying my mother always uses. It goes like this: 'The best days end with dirty clothes.' Natalie has been having a very good day today, which is why her clothes are really, really dirty. But you know what? They aren't her good clothes, and luckily, Mrs. M stocks plenty of my mother's lavender soap to clean up when the day is done."

Pam's blue-eyed look of indignation conveyed the impression of entitled royalty. Melissa was right; Pam Lyndon was as high and mighty as a duchess. "You"—Pam rudely pointed a finger at Willow's chest—"will have nothing to do with my granddaughter. Is that clear? You've already made enough trouble for my family."

Oh boy, there was that word again. But this time Willow embraced it. "Oh, yes, I am a troublemaker. I make the kind of trouble that brings people together to have a good time and paint the inn at the same time. And as for Natalie, no, I have no intention of staying away from her. I'm her godmother, and while I admit that I've been absent for a while, I'm back now, and I take my responsibility seriously." She snapped her spine, planted her hands on her hips, and prepared herself for a catfight if Pam Lyndon wanted one.

But just then Natalie came running across the lawn to Willow's side. She tugged on Willow's sweatshirt. "Miss Willow, Miss Willow," she said.

Willow looked down at the beautiful child who was more or less covered in green paint from her nose to her toes. "Natalie, not now. I'm—"

"Are you really and truly my fairy godmother? Can you turn the pumpkin into a carriage? Can you make my wishes come true?"

Behind her someone giggled. The laugh stopped abruptly, followed by a momentary silence, which was broken by a warm, silky laugh that belonged to David Lyndon himself.

Willow looked up, only to realize that she was standing right next to him. How odd to see him laughing instead of sulking and grumping. The sound of his laughter sent Willow's heart soaring.

"I'd like to see you turn a pumpkin into a carriage," he said through his laughter as he crossed his arms over his chest. "I bet you could do it too."

"Can you really?" Natalie jumped up and down on her paint-splattered sneakers.

"Do not encourage her," Pam said, then stared down at her granddaughter. "You're far too old to believe in silly fairytales, Natalie. Ms. Petersen is not your fairy godmother. She can't do much of anything, really, except make trouble. You shouldn't listen to one word she says. She doesn't tell the truth."

And just like that, Willow's bravado disappeared. How many times would people call her a liar just because she told a secret Restero didn't want told? The world was not a fair place, and she wasn't a fairy godmother. Hell, she wasn't much of an ordinary godmother either. She couldn't work magic, and given that she'd been absent most of Natalie's life, she really didn't have any right to tell Pam Lyndon how to raise her grandchild.

She'd overstepped. She'd let her anger and her growing affection for Natalie (and David) warp her judgment.

Making a scene wouldn't help Natalie. In this town, people challenged Pam Lyndon at their peril.

"Excuse me," she said, stepping around Pam. She walked calmly until she reached the edge of the woods, and then she broke into a run. She was out of breath by the time she reached the meadow adjacent to the Laurel Chapel. She fell down onto her knees, sank into the coarse brown grass, buried her head in her hands, and bawled her eyes out.

Is this what Shelly had had to contend with? Willow had heard enough from her friend to know that being David's wife hadn't always been the fairytale Shelly had once believed in.

David Lyndon was a handsome and appealing man, but he was also grumpy and Scroogy and he let his mother run roughshod over his daughter. He wasn't a prince. He hadn't slain any dragons or rescued any damsels.

This was the problem with modern princes. They could awaken a woman with their kisses, but the rest of the prince thing was utterly beyond them.

Chapter 11————————————

David's laughter died the moment Willow squared her shoulders and marched off into the woods. Mother had managed to cut her down to size in about a nanosecond, and that pissed him off.

"Why are you here?" he asked, putting his hand on Natalie's shoulder to keep her from scampering off into the woods after her fairy godmother.

"Roxy stopped by, and I thought it would be fun for you and Natalie to join us at the Red Fern Inn for tea or cocktails."

David doubted that Roxy had just "dropped by." Mother had been shoving Roxy in his face for several weeks now. And if Mother had really wanted to meet for drinks somewhere, she would have called or texted. No, she had used Roxy as an excuse to check up on the status of the paint party. Mother was probably hoping Willow's party would fail, and that Jeff and Melissa would change their minds when they realized how dilapidated the inn had become.

"What on earth made you think that I could join you for cocktails today? You knew today was the paint party."

"David, dear, I didn't expect you or Natalie to be painting. Really. If Jeff and Melissa want to get married here in this...place, well, I suppose no one can stop them. But I didn't really expect you to help them. To be honest, I expected you to go fishing this morning."

"Mother, like it or not, this is my house, and that makes me the official host of Jeff and Melissa's wedding reception. You need to accept both of these facts."

"David, I know this is your house, but not by choice. I mean you—"

"I chose to marry Shelly. That wasn't a mistake." He fingered his ring.

"Well, whatever, you know what I mean. Charlotte's Grove is your home. It's the house you'll inherit one day. This place is merely a liability you're planning to sell."

He could hardly argue that point, so he didn't. He let his mother rant on.

"I can understand why you decided to help your cousin. After all, you are both members of the same family. But I will never understand why you hired *that woman*. You know she has a terrible—"

"Don't," he said, his voice going hard.

"Don't what?"

"Say what you were about to say. I don't want to hear about Willow Petersen's reputation."

"Well, you should. Have you even bothered to read what they're saying about her in the *Wall Street Journal*?

David, her father was that horrible punk-rock person who killed himself. And we all know what her mother is like."

"Yep, we sure do," Linda said from somewhere behind him. "And trust me, Lucas was a good man. A little confused, but his heart was made of gold."

Mother sniffed. "David, really? I can't believe you're spending time with these people."

"Why? You're the one who is always telling me I need to get out and connect with the people if I'm going to run for Congress. So, here I am, connecting with folks. I want you to look around at the people assembled here. Some of these people are Jeff and Melissa's friends. Some of them are Poppy's friends. Some of them are friends of the inn. Willow got them all here together. And that's a good thing—for Jeff and Melissa and even for me."

"David, really, don't take that tone—"

"Stop. I don't want to hear it." He clamped his mouth shut before he spoke his mind too clearly. He was exhausted by his mother's antics. She had been calling him daily complaining about the wedding, trying to set him up with Roxy, talking trash about Willow, and nagging him constantly about his congressional run whenever it served her purpose.

She glared at him. He glared right back.

"You're behaving like a child," she said.

"No, Mother, I'm behaving like a grown-up." He nudged Natalie behind him and got right up in his mother's face. "It's time for you and Roxy to leave," he whispered.

"David, really, you—"

"What part of 'leave' did you not understand? Get it through your head, Mother, Jeff and Melissa are getting married at Grace Presbyterian and the reception is going to be here, at *my* house."

"David, don't—"

"Go now, before I lose my temper."

They stared at each other, blue eyes to brown, and finally Mother turned around, took Roxy by the arm, and guided her back to the SUV.

"Daddy?" Natalie said in a small voice as Mother peeled out of the parking lot.

He turned and squatted down to be on his daughter's level. "Don't worry about what Grandmother said. You don't have to stay clean all the time. I'm very proud of you for all the painting you've done. And we have more to do. Why don't you help Melissa organize these folks to get busy painting the outside while I go find Miss Willow and tell her I'm sorry about what Grandmother said to her?"

"Is she really my fairy godmother?"

The tight coil of anger eased a little. He even managed a smile that felt rusty and out of shape. Maybe he needed to practice smiling more. He gave Natalie a little kiss on one paint-smeared cheek. "Miss Willow is your godmother, sweetheart. She's not a fairy, and I don't think she can do magic like changing pumpkins into carriages or mice into horses."

"Yes, but she's going to get me a beautiful green dress with a hood."

"Yes, I guess she is."

"So that's sort of like a fairy godmother, right?"

"Uh..."

Melissa came to his rescue. She stepped down from the portico and squatted down too. "Yes, Natalie, it's exactly like what a godmother does. And while Willow isn't exactly a fairy, she's definitely magical."

David opened his mouth to argue, but when Natalie's face lit up, he shut it tight.

"Really?" his daughter asked, her big brown eyes wide.

"Absolutely," Melissa said. "She's more than that; she's a miracle worker. Now, why don't you come help me paint? I'll paint the tall parts and you can paint the short parts. How does that sound?"

Melissa stood up and gave David a big smile. "Thank you," she said. "For standing up to Pam and for hosting my wedding, and for hiring Willow too. She's been amazing, David." Melissa glanced at the woods. "You should go find her and bring her back. What your mother said to her was mean."

David nodded. "I'll be back in a minute. In the meantime, you're in charge." He glanced up at the sky; clouds were beginning to roll in. "We need to finish before the rain comes."

"I've got this," Melissa said. "You go find Willow and bring her back. Tell her we all love her."

We all love her. The thought pounded in David's brain as he turned and jogged through the woods. Did he love her? No, certainly not in *that* way. But Willow had been a friend for a long time. And recently she had gotten way deep under his skin.

He knew the way to Laurel Chapel this time. In early winter, the meadow stretched away brown and dead, punctuated by dry wildflowers. The cemetery looked dark and dreary as the clouds rolled in. The chapel itself brooded like some ancient relic out on an English moor.

Willow wasn't hiding inside the chapel like Natalie

had done. So it took him a moment to find her, lying face-down in the grass.

"Willow!" He said her name sharply. Like everything here, she looked dead. He fell down on his knees by her side. "Are you okay?"

She turned her head in his direction, her eyes puffy, her nose red. She'd been crying. Hard. The look on her face left him feeling hollow and angry at the same time. How could the mother he loved be so cruel?

"Willow," he said, fighting through the anger to find an island of calm. He pulled his handkerchief from this pocket. "Here, blow your nose."

She rolled over and stared up at a sky that had turned from bright endless blue into rolls of gray flannel. "Of course you carry a handkerchief," she said, bypassing his offering and wiping her nose on the sleeve of her sweat-shirt.

He tucked his handkerchief back into his pocket. Willow had always been good at drawing lines between them, of pushing him away. She'd been doing that all week, and he understood why. But suddenly he was exhausted by it.

"Come on, sit up. Mother's gone, and I've been dep-utized to bring you back. Melissa told me to say that everyone loves you."

She barked a laugh and curled up from the ground, blades of dry grass sticking to her shirt and tangling in her honey-colored hair. He reached to brush the grass away, and a carnal heat surged through him the moment his palm slid through her hair. He inhaled sharply, reveling in the erotic rush. He deepened his touch, tangling his fin-gers where once the blades of grass had been. He cupped her skull and drew her toward him.

He expected her to push him away. Instead, she stretched into his touch like a cat demanding attention. He indulged her, stroking and fondling as she pressed against his hand.

A deep longing settled down in his gut, prickling along his back and down to his butt. Arousal. He'd forgotten how good it felt, and like a crazy teenager, he wasn't about to stop now. She'd initiated that little nothing of a kiss the other night at the Jaybird, and she'd been running from him ever since. If he wanted more, he would have to take it.

He slanted his mouth across hers.

Oh, man, she had killer lips. Soft, plump, mobile, sexy. He explored her mouth with his tongue and then his teeth. He wanted her mouth on his body, and she obliged, nipping his cheek, kissing down his neck, and then coming back, opening for him.

He stopped thinking, stopped worrying, stopped trying to resist. He wanted this woman in the worst way. And he would have her.

He pushed her back onto the grass. She fell willingly, and he covered her body with his own.

David Lyndon smelled like an exotic spice that came from a faraway place: piquant and unique and hot. So very hot. All of him, his mouth, his stubble, his scent made her a little crazy.

And then he kissed along her jaw and laved the spot right below her earlobe.

"Oh, yeah, right there," she whispered, when he hit the magic spot that made her whole body flash to attention.

She could have sworn she heard a rumble of laughter, or maybe it was just the earth moving or something. He pressed his hips against her, and there was no doubt that David Lyndon was enjoying himself. And just thinking about David being hard and naked turned her on a little bit more. She wanted to strip him bare and ride him.

But wait, that would be stupid. And dumb. And complicated. And wrong.

Okay, maybe not wrong, exactly, but not right either.

Her brain was making a valiant effort to take over from the hormones that had suddenly found themselves in control. And for an instant her brain almost won the battle.

But then David touched her nipple through the fabric of her old sweatshirt and thinking became impossible and highly overrated. Except for those thoughts about getting him naked.

She found the edge of his sweatshirt and pulled it up. Oh, yeah, that was better, his skin was so hot and silky smooth. But touching him unleashed a maelstrom of want. She wanted to feel his warm body sliding across more than her hands. She wanted him to sit up so she could take the sweatshirt off. She wanted to roll him in the grass until he begged for mercy.

She'd never rolled in the grass with anyone before. And suddenly a tumble in the grass moved up to number one on her bucket list.

Oh, crap, was that a raindrop? It *was*. There was another one.

A second later the unseasonably sunny November day turned bad. Abysmally bad.

"Crap," David said as the skies opened up. He grabbed her by the hand and tugged her from the ground. They were soaked to the skin by the time they found shelter in the one corner of the chapel where the roof remained intact.

They stood facing each other in the storm gloom. David's hair hung over his forehead in a wet tangle, and the look in his dark eyes said it all. Like her, he'd come to his senses. The cloudburst had definitely put a chill on the mood.

"Uh, um, I didn't come here intending to do that," he said.

"Neither did I," she said.

They stared while the rain beat down heavily on the roof above them. A cold wind rattled the trees and made Willow's skin pucker. She wrapped her arms around herself, a small part of her wanting David to pull her toward him again and envelop her in all his masculine warmth.

But it wasn't going to happen, and that was probably wise.

"I'm so sorry," he said, looking away through the broken window at the sudden storm, then down at his sneakers. Anywhere but directly at her. "I came here to apologize for what my mother said. And the dumb things I said this morning. I didn't intend—"

"It's not your place to apologize for your mother. She needs to apologize for herself. Not that I ever expect her to do anything like that."

He looked up then, water dripping down the side of his face. She wanted to push his hair back, dry that trickle that almost looked like tears. "Why do you say that?"

"Your mother doesn't consider me worthy of an apology. Hell, she probably believes what she said. There are plenty of people out there who believe that I purposefully set out to ruin Restero's reputation because Corbin Martinson jilted me and I wanted to get a big payback from him."

"You were involved with Martinson?"

"Come on, David. I know you read the exposé in the *Wall Street Journal*."

"I don't think so. I'm not a big fan of the *Journal*. And even if I were, I'd rather hear your side of the story."

"I was in love with Corbin, okay? I worshipped the ground he walked on. He was my mentor and then my lover and I thought... Well, stupid me, I thought he loved me. But I learned pretty quick that wasn't the case when I discovered that Restero had knowingly sold defective hip replacements. Corbin was the first person I went to with that information. And he was also the first person to tell me to shut up about it.

"And you know what? I *did* shut up about it, because I stupidly thought Corbin was going to fix the problem. But he didn't. Instead, he covered things up. So I had to go to the Feds and tell them the whole story. I needed to do something about all those patients who will need additional surgery when their Restero hips fail. I owe each and every one of those people an apology. I may have ultimately told the truth, but before that, I told a lie. It was a lie of omission, but it was still a lie. And I lied because I loved a man who wasn't worthy of love."

"Do you still love him?"

She wasn't about to answer that question. "Look, let's not talk about Corbin, okay? Let's talk about you and me. I don't want to be attracted to you. It's crazy. It's wrong."

"Is it?"

"You're Shelly's husband. It feels wrong. And besides,

your mother punctuated the point this afternoon. We come from different worlds and we're going different places in our lives. Us getting together, even for a quick little affair, would be complicated. So let's just say that we both got a little out of control and then came to our senses, okay? I don't know about you, but I for one am not looking for a roll in the grass with you." Although ten minutes ago that was exactly what she'd wanted.

"Holding out for true love, huh?" he asked, that patrician eyebrow of his arching just so.

"True love? Really? Geez, you princes are all alike, aren't you?"

"What's that supposed to mean?"

"It means that I'm not Shelly, David. She believed in fairytales. I never have."

She turned her back on him and left the sheltered corner of the chapel. It was a long, cold, wet trek back to the inn. Luckily, David had the good sense to give her a head start.

"Now, Poppy, I don't want you worrying about the paint on the portico," Walter said late in the day after all of the volunteers had departed. Poppy and Walter were alone in the solarium together drinking cocktails—a bourbon on ice for him and a gin and tonic for her. David and Natalie had gone home to the caretaker's cottage to clean up. David was taking Natalie up to Charlotte's Grove for dinner as a peacemaking gesture.

Willow had come back from her walk soaked to the skin, and Poppy had told Linda to take her home. The bridge club offered to help with the cleanup. Faye and Harlan, Viola and Bud, and the Ingrams had left fifteen minutes ago.

The party had been a complete success as far as the inside painting was concerned. But the grand portico looked like it had cancer, with its splotches of scraped paint.

"We'll get it finished," Walter said. "It was just bad luck that the weather turned so sudden. But you know how it is this time of year. It can't make up its mind whether it's winter or fall."

"I'm not worried about getting the house painted, Walter. Although I imagine Melissa is having a fit. I suppose you care, since you're the listing agent."

"Now, don't be that way, Poppy."

She sighed. "I'm sorry. The truth is, it was fun today seeing the inn come alive with people again. I'm so tired of living in this house as if it were a mausoleum. You know, I don't really care if David sells the place."

"That's a lie too." He put his drink on the coffee table. "You're just grumpy because your plan to match up David and Willow fell apart on you."

"Well, you didn't help it any when you encouraged Willow to stay while David drove off to get the pizzas."

"Sorry. I wasn't yet in the loop. I guess it's because I don't have Barbara anymore to fill me in on the gossip. You should have given me a full explanation before the fact."

"Sorry. I assumed Harlan had clued you in."

He chuckled. "Men are not like women. We don't fill each other in that way."

She let go of a long, tired sigh before speaking again.

"You know, I really thought David might be interested in Willow, but the feelings aren't mutual. Oh well. It's probably for the best. How could David ever marry someone who showed such utter contempt for his mother?"

"If you ask me, that's precisely the kind of woman he needs."

"Walter, really, you know better. Pam made Shelly's life difficult, and Shelly got very good at going with the flow. I don't ever see Willow doing that. She's too much like her mother. She's a natural-born boat rocker."

Walter reached over and took her hand where it rested on the arm of the rocking chair. His touch confused her. Why was he doing this? Was it because he wanted to reassure her, friend to friend? Or was there something else? They had been slow dancing to Paul McCartney when Pam had ruined the party. She might be an old lady, but she had been enjoying the sensation of Walter's arms around her.

Foolish woman. He was too young for her.

She tried to pull her hand away, but Walter was having none of that. He laced his fingers with hers, and she let him do it. Suddenly she felt like the young girl she'd once been, sitting out on her mother's porch swing, letting Bobby whatever his last name was kiss her for the first time.

Who knew an old lady could still feel that crazy, adolescent feeling just by holding hands with a man.

"I don't mean to be smug," Walter said, "but you've got it all wrong. What I saw today was David telling his mother to take a long walk off a short pier. And then the man ran off after Willow like he was deeply concerned about the ugly things his mother had said to her."

"Well, yes, I saw that. And if they'd come back together, I might still have some hope. But they didn't come back together. She came back and he followed, as if she'd given him a piece of her mind and walked away from him. Which, basically, is exactly what she did all day. I don't think she's playing hard to get, Walter. I think she actively dislikes him."

"I wouldn't go that far."

"Well, what else? I can almost guess what's going through her mind. She knew all about Shelly's marriage. Who would want to sign up for that? Even I have to walk on tiptoes not to offend Pam Lyndon. She's a bully, but she's a powerful bully."

"I have only one thing to say to you, Poppy Marchand."

"What's that?"

"Stop living in fear."

She turned in her chair, her hand still firmly connected to his. He had nice, big hands, warm and calloused. "What on earth are you talking about?"

"First of all, you shouldn't be tiptoeing around Pam Lyndon. Who elected her the boss, anyway? And second, I'm saying that you and Willow Petersen are both singing from the same hymnal. You've both got interested suitors knocking at your door, and you are both running like scared jackrabbits."

This time she pulled her hand away from his. "What are you talking about?"

"You and me. You have been running from me for almost two years. And why? Because you have some idea in your head that I'm not old enough for you, or maybe you're too old for me. Or maybe you think that if you aren't slavishly devoted to Natalie and her father, they might kick you out on the street. Whatever it is doesn't matter. It's an excuse for not living the life you want to lead."

Walter stood up, reached down, and pulled Poppy from her rocking chair. "Let's get out of these rockers, shall we?" He moved in. "You think I'm too young for you, but the truth is I'm getting too old to chase you. How about stopping for a minute and gathering a few rosebuds? How about not worrying about what people think and just doing what you want to do?"

She laughed in spite of herself. "My rosebud days are long gone, Walter. Don't be silly."

"I don't think so," he said, and then he cocked his head, moved in, and gave her a kiss that was definitely not an old-lady kiss. It made Poppy remember that she was a woman, not some empty vessel where once a woman had lived.

Chapter 12————————————

The rainstorm that brought David and Willow back to their senses on the day of the paint party heralded a change in the weather. Willow went back to giving David the cold shoulder and he let her, despite the fact that he couldn't manage to get her or their brief roll in the hay out of his mind.

Walter Braden and Harlan Appleby managed to get the last of the exterior painting done, but they'd frozen their butts doing it. And then it snowed on Thanksgiving Day, enough to leave the landscape with a thin white icing. The cold suited David as he and Natalie walked from the caretaker's cottage to the big house to collect Poppy for the drive up the hill to Thanksgiving dinner at Charlotte's Grove.

Poppy was waiting for them in the lobby dressed in a pair of gray flannel slacks and a black twinset—far too casual for the usual gathering up the hill. "I know I'm not dressed up, David," Poppy said. "You can stop looking so shocked. The truth is, I'm not coming with you."

"But you always—"

"No, I don't always have Thanksgiving at Charlotte's Grove. That's a recent development. Once upon a time, I hosted people here at the inn. Those were wonderful gatherings, back when Shelly was a girl and Craig was still alive," she said in a tremulous voice.

"Everyone expects you at Charlotte's Grove."

"Do they? Really?"

"Of course they do."

"Well, I'm sorry to disappoint them." She paused for an instant, as if she was considering her next words carefully. "David, the thing is, I've begun to see that doing what is expected of me is a terrible way to lead my life. So I've decided to do the unexpected, even if it does sometimes disappoint others. And if you want my advice, which of course you don't, you might think about doing the same thing."

"What's that supposed to mean?"

She shrugged. "Just that I know you were invited to Jeff and Melissa's. Why don't you come with me? I'm going there with Walter."

Damn. Mother wasn't any happier about Jeff's alternate Thanksgiving plans than she was about the alternate wedding. Poppy's support of Jeff was like a defection in a covert family war.

He couldn't follow suit. He didn't even want to. He wanted to make peace. "Poppy, you know darn well my presence is required at Charlotte's Grove."

Poppy grunted a laugh. "David, you should listen to yourself sometimes. Life is too short to spend it going places where your presence is *required*. Why not go where you want to go?" She gave him a wink, which was something Poppy never did. What was up with that?

"One Thanksgiving is the same as another, and I have fences to mend."

She shook her head. "Oh, you poor man. Why don't you just screw up your courage and do what you want for once in your life?"

"And what's that?"

"Well, I don't know. But here's a suggestion: You could gate-crash Linda Petersen's Thanksgiving. That might be all sorts of fun, not that Linda will be cooking any turkey. But I expect Willow would be happy to see you."

His face burned, and Poppy got a sly look on her face. He obviously hadn't fooled his mother-in-law. "You're being droll, aren't you?"

She snorted a laugh. "No, David, I'm utterly serious. You need to stop mourning Shelly and get on with your life."

He touched his wedding band, but the guilt failed to stir inside of him, which, in turn, confused and confounded him. He was comfortable with his guilt. Stepping out of it required taking risks with more than just his heart. He had to think about Natalie, and his congressional race, and so many complicating factors.

His libido wanted to rush right in and drag Willow off to some hotel where they could finish what they'd started out in the meadow. He longed for that. He dreamed about it. It would not leave his mind. But he was not a slave to his libido.

Luckily the doorbell sounded, and he escaped having to explain himself to his dead wife's mother.

Natalie opened the door to reveal Walter Braden wearing a tweed jacket, a striped tie, and a recent haircut. The scent of Old Spice drifted into the foyer on the November wind. "Hey, beautiful," he said, grinning at Poppy. "It's starting to snow again. So bundle up. I left the car running."

Poppy pulled on her black cloth coat and a bright red and green scarf that had Santa faces all over it. "Bye, precious," she said, leaning down to give Natalie a kiss. "You look beautiful in your new dress. Be good."

Natalie frowned and then looked up at David with a face that could melt the strongest resolve. "Can't we go with Grammy and Mr. Walter? Please, Daddy, it would be so fun."

"No. We're going to Grandmother's. Uncle Jamie will be there. I know you'll like that."

Natalie adored her great-uncle, but the look on her face told him that she adored Melissa and Jeff almost as much. Damn, he hated being in the middle of this family tug-of-war.

Fifteen minutes later he arrived at Charlotte's Grove, which, as usual, was draped end-to-end in Christmas cheer and historically accurate holiday decor. The windows and doors were outlined in pine roping. Small holly wreaths hung on every window. A swag of mixed evergreens, punctuated by red and green apples, two pineapples, and a garland of cranberries and lemons hung on the transom above the front doors. Electric candles burned in every window.

All that greenery, coupled with Poppy's defection, soured his mood further. He needed a good stiff bourbon.

Heather was waiting for him in the front hall. She gave

him a sisterly hug and a kiss on his cheek, then asked, "Where's Poppy?"

He leaned over to help Natalie with her coat. "She's at Jeff and Melissa's."

Heather's eyes widened. "Oh no. Mother's not going to like that."

"Well, maybe it's time for Mother to realize she's not in charge of the world." The words slipped out before he could catch them. He had a feeling Poppy might approve of them, which was mildly disturbing.

"Uh-oh, you're in a foul mood," Heather said, her dark eyes warm with understanding. "By the way, touché on the way you handled the school. That was frigging brilliant."

A part of him wanted to give credit to Willow for the idea, but he held his tongue.

"Uncle Jamie's grumpy too."

"Really? He's never grumpy."

Heather rolled her eyes. "Apparently he and Amy had a ginormous fight about her credit-card bills. Cousin Amy isn't speaking to her father, and he's feeling guilty, which means, of course, he'll pay her bills and she'll never learn anything."

"Well, it's his own fault. You know, if Mother wants a project, maybe she should go looking for a rich husband for cousin Amy."

Heather giggled. "I think she already has. Edward brought his friend Grady here tonight, and I understand he's a hedge fund manager."

"I don't know whether to be happy or sad for Amy."

"Be happy. Amy needs a rich husband. Also, you should know that Andrew is brooding, so don't say anything about Valerie Evans, okay?"

"Andrew always broods. And who is Valerie who-ever?"

"His girlfriend for the last eight months. Where have you been? Everyone thought for sure they were going to get married. She dumped him for some guy in the air force. So be nice. You know how sensitive he is." Heather grinned and then dropped down to give Natalie a big hug. "Hey, Natty Girl, you look fabulous. Did your grammy make you that dress?"

Natalie shook her head. "No. My fairy godmother gave it to me. She said she found it at the Haggle Shop, when she was there looking for old lace for Jeff and Melissa's wedding decorations. She said it was waiting just for me. Like magic." She ran her hand over the fabric's nap. "It's soft."

"What's this about the Haggle Shop? Hello, David. Where's Poppy?" Mother appeared in the foyer, Roxy Kopp trailing after her the way she always did. Of course Roxy was here. She and her father were perennial atten-dees at the Lyndon family Thanksgiving.

Before David could explain that Poppy had abandoned ship, Natalie said, "Miss Willow found my dress at the Haggle Shop. She said it was just waiting for me like magic. And Grammy is having Thanksgiving with Melissa and Jeff and Mr. Walter. I wanted to go with her, but I couldn't 'cause I'm a Lyndon and I have to come here for Thanksgiving." Natalie made Thanksgiv-ing sound like a dreaded obligation.

Which was exactly how David had described it before they'd left the inn. He was an idiot. He should have known Natalie would repeat everything he said.

A thunderous expression filled Mother's face, so

David gave her a quick kiss on the cheek before she could say something unkind about Natalie's secondhand dress or holiday attitude. As he pulled away, he whispered, "Don't say a word about the dress or Willow or Poppy. Let's just try to be thankful that we're all here together."

"But she needs to learn—"

He held up his finger. "One word and I'm out of here."

"You wouldn't dare."

"Look, Mother, it's Thanksgiving. I'm here with Natalie. She's appropriately dressed. Why don't you try to look at the positives?"

"David, this sudden sarcasm is unattractive. Especially in a man who's planning to run for Congress."

He felt a momentary pang of pity for his mother. She'd been born into a political family, and she truly saw everything in life through that lens. He loved her, but she was so wrapped up with her own myopic view of the world that she never saw the wreckage she left in her wake.

"C'mon, you guys," Heather said, "bury the hatchet, okay? And not in each other's heads. Let's get some adult beverages and watch the Redskins lose to the Cowboys one more time." His sister draped her arm across David's shoulders, effectively blocking Roxy's move toward him. Heather gave him a warm squeeze filled with genuine affection.

You had to admire Heather. She had her finger on the pulse of the family and managed to negotiate all the drama with an ease that she'd inherited from Dad. Dad was a master at smoothing over all the feathers that Mother regularly ruffled.

They headed for the den, and Natalie made a beeline for Uncle Jamie, who didn't appear to be all that grumpy.

Jamie complimented Natalie on her pretty dress, listened to her story about her fairy godmother, and then plopped her on his knee as if she were his granddaughter.

Heather and Mother got pulled away by Aunt Julie, who was having a heated political debate with Laurie Wilson, Brandon Kopp's fiancée, about funding women's health care—a topic both Mother and Heather were more than passionate about.

Cousin Andrew was behind the bar, nursing his broken heart by handing out drinks. Edward and Amy were chatting with a tall stranger with a receding hairline who must be Grady the hedge fund manager.

Andrew put a draft beer into David's hand just as Dad called from across the room, where he was hanging out with Uncle Charles and August Kopp.

Oh boy, just what David needed, shop talk with his law partners. He was about to turn around and pretend he hadn't seen his dad, when Roxy struck with the speed of a boa constrictor. She coiled herself around his arm and squeezed. "David, I'm so sorry you couldn't join us for drinks last Saturday."

"David," his dad called again, waving his arm, "come here. We want to talk to you."

So much for pretending he hadn't seen Dad.

Roxy pressed against him and said, "Go talk to Daddy, please. He's been anxious to speak with you all day. Once he gets whatever it is off his chest, you and I can find somewhere more quiet." She gave him one of her come-hither smiles and shoved her boobs in his face. He looked. He was a guy. But her boobs did nothing for him. In fact, nothing about Roxanne Kopp attracted him. Not. One. Thing. She was not the woman he wanted.

He let Roxy drag him across the room.

"David," August said, slapping him on the back when they arrived. "I see Roxy has you all wrapped up. But before you two get too comfortable, I wanted to talk to you about something important."

"Sure, what?"

"What's this I hear from Charles about you making all kinds of calls to the Jefferson County Council about the Liberty Run park project?"

"Since when do you care about Jefferson County parkland?" David asked.

August's mouth twitched. Was he amused or ticked off? It was hard to tell. "I've heard that you're pissing off constituents," August said, then took a sip of what looked like bourbon on the rocks.

"I don't have any constituents. I don't hold public office at the moment."

"The park is popular," Uncle Charles said.

"I imagine it is. But to build the park, the county has to take Dusty McNeil's land—land his family has owned since before the Revolution. And Dusty has plans for that land. He's been saving his money, working hard, and dealing with a difficult father. How would you feel, Uncle Charles, if the county decided to take away Charlotte's Grove because they thought it would make a great park with access to the Appalachian Trail and fishing?"

"Don't be ridiculous. We aren't maintaining an eyesore."

"No, we're not. But the county could take our land if they wanted to, and we both know it would be legal. But the county wouldn't do that to us, because of who we are."

Charles frowned. "It isn't the same, David, and you

know it. Dusty McNeil is never going to do anything with that land. He has no resources."

"So?" David said. "That's a reason to go after his land? You've just made my point."

"Look, you can't be making phone calls on McNeil's behalf. Bill Cummins is definitely going to give you a primary challenge. You don't want to give him any ammunition."

"By the way," Dad interrupted, "that was a brilliant move, calling all the parents in Natalie's class. I'm sure you won a few votes there. And that wasn't a federal issue either."

As usual, Dad was trying to tone down the rhetoric. But David didn't want to tone it down. "Look, Dad, Uncle Charles, Dusty is my friend. He's asked for my help."

"Did he retain you?"

Not exactly. But he had asked for legal advice. "Yes," David said.

"You can't be serious," Uncle Charles said. "You need to recuse yourself from this, David. It's political suicide."

"No, Uncle Charles, I won't and I can't."

Roxy tightened her grip, no doubt because she thought she could pull David back from the brink. But it was too late for that. He'd made up his mind. If it came to a choice between a new park for Jefferson County and his friendship with Dusty McNeil, he'd choose Dusty every time.

"Son, what's gotten into you?" Dad pulled him by the shoulder. "Your mother says you've been acting out recently. But this isn't the place to draw lines in the sand. The family is even considering an endowment to the Historical Society that will ensure the land is preserved the way it should be."

Dad looked genuinely concerned, but that look in his father's eyes didn't move David an inch. "So basically you're saying that this is Mother's thing and I should just get with the program."

"Of course your mother is involved. She's chair of the Historical Society."

Dad clearly missed the point, didn't he? For him politics, not friendship, came first. It was just like Heather and Hale not understanding that Natalie was a higher priority than any stupid campaign pledge.

Damnit. He didn't want to be here. Not for one more minute. He didn't want to endure an evening of Roxy hanging on his arm, or Mother disapproving of Natalie's dress and behavior, or Dad giving him endless advice on election politics.

He just wanted to eat his turkey and try to be thankful. But that wasn't going to happen here, was it? Poppy was right; this was the place he'd come because it was expected. It wasn't where he really wanted to be.

He turned and spied Natalie giggling as Uncle Jamie did his corny missing-thumb trick. "Natalie," he said sharply, "come on. We're leaving."

"What?" Half a dozen heads turned in David's direction. He did his best to ignore the astonishment on the faces of his cousins.

"David, don't be childish," Dad said behind him.

"Are we going to Jeff and Melissa's?" Natalie asked, her face lit up from the inside. The joy he saw there opened up David's heart a tiny crack, big enough for something warm and wonderful to come spilling into him. He wanted to see that joy on his daughter's face more often.

"Yes." He said the word and a weight lifted from his shoulders.

Natalie scrambled from Jamie's lap, oblivious to the disappointment on her great-uncle's face. She hurried across the room toward David. "Do you think Miss Willow will be there?" she asked in a voice everyone heard.

David took his daughter's hand. "I don't think so, sweetheart. But Melissa and Arwen will be." He headed for the front hall closet and their winter coats.

"David, what on earth are you doing?" Mother asked, her voice shrill.

He didn't reply because he didn't trust himself to speak aloud. He didn't want to hurt Mother or Dad or anyone in the family. He loved them.

But Poppy was right. And Willow had helped him to see the truth. For too long, everything associated with the family felt more like an obligation than a joy. And he was tired of being grumpy all the time.

Mother tried to stop him from leaving. Dad too. Even Heather had a word or two to say. But he shut them out as he bundled Natalie up. He left them all standing in the front foyer.

Before he fired up the Lexus's engines, he looked down at his left hand. He'd loved Shelly. She'd been his friend for years before they married.

And Willow was right, if she were alive right now, she would be four-square behind helping Dusty, behind supporting Melissa and Jeff. If she were alive, they would probably all be having Thanksgiving together at the inn, instead of Melissa's tiny apartment above the bookshop.

If she were alive. But she wasn't here anymore, except

in memory. And no amount of grieving her would ever bring her back.

He tugged at the band. It took a little work to get it off over his knuckle. It finally came free, and he dropped it into the center console, where it got lost amid the random pocket change, a pack of tissues, a phone charging cord, and a roll of antacid tablets.

Snow was flurrying when Willow parked her ancient Honda on Liberty Avenue half a block from the bookstore. Dusk had fallen, and the warm glow of the wrought-iron streetlamps gave downtown Shenandoah Falls the sentimental look of a Thomas Kinkade painting. Every lamp on the street sported a pine wreath with a big red bow and lots of white twinkly lights.

Willow sat in her car enjoying the snow and the view and a feeling of peace in her heart that had been missing for a long time.

Tonight she would be spending Thanksgiving with friends—real friends who didn't care about the stuff Restero spewed in its PR campaign against her. Friends like Mrs. M and Dusty, who were practically family. Friends like Jeff and Melissa and Courtney and Arwen, who made her feel as if she was a part of something extraordinary and important.

Fixing up the inn. Planning Jeff and Melissa's wedding.

A year ago she would have looked down on these tasks. She would have thought, mistakenly, that her job at Restero was more important than what she was doing now.

Jeff and Melissa's wedding may have split the Lyndon family into two camps, but it had also brought a lot of people together. And when the big day finally arrived, she truly hoped that everyone would see that the wedding was special. Maybe not big or extravagant, but special.

She couldn't wait for that moment when Melissa walked down the aisle wearing the fabulous white velvet dress that Willow had finally found at a store in Houston. Melissa would look like a fairytale character in that dress.

How could Willow not spend Thanksgiving with the people who had given her a chance to pull herself up from despair? She'd tried to get Mom and Juni to come too—the invitation had been for everyone in the Petersen household—but Mom insisted on a vegan dinner. And Juni, the sweet girl she had always been, sent Willow here and told her not to feel one iota of guilt.

So she wouldn't. She unbuckled her seat belt and was just getting out of the car when a big, black Lexus SUV pulled to the curb right in front of her.

She knew this car because she'd been specifically avoiding it for days. A flash of heat traveled over every square inch of her skin before David opened the door and got out. The Prince of Shenandoah Falls had arrived in his pricey carriage, looking good enough to eat.

And Willow was hungry.

The thought brought her back to standing in the rain that day, telling him that what she felt for him was wrong.

Was it wrong? It was so strong. So unexpected.

And yet if she were counting blessings and friends, she'd have to number him among them, wouldn't she?

"Hey," he said, his voice low as the snow caught in his hair like little sparkles.

"Um, what are you doing here? Mrs. M said you were planning to have Thanksgiving with your family up on the hill." She shut her car door but didn't look away from him.

His lips might have twitched into a smile. It was hard to tell in the semi-dark. "Poppy told me that you were celebrating with your family down in the valley."

She shrugged. "I might have said that, but I decided at the last minute to come here. I'm not a very good vegan."

He gave a short nod as he opened the back door and helped Natalie with her seat belt. The little girl scrambled out of the car and ran toward Willow with her arms out and her red hair flying.

Here was another blessing—maybe the biggest one of all. Willow bent down to receive a hug that was large and warm and fed something inside her heart that she couldn't even name. For a brief instant she buried her nose in Natalie's scalp and drank in the scent of baby shampoo as if it were the most expensive perfume in the world.

The girl pulled away and started talking a mile a minute. "Thank you so much for my magic dress. Everyone said it was pretty. Even Aunt Heather said so. But I'm not sure Grandmother is too happy because we didn't stay for dinner and we sort of should have 'cause Lyndons always have Thanksgiving at Charlotte's Grove. But I guess we're not doing that this year. We're having it with you and I'm really glad."

Willow looked up at David as Natalie continued to babble on about Uncle Jamie and Aunt Heather and cousin Andrew, who apparently had just been dumped by a girlfriend, and someone named Amy who was a spoiled brat.

David's mouth twitched again, and the lamplight caught fire in his dark eyes. When Natalie paused for breath, he said, "As you can see, we started out at Charlotte's Grove, and there's always a ton of family gossip whenever we all get together. But we're here now, so I guess we qualify as holiday party hoppers."

That brought a smile to Willow's lips. "What happened to 'bah humbug' and 'I don't want to be bothered with the holidays'?"

"You did," he said, his gaze hot enough to melt the snow before it reached the ground.

"I'm thankful for my new fairy godmother," Natalie said with a gigantic smile on her face as she looked up at Willow, who was sitting right next to her at the collection of card tables that had been shoved together to handle the overflow crowd at Melissa's small apartment above the bookstore.

The candlelight from two dozen pumpkin-scented candles reflected in Natalie's eyes, and it was all David could do to keep tears from forming in his eyes. Natalie was having the time of her life here, not because anyone had spoiled her, but quite the opposite. She'd been put to work, helping Poppy and Willow mash potatoes and setting the expanded table.

Melissa and her friends had doted on her, but in a way that made it clear she was valued for her beautiful self, not some arbitrary behavior that was expected of her. And here she was, grinning up at Willow, who, he suddenly realized, had tears in her eyes.

She gave Natalie a hug and wiped her eyes.

"It's your turn, Willow," Jeff said. "No one eats until they share."

Willow looked around the table, her gaze stalling a little when it reached him. She was so beautiful with the candlelight glinting in her eyes. He reflexively touched the third finger of his left hand and found it naked.

Right. He'd taken off his ring.

"Ever since I lost my job at Restero and they started saying all this horrible stuff about me, I've felt, I don't know, like I'm a big failure. Like I'm a beggar at the door.

"But how can that be true, if I have friends like you guys? You're the best, all of you. I really mean it. I'm so thankful for every person sitting at this table." Her voice wavered and the tears overflowed and her mascara started to run. "Oh, God, look at me. I'm a mess. I've definitely had too much wine."

Dusty, who was sitting beside her, draped his arm over her shoulder and pulled her into a big hug. "Well, honey," he said, "I for one am thankful that you're back in town."

"Oh, stop it," Willow said, pushing away from him and using her napkin to wipe her tears.

Dusty laughed. "Well, yeah, you're right, I'm mostly thankful that David has agreed to help me fight Jefferson County." Dusty hoisted his beer. "Thanks, man," he said in a heartfelt voice.

"You're welcome," David said out loud, even though what he really wanted to say was, "Take your hands off that woman; she's mine." He hadn't realized just how possessive he felt about Willow until that moment.

"Well," Melissa said, since she was next, "I'm thankful

for both Willow and David, because without them I'd be organizing a trip to Vegas right now. You guys have been great." She hoisted her wineglass, and everyone drank again.

"Your turn, cousin," Jeff said.

Damn this was hard, especially since he realized that he'd been walking around in a funk for a long, long time. "I'm thankful to be here," he said aloud. But inside he was thinking, *I'm glad I took off my wedding ring.* He kept his gaze on Willow and let himself enjoy the view.

"I am also glad not to be stuck up the hill," Jeff said, raising his glass. "Here's to *not* spending Thanksgiving with the family."

"Hear, hear," Gracie Teague said. "I'm thankful for my adopted family—all y'all, but especially Melissa. Hon, I'm so proud of you and so thankful that you've decided to move back here permanently." She dashed a tear from her eye too.

"And I'm thankful that Gracie cooked this dinner, because if it had been left to Melissa and me, we might be eating mac and cheese from a box," Jeff said. "Let's eat."

They ate without Mother telling anyone to keep their elbows off the table. Without Dad dominating the conversation with political talk or Uncle Charles trying to talk shop about the various cases the firm was working on. Instead they talked about books and movies mostly, leaving David seriously out of the loop because he didn't read fiction and he hadn't been to a movie in ages. But that was fine, because he had never been a great dinner conversationalist. He contented himself with watching Willow eat.

She knew he was watching, because every once in a while she would look his way and their gazes would connect. When that happened, the desire would sizzle along his synapses.

"You guys," Courtney said as she came into the dining room carrying pumpkin and pecan pies, "it's snowing hard outside."

Jeff stood up and pulled the blind away from the window. "Wow, it's accumulating, even on the road."

Willow stood up and had to touch the wall to stay steady. "Uh-oh," she said. "Walter, you shouldn't have kept filling my wineglass like that. How much is on the road?"

Jeff shrugged. "Maybe two inches, but it's still snowing hard. Were they calling for this much?"

"I don't think so," Walter said. "And don't worry, Willow. I'll drive you home."

She sat down with a *thump* and put her elbow on the table in order to prop her head. "Thanks, Walter. I'm so looking forward to going home and getting a lecture about eating meat. I'm really sorry Mom boycotted your party, Melissa."

Dusty laughed. "Wouldn't be the first time your mom boycotted something."

"And your mother...Shoot, I'm too tipsy to think of anything clever."

Poppy spoke up then. "Willow, why don't you take one of the rooms upstairs at the inn until after the wedding? I mean, you're at the inn every day, we have plenty of room, and we don't do vegan at the inn."

"That's a fantastic idea," David said. Poppy had the temerity to give him a big smile. The woman was as bad as Mother when it came to playing matchmaker. Only in this case, he was definitely interested. And he was tired of Willow's avoidance tactics.

Willow turned toward him, cocking her head, her gaze zooming in on his left hand. "You've..." An attractive blush crept up her cheeks, and she didn't finish the rest of her sentence. He lifted his eyebrow and swore her green eyes darkened.

She must have read his intentions because she squared her shoulders in that way of hers and said, "That's so generous of you guys. I've always wanted to spend the night at Eagle Hill Manor. I don't suppose you'd let me stay in the Churchill Suite, would you?"

Poppy, who he now realized had been manipulating him for some time, gave a large, theatrical shrug. "Why not?" she said, grinning in Walter's direction. "No one else is sleeping in there right at the moment."

The Churchill Suite was a corner room with windows on three sides that provided an expansive view of the snow-covered woods and, during daylight hours, the ruins of the old Laurel Chapel. The room's walls had not been repainted during the paint party, and the red paint had faded over the years, as had the gold and red brocade curtains and bed hangings.

But the period four-poster, mahogany bed was gorgeous.

Willow had dreamed of sleeping in that bed since she was a child of six. It was, as far as she could imagine, the most romantic bed she'd ever seen. With its tall mattress and feather comforter, it seemed like a bed fit for a princess.

Standing here in the room, all grown-up and slightly tipsy from too much wine, she was willing to concede that there had been moments when she'd gotten tired of playing the prince in Shelly's endless princess games. Every girl, especially the ones from the wrong side of the tracks, indulged in a certain amount of Cinderella fantasy, bankrupt and anti-feminist as those fantasies might be.

She was having one of those fantasies about Prince David when a knock came on the door that sent her hormones racing. David had said good night at the inn's door as he and Natalie headed off to the caretaker's cottage. She hadn't expected him to come looking for her after he put Natalie to bed.

"It's me, dear," Mrs. M said, sending Willow's emotions tumbling in an entirely different direction.

Willow opened the door, and Mrs. M brought in an armload of fluffy white towels, guest-size hand soap from Serenity Farm, shampoo, and toothpaste, along with a new toothbrush still in its packaging. "We still have a small store of guest amenities," she said.

She dropped the towels on the bed, turned, and gathered Willow up into her arms for a long, hard hug. When she pulled back, her eyes were wet. "I didn't say it tonight but, dear girl, I am so thankful you've returned to us. I want to apologize for being a foolish old woman when you first talked to me about trying to bring this place back to life." She cupped Willow's cheek the way a mother might. "Thank you. For everything. For what you've done for the inn, and for Natalie, and most especially for what you've accomplished with David."

"Accomplished?" It seemed an odd word, as if David were some sort of project, like the inn itself.

Mrs. M grinned at her. "Oh, I think you know what I'm talking about. I'm sure you noticed that he wasn't wearing his wedding ring today."

Willow nodded. "I would have thought you'd be sad about that."

Mrs. M shook her head. "No, dear, I'm not. I've lost a spouse, too, and I'm coming to realize that living in the past isn't healthy. You and Walter have helped me see that. All that trouble you've had with Restero could have broken you. You could have become bitter or jaded, but you haven't. You just keep going. You're like a breath of fresh air blowing through these dusty halls."

"Thank you, Mrs. M," Willow said, her voice a little wobbly. All her life she'd wanted to earn Mrs. M's respect because Poppy Marchand was exactly the kind of mother she'd always wanted. Hell, Poppy Marchand was the kind of woman she aspired to be.

"Thank you, especially, for inviting me to stay here for a little while, and in the Churchill Suite. I've wanted to sleep here for years and years. I even painted my bedroom at the farm a bright red, just so I could pretend."

Mrs. M laughed. "Well, it is a grand room. Enjoy it, my dear. It won't be for very long."

The wonderful, warm, slightly tipsy high Willow had been riding vanished. "I know. But at least I can check this off my list."

"With all this work you've been putting into the inn and the wedding reception, how are you doing finding investors for your plan?"

Willow shook her head. "Not well, unfortunately." The wine was suddenly giving her a headache.

"I'm sorry." Mrs. M gave her another quick hug. "But you know that old saying, don't you, about God and windows?"

Willow shook her head. "Mrs. M, you know my mother doesn't believe in God or organized religion."

"Well, it's the one about whenever God closes a door He opens a window. And that's the thing. Maybe you weren't ever meant to own the inn. Maybe something better will come along."

Willow couldn't think of what that might possibly be, because the more she worked on bringing the inn back to life and planning Melissa's wedding reception, the more she wanted to do that for a living. "I guess," she said without enthusiasm.

"Well, you think about it, okay? Now have a good sleep. I'll see you in the morning."

Chapter 13————————————

"You're moving in with that man?" Mom asked on Friday morning as Willow stood in her dormer bedroom packing a suitcase.

"I'm not moving in with a man, Mom," she said, although, truly, if David wanted to sneak into the Churchill Suite one night, she'd probably let him. "I'm just moving into the inn. On a temporary basis. It will be easier this way." She didn't say a word about the fact that Mrs. M wasn't a vegan.

"You're falling for him, aren't you?" Mom said from her station at the doorway. She was in full-out Mom mode, which meant that it didn't matter what Willow said; Mom would hear what she wanted to hear.

"I am not." She kept her head down, folding jeans and putting them into her suitcase. "He's my boss. That's it. He hired me to do—"

"Don't lie. I don't particularly care if you lie to me, but don't lie to yourself. I can see the way your eyes light up every time his name is mentioned. And I saw the way he looked at you the other day at the painting party. I even understand how attractive one of those Lyndons can be—all alpha male and in charge. It's seductive."

Willow tucked her UVA sweatshirt into the suitcase and then looked up at Mom. "But he's not like that. I mean he does sometimes behave as if he's entitled. But if I compare David to Corbin, it's like they're in two different leagues. Corbin had an ego the size of Alaska. But David doesn't. Not really. He can be very..."

"Charming," Mom said, putting her hands on her hips.

"No, not really. He's not very charming, actually. To be honest, he's..." She stopped talking while she thought about it. She'd known David for years and years. He hadn't changed. He'd come down from the hill to go fishing, but once he'd arrived he'd been utterly tongue-tied.

"To be honest, he's kind of shy," she said, the thought becoming a revelation. David was shy. Which made his potential run for Congress utterly absurd. He'd be miserable as a congressman, constantly making cold calls looking for campaign contributions.

Had Shelly understood this? Probably. Maybe that's why she threw herself into the inn renovations. Maybe she'd hoped or prayed that one day she could get David to see the light. Maybe she'd just wanted to give him a soft place to land, when he figured it out.

"Look," Mom said, pulling Willow from these revelations, "if you move into the inn, people are going to talk about you. They won't say nice things. The truth is, baby doll, you will never be the kind of woman the people in this town want to see with David Lyndon."

Mom's words were like a physical blow. Willow slammed down the suitcase lid and lashed out. "What exactly makes me so inferior? Why is it that when I ask for more, everyone feels the need to punish me? And as for reputations, you're a fine one to be talking to me about where, and with whom, I sleep."

Mom wasn't fazed at all by Willow's words. She stood there in the doorway and actually smiled. "Baby, it's perfectly all right to ask for more, but in my experience you will rarely get it unless you take it for yourself. The Lyndons sure aren't going to show you any charity. And don't twist my words. I didn't mean that you weren't worthy of David Lyndon. You are. I'm just saying that he won't ever see you as being worthy of him. And I'm certain his people won't either."

It was so annoying when Mom spoke the truth. "Don't you think I know that?" Willow's voice betrayed her emotions.

"Then don't move out."

But how could she not go? On some level, she'd been wanting this all her life, and it had as much to do with Mrs. M as it did David.

She took a step forward and opened her arms for her mother. "I've got to go. But it's only temporary."

Mom hesitated, as if she didn't understand why Willow was standing there with open arms. So instead of waiting for Mom to give her that big hug, Willow just moved in and gave Mom the hug she'd always needed.

Mom actually returned it, patting her back. "It's only temporary," Willow repeated. "Besides, I'm never going to raise the money to buy the place. I've exhausted every possible investor on my short and long lists. So I'll be back after Jeff and Melissa's wedding."

Mom nodded and whispered, "I'll miss you."

"Will you?"

"Of course I will. I know it took a disaster to get you to come home, baby girl, but I'm glad you're back. And I hope you won't be blowing off the County Council meeting on Monday. They'll be taking public comment about this park proposal, and I've organized a big protest."

"Yeah, I'll be there. Dusty is a friend. I'll even carry a sign."

"Well, I'm glad to hear that, because the Lyndons are on the opposite side of this issue."

"Not all of them, Mom. David has agreed to represent Dusty, not only at the council meeting, but in court if it comes to that. He told us that last night at Jeff and Melissa's."

Mom's eyes widened. "Really?"

"Yeah. It pretty much blew everyone's mind when he said it. Of course, it was a huge surprise that he and Natalie showed up there at all."

Mom blinked a few times. "Baby doll, be careful. Some of those Lyndons will fool you into thinking they're regular guys. But when it comes right down to it, they aren't."

There was a note of sorrow in Mom's voice that had Willow putting two and two together and coming up with an odd number. "Mom, are you telling me you had an affair with one of those Lyndons, as you call them?"

Her mother's silence was all the answer Willow needed.

"Oh my God, Mom, you didn't. Which one? Not Mark Lyndon. I can't see him ever cheating on Pam."

Mom looked away. "I didn't say anything about having an affair with any of them. All I said was be careful with your heart."

Mom turned around and stalked from the room, leaving a boatload of unanswered questions in her wake.

David stood at the front of the Jefferson County Council meeting room and found himself thinking that the room needed just a little bit of Christmas tinsel or even a menorah to relieve the relentless gray. No doubt this was Willow's doing.

He'd never really noticed the grayness before or how the only decorations in the room were the public service posters urging people to get their flu shots and wash their hands. No wonder he'd had trouble staying awake during meetings.

David turned his attention to the audience that had gathered this Tuesday evening for the hearing. It was an overflow crowd. The early birds occupied uncomfortable molded plastic seats, and the late arrivals stood at the back of the room. The vast majority of those standing were women of a certain age. All of them carried handmade signs with slogans ranging from SAVE OUR PRIVATE FISHING RIGHTS to DOWN WITH THE IMPERIALISTS.

Linda Petersen carried that one, and David had no idea what imperialism had to do with an eminent domain case, but he had to hand it to Linda; she'd turned out an impressive crowd of sixtysomething ladies in support of Dusty's property rights.

Willow was there too. She'd ditched her usual corporate look for a light blue, partially unbuttoned Henley T-shirt and a pair of jeans that showed off her curves. David's fingers itched to undo a few more of those buttons and have a look. This was nothing new.

When Poppy had first suggested the idea of Willow staying at the inn, he'd almost jumped for joy. She would be there, within reach. He would find a way to finish what they'd started out in the meadow by Laurel Chapel. But after a week of having meals with her and bumping into her at odd moments, he'd come to realize that starting an affair with Willow was a lot more complicated than he'd first thought.

First of all, he'd come to the stunning and somewhat humbling realization that he'd never actually pursued a woman before. He and Shelly had met when they were sixteen—half a lifetime ago. He really didn't know how to go about suggesting an assignation. And after the way she'd run away from him the day of the paint party, he didn't exactly feel confident about his romantic skill set.

And then there was Natalie. She got in the way. All the time. It wasn't as if he could sneak up into Willow's room and suggest an assignation. Natalie lived at the inn too.

Not to mention Poppy.

The cat-and-mouse game was driving him insane. He had a plan to bring it to an end. Natalie was staying overnight tonight at Uncle Jamie's house because Poppy had bridge and David and Mother would be here at the hearing doing public battle with each other. David aimed to get Willow alone after the hearing.

And he hoped he could convince her to take a chance on him.

He shifted his gaze to the dais at the front of the room. Bill Cummins was there, staring at him like a piranha. Bill was going to run; there were no two ways about it. Hale's hope for avoiding a primary challenge was in vain.

Mother was up there in front, too, schmoozing Brian Stanthorp, the man who had assumed the chairman's seat when David resigned from the council after Shelly's death. Mother and the Jefferson County Historical Society had brought all kinds of exhibits and charts and photos, which were arranged on easels at the front of the room.

Dusty came up behind David and gave him a pat on the shoulder. "Are you sure about this? Because I had a parking-lot encounter with your mother, and she looked like she had a whole hive of bees up her backside."

"What did she say?"

"Not one word, to tell you the truth. It was that look that said it all."

"I'm sorry."

Dusty shrugged. "Parents. We don't get to pick 'em."

Just then Chairman Stanthorp asked everyone to take their seats. Almost immediately Linda and her cohorts began to shake their signs and chant, "Hands off our land." The noise reverberated around the room.

"Quiet, please," the chair said in a patient tone as the noise escalated. "I said quiet," he said again in a louder voice, his face going red.

When this only served to increase Linda's volume, Brian stood up and bellowed, "Linda, shut the hell up.

We're just having a hearing here. It's not the end of the world."

The words bounced right off Linda and her protesters.

Dusty grinned. "I'm liking this."

"Don't get too cocky. Linda is technically disturbing the peace," David said, standing up and heading toward the back of the room, where Linda, flanked by the sexy and adorable Willow, was urging her troops on. The protesters looked like they were having the time of their lives.

He'd gotten halfway across the room when Chief LaRue came through the room's back door, followed by three of his deputies.

"Have the protesters removed," Stanthorp directed.

"Uh, yessir, but where do you want me to put them?" Chief LaRue asked.

"In jail."

"But—"

"You heard the man, Paul." Mother popped up from her seat in the front row. "Put all of them in jail. They are disrupting a meeting. At the very least they should be charged with disorderly conduct."

"Wait," David said, "if I can—"

"You have nothing of worth to say here, David," Bill Cummins said, giving him a cheesy grin. "And I'm just dying to watch you explain your position when we debate next year."

"Bill, please," Brian said. "Let's keep election politics out of this." The chair turned toward the chief of police. "Arrest them, Paul, please."

"You all are under arrest. I mean it," Chief LaRue said in a menacing voice that drew *boo*s and cat calls. At

Linda's direction, the protesters sat down on the floor and continued to shout, "Save our land."

Chief LaRue gave David a disgusted look with a little sympathetic shake of his head. This would never have happened on David's watch. He'd always tried to bring in all sides of any issue and work out a compromise. Linda had never given him any kind of problem back when he was the chairman of the County Council.

Paul looked uncomfortable, but he did as he was told. He turned and directed his deputies to haul the ladies out. It almost broke David's heart to see Linda and a dozen gray-haired senior citizens get dragged from the hearing room.

Willow found herself in the Shenandoah Falls jail, which was located in the same space as the police department in the county building two floors down from the commission's hearing room. The department had three holding cells, but there were more prisoners than could reasonably fit, so some of the protesters, including Mom, were sent across the street to the Jefferson County Detention Facility.

Willow hoped those jail cells were more appealing than the city jail, which was dark and smelly and raised a deep fear in her that probably came from binge watching television shows like *Orange Is the New Black*.

At least Willow wasn't alone. Mom's friends from Colonial Acres, Leslie, Susan, and Alice, shared her cell. They were an island of calm, but there was a chance none of these sixtysomething ladies truly understood the seriousness of the situation. They seemed to be living in the past.

"I haven't had so much fun since we took over Columbia University back in sixty-eight," Alice said as she made herself comfortable on one of the narrow bunks that passed for a bed. It was hard to see Alice as a hippie protester, especially since she was dressed in a pair of frumpy tan knit pants and brightly flowered blouse that was just a tiny bit small for her large breasts. Her wire-rimmed half-glasses completed the grandmotherly look.

"I wonder if we'll be strip-searched," Susan asked in a voice that didn't sound in the least apprehensive.

"Don't listen to them," Leslie said, giving Willow a friendly pat on the back. "We're not going to be strip-searched or booked or arraigned. Chief LaRue is a sensible man. He'll probably wait until the hearing is over and let us go with a warning. If he was really serious, they would send someone in to question us, take our names, addresses, and social security numbers, and—"

"I am not giving anyone my social security number," Susan said.

"It's all right, hon. You won't have to." Leslie leaned toward Willow. "Susan's getting a little vague in the head these days, poor thing. But, as I was saying, they aren't really serious. I mean, they let us keep our knitting, including the needles." She held up a tote bag that came from Ewe and Me, the yarn store in town.

"We could probably use the needles to stage a break-out," Susan said.

"I think I'd rather knit," Alice responded.

For the next thirty minutes, Willow's cellmates knitted and gossiped about their neighbors, while Willow paced and worried about whether she would have to spend the night here, whether getting arrested would further diminish her reputation.

She was worrying herself sick when Deputy Pierce came back, pointed at her, and unlocked the door. "You're free."

He gave the rest of the ladies a serious stare. "Not you, just her."

"Why not?" Leslie asked. "All we did was chant and carry signs."

He shrugged. "Chief said he's getting tired of locking you ladies up for civil disobedience. He said y'all think it's a game or something. He's thinking about charging y'all."

The ladies smiled, and Susan said, "Oh, goody. That sounds like fun."

The deputy let go of a long-suffering sigh, and Willow had to stifle the urge to apologize. Why was that? Mom was in the right here, and Susan, Alice, and Leslie, wacky as they might be, were also right to stand up for Dusty. "I want to stay here," she said in a show of solidarity.

The deputy rolled his big baby blues. "I'm sorry, but you can't. You have been released, and I can't let you stay. Besides, you don't look like the kind of person who enjoys sitting around a jail knitting baby booties for your grandkids."

"Oh, don't worry about us, Willow," Leslie said. "We'll be out of here in no time. You go on. We're fine."

Willow had no other choice, so she stepped through the door, but before she followed the deputy out of the jail, she turned toward her cellmates. "Solidarity, ladies," she said, making a fist.

"Right on," said Alice. Susan waved vaguely.

It was a short walk to the main squad room, where she found David waiting for her. He looked very lawyerish in his dark suit, white shirt, and striped tie. Had he paid her bail? Or had he talked her out of jail?

Why was he here at all?

Didn't he realize the mass arrest had been orchestrated by Stanthorp and that smarmy Commissioner Cummins? Mom had told her that Cummins was planning to challenge David in the primary election next spring. The big public debate over the park was sure to be an issue now. He'd do so much better staying far, far away from her.

But he hadn't stayed away, had he? He'd come. And he'd bailed her out.

The cobwebs that had been gathering around her heart since Corbin's betrayal shook loose. David was a rich, powerful, smart man, but he wasn't at all like Corbin. Not in the least.

"David," she said in a voice suddenly choked with emotion. "You rescued me."

A little smile lifted the corner of his mouth. "You didn't think I'd let you spend the night in jail, did you?"

She didn't know what she thought. But she took a running start and threw herself right into his arms.

Like any prince worth his salt, he caught her. And then he thoroughly kissed her. He didn't even seem to care that the whole Shenandoah Falls police force—all four of them—were looking on with interest.

Chapter 14————————————————

Oh yeah, this was better. Much, much better. He probably wouldn't have kissed her here in the main squad room with Chief LaRue and his deputies looking on, but, hey, she started it.

And he was not about to stop it. Oh, no. Not when she threw her arms around his neck like that. Not when she opened her mouth and let him in. Not when their tongues touched, unleashing a conflagration of lust that had been building for days. Maybe even weeks.

He put his hand on the small of her back and pulled her as close as he could. Her soft round curves seemed to fit against him perfectly as he pressed her close, his hands exploring her backbone.

The blood that was left in his brain pounded with his heartbeat. The rest went south. He was ready to strip her naked right there until...

"Geez, you guys, get a room," Chief LaRue said, and

somehow the words managed to pierce David's sex-fogged brain.

He came up for air with an inarticulate sound only to find the chief standing there with his big arms crossed over his big belly and a look of utter disgust on his face.

Willow turned and gave him a brilliant smile. "Sorry, Chief. I was just happy to see him. I'm not cut out for a life of crime."

The chief was impervious to her charms. "Glad to hear it. Now, if you'd be kind enough to leave the premises, it would make my day."

"Uh, about Mom?"

"She's in the county lockup. I'm keeping her there overnight." He scowled.

"Are you charging her?" David asked.

"I'm thinking about it."

"You can't hold—"

"Son, you may be a Lyndon, but I'm tired to death of Linda Petersen. She's a troublemaker and a royal pain in my backside. Maybe if she spent the night in the county lockup, she'd quit making mountains out of molehills."

"You think Dusty losing his land is a molehill?" David asked, suddenly deeply annoyed at Paul LaRue, who was a decent man most of the time.

"Well, I, uh—"

Willow tugged on David's arm. "Don't argue with him, okay? Mom can take care of herself. And spending a night in jail will probably make her day." She smiled at the chief.

He scowled back. "You think?" he asked.

She nodded. "If you keep her overnight, she'll just make a bigger mountain out of this molehill. You know?"

The chief sighed. "Thanks for that free advice. Now get out of here, both of you." He turned his back on them, and Willow took David's hand in hers. Her fingers, long, slender, slightly cool, felt perfect wrapped around his palm. She pulled him away from the chief into the elevator lobby, where she hit the down button.

"He can't hold her without charging her," David said. "It's not legal."

Willow put the fingers of her free hand over his lips. He had to stifle the urge to suck on them. "We have a choice," she said, her green eyes going serious. "We can get all legal and go fight the injustice of it all. Or..." She let the word draw out.

The elevator came with a *ding*. She pulled him into it. "Or I could hit the stop button."

He laughed. "Are you suggesting elevator sex in the county building?"

She gave him a wicked smile. "Maybe." She turned, her finger hovering over the stop button.

He pulled her back. "I don't want elevator sex, Willow."

Her smile faded. "Oh?"

He ran his hand over her hair. The texture was erotic as hell. "I have other plans for this evening."

Her eyes got wide and kind of sad. "Oh?"

"You see, Natalie is at Uncle Jamie's. Poppy is off with her bridge club. And that means..." He paused dramatically as the elevator doors opened. "The inn is deserted."

"Oh?"

He pulled her from the elevator, then turned her to face him, with his hands on her shoulders. "I want you."

"Oh." She seemed to be stuck on that one word.

"I do. I know we're both kind of hung up on the fact that Shelly and I were together. But Shelly's gone—"

Damn, he didn't want to talk about Shelly, but maybe they had to talk about her before either of them could move on.

She touched his hair. He wanted to press into that touch. "David, I loved Shelly like a sister. You loved Shelly as your wife. Why don't we just leave it there? We both miss her. But she's not ever coming back, and you have a whole life ahead of you."

"I loved her with all my heart. But it doesn't change the way I want you. Do you understand what I'm saying?"

"I do. And believe me, I'm not looking for anything permanent. With anyone. But if you wanted to go back to the inn and make use of the Churchill room, I wouldn't stop you."

They held hands as they entered the Churchill room. It was sort of romantic.

Willow stepped on that thought. There was nothing romantic about this hookup, even if the high four-poster bed with its feather comforter was possibly the most romantic spot for a tryst that Willow could imagine.

But he'd been clear. His words were unmistakable in their meaning. He wanted her. He wanted to take the first step of leaving Shelly behind. That's all this was about. And maybe she could help him take that step. He needed to let go.

So they weren't a forever kind of the thing. Just for now. And that was probably enough.

He switched on the bedside lamp. It cast a warm glow over the red walls and sparked in the golden threads on the bed hangings.

He turned, loosening his tie, the movement so incredibly male, the moment so strangely intimate. She'd known David for decades, and yet this intimacy was something new.

He tossed his tie on the back of the wing chair and stepped toward her, the light flashing in his dark eyes. When he reached her, he didn't immediately pull her into an embrace. Instead he swept his gaze over her, his dark eyes growing darker by the minute.

"You are stunning," he said under his breath as he stepped forward and unbuttoned the last two buttons on her T-shirt. "I've been wanting to do that all night."

He pressed his fingers to the skin at her clavicle, the touch sending shivers through her as he moved his hand, featherlight, up her throat until he captured her head in his palm.

He pulled her into a kiss that was at first almost tender, but grew into something else again. His lips, teeth, tongue demanded something of her, and she gave it up willingly.

A deep, deep hunger roiled in her belly as she threaded her hands through his hair, as his stubble rasped over her cheeks, as the hard muscles of his body pressed up against her.

His mouth moved away from hers as he licked and nipped and kissed his way to the hollow of her neck. And when he found that spot right below her ear, her body went frantic.

This wasn't enough. His mouth was talented, but he

was moving way too slow. Was he trying to be tender? Was he trying to turn this into something it wasn't?

She didn't know the answer to those questions. She just knew that she wanted so much more than tenderness. She wanted to be possessed.

She pressed into him, running her hands under the shoulders of his jacket, until he lost the garment on the Persian rug. Then she attacked the buttons of his shirt as she let him work his magic on her mouth and jaw and neck.

Before she could get the shirt off him, he made a move on her breast, and she had to stop for a moment to enjoy his touch. The man knew what he was doing.

She needed more. So she pushed his hands away and pulled the T-shirt over her head. She didn't play coy. She unhooked the back fastener of her bra as well.

If he wanted to play, she was going to give him unfettered access.

He went back to work with his fingers and his mouth, while she managed to get all the buttons on his shirt undone. The shirt hit the floor, but he was still wearing a T-shirt.

Damn.

"Take that off," she commanded.

His mouth twitched. "Yes, ma'am. Anything else?" he murmured.

She glanced down at his suit pants.

His smile widened as he unbuckled his belt. He lost the pants, boxers, dress shoes, and socks in a real hot hurry.

"Your turn," he said, standing there looking glorious and fully aroused.

She stripped. He watched. His gaze made her skin

ache until he stepped forward and embraced her, chest to breast, hip to hip, sex to sex.

Yes. That's what she needed. His touch. Everywhere.

They managed to make it into the bed, tossing throw pillows in every direction, kicking the down comforter aside. She rolled onto her back and pulled him close.

This. His weight, the warmth of his body, the featherlight touch of his breath. And, finally, when she could stand it no longer, the long, hard length of him.

Filling her. Taking her. Possessing her.

David watched the sky turn pale, predawn gray. Willow nestled against him, warm, safe, sexy even in sleep. The scent of her enveloped him as he listened to her deep breathing. He wanted this moment to last forever.

But the sun would be up soon, and there were things that needed doing. He didn't have to check his watch to know that it was a little before seven. On a normal Wednesday, this would be the time he'd begin the process of prying Natalie out of her bed. Like her mother, his daughter was most definitely not a morning person.

Shelly. The thought intruded on this quiet moment.

He waited for the guilt, but it didn't come. Had he moved on?

Maybe.

He eased away from Willow, propped his head, and watched her sleep. She was stunning and hot, and he'd loved making love to her. He wanted to do it again. Being with her made him feel free, unfettered, light, alive. He didn't know how, but she'd worked a change in him. She was his saving grace.

Last night, when they'd been making love and he'd looked deep into her eyes, he'd seen a reflection of himself that blew him away. She saw him as some kind of hero. In her arms, he was transformed into a braver man than the one who had loved Shelly. A kinder man. A truer man.

All because Willow believed he could be these things. She'd as much as said it last night after the lovemaking, in those moments when people whisper things that they often forget the morning after.

But he wasn't going to forget. Not ever. He was going to work at being that better man. First he'd make her breakfast. Then he'd call in sick and spend the day helping her decorate Eagle Hill Manor like it was Santa Claus's house. And tonight he'd figure out some way to share her bed again.

He eased from the bed, found his pants, and headed down to the kitchen. He started some coffee and had just cracked a couple of eggs when the kitchen door opened. Poppy was the only person who used the kitchen door on a regular basis because her bedroom was at the back of the house and the door gave her a private entrance.

He looked up as she entered the room. She wore the same clothing she'd been wearing last night when she'd left for her bridge club. She looked rosy-cheeked, which could be the result of the chilly temperature outside or something else altogether.

She stopped dead in her tracks, her gaze sweeping across his unshaved face, naked chest, and shoeless state. He'd obviously not walked from the caretaker's cottage.

They stared at each other for a long moment before the corner of Poppy's mouth turned up just slightly. "Well, I didn't expect to have company in my walk of shame."

His face grew hot. Here was the guilt he'd been waiting for. Finally.

Damn. What could he possibly say to Shelly's mother? He didn't know where to start. So, coward that he was, he turned back to whipping up the eggs and asked, "You want some breakfast?"

"No, thank you. I've already had some. Walter is an early riser." She took several steps into the room and stood there hesitating, as if she was waiting for his explanation. It occurred to him that he could demand an explanation of his own, but he had no desire to do that. Any idiot could see that she and Walter had a little romance going. He was happy for her.

She finally spoke. "David, it's fine. Really. I'm not in the least upset. In fact, I've been hoping this would happen."

He looked up. "Hoping for what?"

She smiled. "For you and Willow. Dear boy, you need to move on. So do I. It's not easy losing a spouse. I haven't said it before, but I was very happy when you took off your wedding band."

He nodded, tears suddenly filling his eyes. Damn. He looked down again. "Thanks. I . . ." He ran out of words.

"I know. You don't have to say anything. I understand. I really do." She put the paper on the stainless-steel counter. "I also know what a private man you are, and I'm afraid that this affair you've started with Willow has become common knowledge."

He looked up again, just as she shoved the paper across the counter. "Take a look at the front page."

He looked. His gut clenched. There was Willow being led off in handcuffs big as life on the front page above the fold. Below it was a second photo of that moment in the police station when Willow had thrown herself into his arms. Someone in the SFPD had caught them in the act. The photograph was sharp and clear and there could be no doubt that David was enjoying the hell out of the kiss Willow was laying on him.

The main headline read: PROTESTERS DISRUPT HEARING, which was to be expected, but the subhead said, CONGRESSIONAL HOPEFUL OPPOSES PARK, THEN KISSES TROUBLEMAKER.

Willow opened her eyes to find pale winter sunlight edging the gold and red curtains of the Churchill Suite. For an instant, in that time between waking and sleeping, a bone-deep happiness filled her. A new day had dawned. It was time to get up and live it to the fullest. A little morning sex would definitely get the day started right.

She took a deep breath, filled with David's unmistakable scent, and reached for him.

He was gone.

She closed her eyes. What an idiot. Of course he'd run.

She remembered the words she'd whispered to him in the immediate afterglow last night. Stuff about how he was sort of a hero for rescuing her from jail, representing Dusty for nothing, and standing up for Jeff. "You better watch out," she'd teased. "Your bah humbug is slipping." Yeah, that's what she'd said. It was almost the truth, because she'd already started thinking about him as a hero. That's how beautiful and moving the sex had been.

Right, Willow, nothing like leading with your heart and then following with your chin. He might be her hero, but she was wise enough to know that a happily-ever-after with Prince David just wasn't in the cards. In the real world, commoners like her never got the royalty on a permanent basis.

The best they could hope for was a tumble in the hay. The rain had fallen on her hayride, but she wasn't complaining. A night of love in the Churchill Suite was more than all right. It was a fantasy come true—with the emphasis on the word "fantasy."

She checked her watch. It was almost seven thirty. She should get up and shower. There was a ton of work to do today. The manor had to be decorated for Christmas, and the bride and her bridesmaids were scheduled for final fittings today at A Stitch in Time.

With the wedding only ten days away, there were so many wedding details to nail down that she didn't have time to get all emotional about her fling with David. She would tuck the memory away and savor it.

She had just pushed herself up in the bed when the door opened. She snatched up the sheet and said "eek," just as David strolled in bearing a big tray filled with something that looked like coffee and breakfast.

In his shirtless state, with beard shadowing his jaw and his hair all tousled, he looked like one of those guys in the local fireman's calendar. Forget breakfast and one-time flings. She wanted to eat *him*. Plus her heart surrendered when she saw the tray he carried. He hadn't run away from the things she'd said last night.

"Hi," he said, his ears an adorable shade of red. He stood there with the morning sun lighting him up like a Greek god.

"Hi," she said, completely unable to hide the smile that tugged her lips.

"You look stunning."

Her turn to blush. She ran her hands through her hair. "I'm sure I look well used."

"Yeah, you do. That's part of the attraction." He came forward and put the tray on the bed. Then he leaned in and kissed her. Thoroughly.

"Let's forget about breakfast," she whispered.

He pushed her back. "No, I think we should eat. And we need to talk."

We need to talk? Whoa. Those were the very last words she ever expected to hear from David's mouth. He was not a big talker.

"About what?" she asked.

He handed her a cup of coffee made exactly the way she liked it. "I'm afraid someone on the SFPD took a picture of us last night, together, kissing. It's on the front page of the *Winchester Daily*. There's also a photo of you being led off in handcuffs and a snotty headline that pissed me off."

She sagged back against the big feather pillows. She didn't know whether to laugh or cry. She'd been worried about this. Apparently he hadn't given one thought to it. If he had, he'd never have bailed her out last night. She took a deep swallow of her coffee and, thus fortified, squared her shoulders. "Well, it was fun while it lasted, huh?"

He cocked his head. "What do you mean?"

"I mean that it was fun, but, you know, that's it."

He blinked at her. "Is that how you feel?"

Oh, boy, how did she feel? For starters, she was falling in love with him and that was ridiculous. Mom was absolutely right about some things. Willow would never be accepted by his family. She was the wrong kind of wife for a man pursuing a political career. She was neither the sweet, adoring wife type, nor the hard, political operator. She was, in a word, trouble, with a capital *T*.

"How did you expect me to feel?" she asked.

"I don't know. You said some things last night that made me think..."

She put her coffee down on the bedside table and then snaked her arms around his neck. "David, last night was amazing. I enjoyed every minute of it. And I mean it when I say that I was really, really thankful when you bailed me out of jail. I don't ever want to be arrested again. So thanks for that. And for making me breakfast. That's so sweet of you. But I know this can't be permanent. And now that the press has latched on, it's going to get ugly.

"So it's okay. I'm good with it. It wasn't ever going to be real, you know. I'm just your bridge to get over Shelly."

He picked up the tray and put it down on the rug. "Come here," he commanded, as he reached for her. He pressed his forehead against hers. "Let's get something clear here. If you think I'm done with you just because of some stupid article in the newspaper, then you need to think again."

"But—"

He ran his hand through her hair, his touch breaking her insides. "I'm so crappy at talking about stuff like this.

I get so tongue-tied. I've never been encouraged to talk about my feelings. You know?"

"Uh, if you don't want to, it's—"

He put his fingers over her mouth. "Just give me a minute to stumble through this, okay? I can see you've got this idea that you being Linda Petersen's daughter is more than I can handle. But you're wrong. I don't care whose daughter you are. I don't care what Restero or the *Winchester Daily* says about you. I don't care about any of that. I care about you. That's it."

His thumb caressed her cheek, and it was all she could do not to break down in tears. Her chin started to tremble and she couldn't make it stop. If he kept talking like this, it would destroy her. "Please, David, I—"

"You don't believe me, do you? I guess that's natural, given the way people in this town have always treated you because of your mother. I know how that stuff works. I know very well how it works."

His words settled down deep inside of her where her heart was so hungry for them. "I love my mom," she said on a shaky voice, "but I hate it when everyone compares me to her. I'm not like her. At all. But everyone expects me to make trouble, even when I'm always trying to be on my best behavior. I'm sorry, David. You should never have rescued me last night."

"Nonsense," he said, brushing away a tear that leaked from her eye. He leaned in and kissed her tenderly. "I'm a really reserved and private person, you know? But even so, I think maybe this newspaper article is a blessing. Now everyone knows about us, and we don't have to hide what's happening between us. We can just let it happen right out loud."

She wrapped her arms around him and rested her head on his shoulder. His body was so hard, and strong, and male. Could she dare to hope that happily-ever-after was possible?

No, maybe it was better not to get that far ahead in her thinking, because his formidable family would never accept the two of them together. But then again, she wasn't falling in love with his family; she was falling in love with him.

Wasn't that the point he was trying to make?

She tipped her head up and kissed his jaw. It wasn't enough. She wanted to drink him in like her morning coffee. She wanted to eat him up for breakfast. And maybe then the hunger at her core would finally be satisfied.

Chapter 15 ———————

Willow had come down from the clouds by the time two o'clock rolled around. The words David said this morning would forever be pressed between the pages of her memory. But it didn't take long for storybook endings to fall apart.

His cell phone started buzzing a little after eight, cutting short their breakfast in bed. His plans for staying home and hanging holly evaporated with the morning mist.

The Lyndons—all of them, including Senator Mark Lyndon himself—had called a family meeting in order to deal with the latest media crisis. David's attendance was mandatory, and even though he'd told her not to worry, she wasn't an idiot. She knew how this would turn out.

So she wasn't in the best frame of mind when she picked up Natalie at Daniel Morgan Elementary. But Natalie, bless her sweet, young heart, was so excited about trying on her new green dress that by the time Willow pulled into the parking lot at A Stitch in Time, her mood had improved.

A Stitch in Time was one of half a dozen businesses located in a nineteenth-century Victorian house that had been converted for commercial use. Reva Daraji owned the business, and according to Yelp, she was the best seamstress in all of Jefferson County. Willow hoped the ratings were real, because every dress she'd ordered was the wrong size. Maybe if she'd had months to plan this wedding she could have gotten dresses closer to the mark, but beggars couldn't be choosers. The bridal gown had come from a shop in Houston. One of the bridesmaids' dresses had come from San Francisco, the other from Chicago, and Natalie's dress had come from New York. It had taken hundreds of phone calls to locate the dresses Melissa and Courtney wanted.

If Deva Daraji could make them fit, all would be well. Otherwise Willow was prepared for tears and tantrums. According to the wedding dress disaster stories she'd studied on the Internet, that's what she could expect.

She was prepared for the worst, but not for the smirks, sly looks, and goofy grins she got from Melissa, Courtney, Arwen, and even Mrs. Daraji herself when she strolled through the seamstress's front door.

"Good afternoon," Mrs. Daraji said, her brown eyes twinkling. "I am thinking you were having a busy, busy day, no?"

Courtney snickered and slapped her hand across her mouth.

"Yes. Very busy," Willow said, glaring at Courtney.

"Yes. Just so." Mrs. Daraji nodded. "And we are all here, no? Who will be coming in first?"

"Can I go, please?" Natalie jumped up and down.

Mrs. Daraji gave the child a wide smile. "Yes, you can, but when we are finishing with you, you will have to be good and patient while I am finishing with the bride and bridesmaids."

Natalie nodded. "I'll be good."

"Come, then, I will help you try on your dress. We will be coming out so everyone can see." She ushered Natalie into a fitting room.

"So," Courtney whispered once they were gone. "What the heck is going on?"

Willow's face flamed. "I was arrested, and he bailed me out. I showed my gratitude."

"Uh-huh. The entire world can see just how grateful you were."

Willow sank into one of the straight-back chairs in the seamstress's front room.

"So?" Courtney said in a wheedling tone.

"So, what?"

"So, did you, you know..."

"That's none of your—"

"Judging by the crisis mode at LL&K this morning, I think we can all assume that you and David went all the way last night," Arwen said. "And you don't have to confirm that. I can see it in the beard burn on your face."

"Look, ladies, can we not—"

"No," Melissa said, folding her arms. "No, we're not going to shut up. Because we're your friends. I know this comes as a surprise to you, Willow, but we've all come to care for you. And, take it from me, you don't want to get involved with a Lyndon unless you've decided you can't live without him."

"Geez, Melissa, you don't have to be so blunt," Courtney said.

"Yeah, I do." Melissa got up, crossed the room, and sat in the chair next to Willow. "Honey," she said, taking Willow's hand in hers. "Do you love him?"

Crap. She didn't want to talk about this. To anyone. It was too new, too fresh, and besides, talking about it would mean she'd have to admit what a stupid idiot she was for falling for Shelly's husband.

"Do you?"

"I..." She shrugged.

Melissa got right up in her face. "Do you?"

"I don't know if it's a forever kind of love," she finally said, "or just a right now kind of love. And don't lecture me. I've already gotten the lecture from Mom and everyone else about how dumb it is to go falling for a person like David. And, please, guys, don't heap a boatload of guilt on me either. I know it all. He's my best friend's husband, for goodness' sake."

"And he's Pam Lyndon's son. So I'm just saying." Melissa squeezed her hand.

Right then something snapped, and David's words from the morning came back at her. "So?" she said, sitting up in her chair. "Why does that change anything? I mean, to hear people talk, it's like the Montagues and the Capulets or something."

"Yeah," Arwen said, "and that worked out so well for Romeo and Juliet."

Melissa put an arm around her. "I can see why you might be falling for him. He's been a prince these last few weeks. But he's not like Jeff. I mean, Jeff wasn't raised as part of the Lyndon family. He doesn't care what they think. He's given up trying to please his father. And he tolerates his mother's friendship with Pam, but he definitely draws the line when Pam starts interfering."

"David isn't like that," Courtney said.

"I know."

"Be careful, hon," Melissa said.

"Yeah," Arwen echoed. "Those people will eat you alive if it serves their political purposes. And—"

"Lookit, lookit," Natalie said in a bright happy voice as she emerged from the back room wearing the most adorable green velvet dress with a matching hooded cloak. The dress was at least one size too big for her, and the hem was dragging the floor, but it didn't matter. The joyous look on Natalie's face was enough to make everyone smile.

And the subject of Willow's relationship with David Lyndon was mercifully dropped. At least for a while.

They were waiting for him—Mother, Dad, and Heather—in the den at Charlotte's Grove. The room was filled with comfortable furniture, and no effort had been made to decorate the room in keeping with the two-hundred-year-old house. This was the family space. It always had been.

There were other rooms at Charlotte's Grove with antiques that had been in the house for generations, but it struck David as he strode onto the dark beige carpet that, although Mother was a stalwart member of the Jefferson County Historical Society, she had never once tried to turn her home into a museum.

Quite unlike Shelly. But then Shelly had always been

trying to keep up with Mother. Hadn't that been part of the problem?

"How could you?" Mother said as he entered the room. "Really, David, it's bad enough that you've decided to represent Dusty McNeil, but to bail that woman out of jail, and..." She threw up her arms in a gesture of complete exasperation.

"Sit down, Pam," Dad said, and Mother sat, turning her gaze out the large windows. "You too." Dad pointed at the wing chair facing Mother's.

David sat down, but he didn't relax.

"I have to say, I'm a little disappointed," Dad said. "You do realize this woman has a reputation?"

"Yes, I do. She blew the whistle on a case of major Medicare fraud. I'd say that's a pretty brave thing for someone to do."

"Come on, you don't actually believe—" Mother started to speak, but Dad put up his hand, and she stopped.

"I do believe her," David said.

"Well, I suppose we can spin it that way," Dad said, turning toward Heather. "What do you think?"

"I think Bill Cummins is going to challenge us to a primary. And I wouldn't be surprised if he used his connections with Chief LaRue to have a raid mounted on Linda Petersen's farm."

"What are you talking about?" David asked.

"Oh my God, you're so naive. Everyone knows she's growing marijuana out there," Mother said on a sniff.

"Mother, I admit that I've heard the rumors running around town for years, but there's a huge difference between gossip and truth. Paul LaRue is a good, honest man. I have a relationship with him too. He's not going to go raid Linda's farm unless he has probable cause. Not if he knows he's being used as part of a dirty campaign trick."

"You don't think so?" Dad asked. "Who do you think took the picture that was in the paper?"

"I have no idea. There were four members of the SFPD in the room when I bailed Willow out."

"Well," Dad said on a cough, "whatever. I'll give Paul a call and make sure there aren't any drug raids. But even if there isn't any pot growing out there, the perception is the reality anyway. People think Linda is a pothead, so naturally you being involved with her daughter is unacceptable."

"You must drop her," Mother said. "She must be fired right away. You can't risk the gossip. Not when we're so close to announcing your candidacy."

"I won't fire her."

"David, be reasonable. The wedding is in just a few days. Melissa can muddle through on her own."

"No."

David got up from his chair even though he knew his parents weren't finished reading him the riot act. But he was finished listening to it. This hysteria was no more and no less than what Willow had predicted.

He didn't know where this thing with Willow was going, but he wouldn't throw it away because of politics.

"I'll take what you have to say under advisement. But if you'll excuse me, I have a busy evening planned. We're putting up a Christmas tree at the inn, and I promised Willow and Natalie that I would help decorate it."

He hurried from the room, but Heather followed him. She caught up to him in the lobby.

"I don't want to hear it, Heather," he said, pulling on his overcoat.

"I wasn't going to tell you to drop Willow, if that's what you think."

"No?"

Heather shook her head. "You've taken off your wedding ring, so naturally I want to know the truth, the whole truth. Was it just a kiss, or is there more?"

"I told you I'm not in a mood to chat."

"So you've slept with her, then?"

He gave her his bulldog stare, but it backfired.

Heather gave his arm a squeeze. "Look, I think it's terrific that you're moving on. But I'm your sister first and a potential constituent second. Let me confer with Hale tonight and see what he thinks. I'll call you in the morning and set up a meeting, okay? And in the meantime, I'll try to make Mother stand down."

Willow had put Dusty in charge of securing Christmas trees for the inn. He came through in spades, showing up with no fewer than three, all of which were freshly cut at the Snicker's Gap Tree Farm in Blumont.

The largest of these trees was set up by the grand staircase that wound its way down to the lobby. Dusty took care of getting the tree in its stand and pruning a few of the wayward branches. Now it was up to Willow to make it beautiful.

She had several boxes of vintage ornaments, plus a few dozen boxes of new decorations that she'd bought from a warehouse that shipped in Christmas decorations from

Asia on the cheap. She'd never had much of a budget for this, but she'd stretched it as far as it could go.

When she and Natalie returned from the dress fittings, they got to work opening ornament boxes while Mrs. M made hot chocolate. The mood was pretty festive, but it turned almost jolly when David came home from his family powwow early and went to work doing the manly job of stringing lights on the fifteen-foot monster.

Mrs. M punched up classic Christmas carols on the inn's sound system. And for a while Willow felt as if she'd truly come home. Natalie was happy. David was happy. Even Mrs. M was happy.

And then the doorbell rang.

Since David and Natalie were busy looking through an old box of ornaments that Shelly had once treasured, Willow answered the door. Pam Lyndon swept into the foyer with a Cruella de Vil frown on her face.

"Hello, Mrs. Lyndon," she said in her best good-girl voice. "We're trimming the tree. I'm sure Natalie would love to have some help from her grandmother."

The scowl on Pam's face deepened. "Don't try to appeal to my better angels. I know what you're doing, and I have no intention of joining your pack of volunteers. You know very well that I disapprove of you and this ridiculous wedding reception you've roped David into hosting. Where is my son?"

She breezed past Willow without even taking off her coat and marched right up to David. "We need to finish our discussion," she said. "You left before things were settled." Mrs. Lyndon gave Willow a killing glance.

"I'm busy, Mother."

"David, do not defy me."

David let go of a long-suffering sigh. "All right, you've got five minutes." He gave Natalie a hug. "I won't be long. I promise. And then we'll hang some of these ornaments. Especially this one." He held up a heart that said "Baby's First Christmas."

He stood up, glanced at Willow and then Mrs. M, and said, "I'll be back." Then he ushered his mother into the library and shut the pocket doors—something that was rarely ever done.

"Should we eavesdrop?" Mrs. M asked.

Willow shook her head, but it didn't matter, because no sooner had the doors closed than Pam Lyndon's voice rose in anger. "You let me think that you and that woman hadn't done anything more than kiss in public, but Heather says there's more. David, since when do you lie to me?"

David's response was too low and quiet to be heard. Mrs. M crossed the room and pressed her ear up against the door. Willow wished she hadn't done that because she didn't want to know what David said. At that moment, her face felt like it was on fire, and her heart had risen into her throat. She expected the ground to open up and swallow her.

"David, don't be stupid," Pam yelled. "I know your father and sister want to smooth things over, but they don't seem to understand the problem. That woman is not good enough for you. She's nothing but a slut, like her mother. She was having an affair with the CEO of that company. Did you know that?"

Again David's response was too quiet to hear, but at least it was cold comfort that she'd told David all about Corbin. David didn't see her as a slut. She knew that in the deepest places of her heart.

And she might have been all right if not for the fact that she glanced toward Natalie. The little girl stood there with her hands balled into fists and a pained expression on her face.

Did Natalie understand what the word "slut" meant? Willow hoped not, for David's sake as much as her own. The little girl didn't need to hear all this ugly stuff.

"Mrs. M," Willow said in a strangled voice as the reality of her situation hit home.

Shelly's mother turned, and Willow nodded in Natalie's direction. "Maybe we should—" Willow began.

But Natalie interrupted. "Why is Grandmother so unhappy?" she asked.

Mrs. M bent down and tucked a strand of red hair behind the child's ear. "I don't know, precious. Sometimes grown-ups can be pretty darn stupid, if you ask me. Why don't we go see if we can find some gingerbread cookies to go with that hot cocoa."

Natalie resisted Mrs. M's tug on her shoulders. "You said 'stupid.' It's not nice to say that word."

"I'm sorry. You're right, but—"

"And Daddy got mad at the teachers and called them stupid too." Natalie took a step toward the door. "And then he had to apologize."

"I know, but he was—"

Natalie shook her head and dodged Mrs. M's hands. She ran to the library door, pulled it open, and marched right into the argument.

"Stop yelling, and stop calling my daddy stupid. That's not a nice word," she yelled at the top of her voice. "I hate it. I hate you. And yelling like that is stupid, stupid, stupid. I wish Mommy was here. She'd make you stop yelling."

Both Willow and Mrs. M reached the library doorway in time to see Natalie's face crumple into tears before she turned and pushed through the French doors, taking off toward the caretaker's cottage.

"See what you've done now?" Pam said in a hard, flat, angry tone. She wasn't looking at David when she said it either, because David had left the room, following his daughter's flight.

Chapter 16

Half an hour later, Willow strode through Serenity Farm's front door to find Mom at the kitchen table eating something that looked kind of gray and vaguely disgusting.

"What is that?" she asked.

"It's eggplant parmigiana. It's delicious. You want some?"

Willow was hungry, but she shook her head. "No. I think I'll pass. Not a big fan of eggplant."

She sat in one of the kitchen chairs.

"So, you're not here for dinner. What's the occasion?" Mom asked.

Willow's face heated. "I'm here to beg a place to sleep. Would it be okay if I moved back into the upstairs bedroom?"

Mom didn't give her any kind of "aw, baby" look. That had never been Mom's way. Mom was a believer in the truth. "So, you got thrown out of Eagle Hill Manor because of that photo, huh?"

"Yup, more or less. I would say that I threw myself out, but only after my integrity was challenged."

"Told ya," Mom said, reaching out to give Willow's shoulder a squeeze. Mom's tone was surprisingly sympathetic.

"Yeah, you did."

"You okay?"

She shook her head and bit her lip to keep it from trembling. "No. I'm not."

"Oh, baby girl," Mom said, and then Willow found herself caught up in her mother's arms, where she proceeded to bawl her eyes out.

It took a good twenty minutes before she'd regained her composure. "Thanks. I needed a good cry. I'm okay now."

"You really care about him, don't you?"

Willow nodded. "I think I love him. But it's never going to work. You were right, and I should have listened to you. And maybe if it was just me and David, I might fight the old biddy over him. But I have to think about Natalie. Pam precipitated this huge scene tonight, and it really upset Natalie."

"So you're here because of the little girl? Not be because David asked you to leave?"

Willow nodded. "She doesn't need her grandmothers squabbling about her father's lover."

"You make it sound very sordid."

"Because it is."

Mom shrugged. "Maybe not so much."

"I thought you told me to stay away from David."

"I did. But mostly because I thought he'd break your heart. It sounds like his mother broke your will."

Great. You could never count on Mom to be consistent in her view of the world. "Well," Willow said, "you can chalk it up to me avoiding the heartbreak before it happens. Isn't that what you said I should do?"

"Oh, I get it now. That totally explains the crying jag. You avoided the heartbreak."

Willow collapsed back in her chair, letting her shoulders sag. "All right. I'm busted. I left. I wasn't tossed out. But it's the right thing to do. And please don't argue with me, okay?"

"Okay. I won't. And you know you're always welcome here, baby doll."

But even if she was welcome, Willow had never really fit here at Serenity Farm. She didn't read auras, she wasn't a musician, she hated eggplant, and she only tolerated farm chores. There was a reason she'd been so anxious to leave this place when she was a kid.

But if she didn't fit here, and she didn't fit with David and Natalie, where the hell did she fit?

Early the next morning, David found himself in his office facing Hale Chandler and Heather. At least neither of them was yelling.

Jesus, he'd never seen his mother so angry. She literally despised Willow, but for reasons he didn't fully understand.

Unfortunately, Mother had no concept of the damage she'd done last night. Not just to David's relationship with Willow (if there was one), but to Natalie. His little girl had cried herself to sleep, and this morning she'd regressed back to the needy child she'd been right after Shelly had died.

Poppy was furious with him for not running after Willow. And Willow had left a note and walked away.

In short, his world was in chaos.

"Do you want this seat, David?" Hale Chandler asked.

David had been asked this question many times, and he'd always said yes. And he'd always known that running for Congress would require sacrifices. He was, after all, a senator's son. He knew what campaigns were like.

But up until right this minute, sacrifice had been merely a concept. Now sacrifice had a name: Willow.

He most definitely did not want to give her up.

"Davie?" Heather sat in the second chair, mostly deferring to her boss.

"Of course I want this," he said. And he meant it. He'd been preparing to run for Congress from the minute he graduated from law school. What else was he good for?

"If you want this," Hale said in his big, gruff, take-no-prisoners voice, "then you have to do several things.

"First"—he raised one fat finger—"you have to endorse this park project. All our polling on this indicates that it's popular with the constituents of this district." He raised the rest of his fingers, palm outward in the quintessential "talk to the hand" gesture. "Not one word, David. I know this is a local issue, but all politics is local. You don't want to be an odd man out on something this popular. And second"—up came two fingers in the victory sign—"you have to distance yourself from this woman Willow Petersen. She's poison for you."

Hale leaned forward and pulled a file out of his attaché case. "Here," he said. "I've had my investigator put together a file on this woman. The opposition will have a field day with this stuff in her background."

David had, of course, heard all this before. Hale Chandler didn't yell, however. He delivered his thoughts on the subject with cool rationality.

David picked up the file and threw it at Hale. "Don't ever do that again," he said through clenched teeth.

Hale scowled at him. "Lose the attitude and stop thinking with your dick."

"I'm not thinking with my dick, thank you. I may be thinking with my heart, though."

"Davie, really?" Heather sounded truly concerned.

He nodded his head. "Really."

"Well, stop," Hale said. "We want you thinking with your brain and not any other part of your anatomy. Are we clear on that?"

David wanted to punch his consultant in the nose. "No, we're not clear."

"Davie, please, just—"

He glared at his sister and his consultant. "Look, if you guys don't want to work for me, then fine. But if you do want to work for me, here are the conditions."

It was his turn to put up a finger. "First, I will not change my position on the park. I intend to continue to represent Dusty McNeil. And if voters in the twelfth district have an issue with me standing up for Dusty and his property rights, then so be it. More important, Dusty is my friend."

Hale's eyes lit up. "Okay. If you explain it like that, I'll give you the park. But you still have a floozy issue."

David jumped up. "Don't you ever call her that again, do you understand? Here's the truth about Willow Petersen. She caught Restero doing something wrong and then covering it up. She pointed a finger and blew the whistle. That takes courage, Hale, more courage than it takes you to shove your stupid file in my face." He leaned forward on his desk.

He had expected Hale to stand up to him, but instead the man smiled. "Most of my clients don't have the balls to stand up to me. I'm impressed. But the woman is still a problem."

Heather spoke. "Davie, did you know that she was having an affair with Corbin Martinson?"

"I did. So what? I was married once, to her best friend. We're both in our thirties. We've had other relationships. It's not a character issue."

Hale leaned forward. "Yes, it is. Martinson is well respected. He says she became a stalker when he ended a short-lived affair. Then she lost perspective and made up a scandal just to get back at him personally."

"And she says something else."

"Davie, your loyalty is admirable, but I'm worried about you. I'm worried she'll break your heart and leave your career in ruins."

"And I just want you to win this election," Hale said in a flat voice. "This is politics, David. If you care about the truth, find another profession."

"And your solution is to have me walk away from someone I've known for a long time. The godmother of my child? Is that your advice?"

"That's my advice."

"You aren't even interested in coming up with something to counter the mud Bill Cummins is going to sling?"

"The best counterpunch would be to tell the opposition that you and this woman are not involved."

"But we are involved."

"Then get uninvolved."

"No."

Hale and Heather both swore under their breath.

"Look, I've known Willow for a long time. She has put herself into hock in order to bring a private legal claim against Restero for knowingly harming Medicare patients. If she wins, they'll have to pay a big fine. If the government joins her suit—and I'm hoping they will—then some of Restero's executives might face criminal charges and jail time. If you take half a minute to really look at this, you'll see she's not a disgruntled employee."

"Voters don't have half a minute," Hale said.

They sat in silence for a long time before David spoke again. "Look, if you guys want to bail on this campaign, that's fine. There are plenty of other people I can hire to provide political advice."

Hale gave him a long, sober look. "David, I like you. I think you'll make a great candidate, precisely because you're standing up for your friends. So I'll make a deal with you. I'll hire that investigator, and we'll see what he turns up on Ms. Petersen and her claims against Restero. But in the meantime, I suggest that you convince Ms. Petersen to give up this lawsuit of hers. If Restero did something wrong, let the government pursue them. That would answer the charges that she's a malcontent and a money-grubber."

David took in a deep breath. "Okay, I see that point. I'll talk to her about it."

"Davie, I think it's wonderful that you've finally moved past Shelly, really. And I'm glad that you've taken off the wedding band and seem to be ready to rejoin the human race. But I just want you to think long and hard about his. Is your heart really involved, or is it just sex? Because if it's just a temporary thing with Willow, it would be crazy to give up your career."

He couldn't answer Heather's question. Except that whatever he felt for Willow went beyond lust. She'd been his friend for a long time. She'd made Natalie laugh again. She'd helped him figure out how to solve the problem at the school. And she'd made Jeff and Melissa so happy.

He cared about her. She'd made him care again. She'd brought him back to the land of the living.

He wasn't going walk away from that.

Poppy, Faye, and Viola sat at a dark corner booth at the Olive Garden restaurant out by the interstate. Poppy had called this emergency meeting after last night's debacle.

"Oh, crap," Viola said, wringing her hands. "After I saw that photograph in the *Winchester Daily* I thought we were on to phase two of our plan. So I had a little conversation with Bryce Summerville about buying Eagle Hill Manor. He's definitely interested. He told me he was going to call Walter today."

"You what?" Poppy said in a voice that carried across the dining room. People turned, and Poppy's face heated.

She needed to remember Natalie's words last night. Yelling was never appropriate.

Viola continued to wring her hands. "That kiss David laid on Willow was hot. I mean, it verified our theory that she was playing hard to get."

"Just waiting to be rescued from the city jail," Faye said on a long, sappy sigh. "That was quite romantic, you know. If he'd rescued me, I would have kissed him too."

"Of course, but one kiss does not cement a lifelong relationship," Poppy said, wondering if the kisses she'd recently shared with Walter were an indication of anything other than her own idiocy.

"You mean that's all it was?" Faye asked, her big gray eyes going round above her half-moon glasses.

Poppy took a sip of her not-very-good wine and tried to compose herself. Thinking about Walter always short-circuited her brain. Right now she needed clarity.

"It wasn't just a kiss, was it?" Viola asked.

Poppy steeled herself. She hated to gossip, but this was an emergency. "No, it was much more than a kiss. They spent the night together. I caught him making breakfast for her the next morning." She neglected to explain exactly how she'd caught him. Nor did she mention the fact that David didn't seem to be suffering any shame for what had transpired the night before last, while Poppy was still trying to come to terms with the fact that a woman her age was capable of having wild and crazy sex.

Viola and Faye sighed in unison.

"Yes." Poppy nodded. "And he appeared to have enjoyed himself until his family gave him a lecture and then his mother followed it up with a hissy fit in which she dredged up every nasty thing anyone has ever said about Willow and her mother." Poppy drummed her fingers on the table. She wanted to drive out to Charlotte's Grove and have a catfight with Pam. A little hair pulling might straighten the woman out. But, of course, Natalie wouldn't be well served by any more yelling or screaming or eye gouging no matter how much Pam deserved it. Someone needed to take that woman to the woodshed and beat some sense into her.

"Maybe we should have thought about that," Faye said. "I mean, with all this controversy over her last job, Willow isn't exactly what I'd call a political wife, you know?"

"I know," Poppy said. "But my gut tells me that she's the kind of wife David wants. And more important than that, she's the kind of *mother* Natalie needs and deserves. I know for certain that Willow has fallen head over heels in love with Natalie, and the child loves her right back. David, I'm not entirely sure of. I think he desires her, but maybe he's not yet fallen all the way."

"Oh." Faye and Viola sighed the word in unison.

"But I just don't see how we get around Pam." She picked up her wine and took another slug. If ever there was a time for drinking, this was it. Her friends stared down at their never-ending pasta bowls. No one had eaten a bite. "David is loyal to his family. He always has been. This was an issue when it came to his marriage."

"So maybe we should back off," Faye said.

"No. This is not the time for retreat. But I don't know what exactly we do next," Poppy said.

They sat in silence for a long while, staring at the food and drinking their wine, until Viola finally spoke. "Well, if Bud were here, he'd say that we need to rebrand Willow."

"Rebrand?"

Viola nodded. "Yup, that's advertising speak for rehabilitating her image."

"I didn't think her image was all that bad to start off with," Faye said. "I mean, her mother is a nutcase, but Willow's okay. Look what she's done for Melissa and Jeff. You can't have lunch at the diner without Gracie singing her praises."

"That's it," Poppy said. "We need to get Gracie's help. Everyone listens to Grace, and she'd do anything for David."

"We can also talk to our church friends. You know, start a little gossip going, only instead of saying bad stuff about Willow, we could say nice stuff. Nothing works faster in this town than the Presbyterian phone tree," Faye said.

"But what, exactly, is the good stuff?" Viola asked.

They stared at each other as the realization dawned on them that they didn't actually know what the good stuff might be. All they'd ever heard about Willow and her mother was bad stuff.

"Well, crap, we ought to know the truth about her if we're going to rebrand her, shouldn't we?" Faye said.

Everyone nodded and took another sip of wine.

"All right," Poppy said after a moment as she moved her pasta bowl aside. "We need to make a plan."

"Another plan?" Viola asked.

Poppy nodded. "Yes, another one. And for starters, we need to figure out all the good stuff about Willow. Faye, I want you to go down to the library and find out everything you can about Willow and that company she used to work for. Don't just read the articles that accuse her of being a malcontent. I'm not sure any of those are fair or balanced."

She paused for a moment. "You know, before you go to the library, have a chat with Jeff. He used to be a reporter. He could probably give you some good advice about digging up the truth."

"I'm on it," Faye said.

"Viola, I want you to talk to Gracie and tell her everything we've been trying to do. We need her help. Pick her brain for ideas. Gracie knows everyone in town. If we want to launch a rebranding effort, she's the right place to start."

"Aye, aye." Viola gave a salute.

"I'm going to talk to Walter and see if we can stall Bryce Summerville. If we can't salvage the romance between David and Willow, then I want to make sure that Willow has a chance to buy Eagle Hill Manor. It will be her consolation prize."

"Does she have the money she needs to buy the place?" Faye asked.

"I don't think so," Poppy said.

"That's a problem. Bryce told me he has the cash for an investment like that. He was really very interested."

"Oh, that's not good. I think maybe we should pray," Faye said.

"Wait. I'm confused." Viola frowned at her empty wineglass. "Should I be praying for David and Willow to fall in love and find acceptance within his family, or should I be praying that Willow finds an investor?"

"Well, for now, maybe we should pray for both," Faye said.

"Yeah, and while we're at it, maybe we should pray that God knows which prayer to answer, because I'm still not convinced that Willow and David can make a happy marriage if she's determined to become an innkeeper and he's determined to run for Congress," Poppy said on a long sigh.

Willow awakened on Thursday and told herself that it was a new day and she could make whatever she wanted out of it. And today she would treat herself to coffee and a Danish at Bean There Done That, which would have two important benefits.

First, she'd avoid eating breakfast at home, which consisted of a spinach and mango smoothie that was about the same color green as the Grinch's complexion. And second, hanging for a while at the coffee shop would delay her in town long enough to avoid having to come face-to-face with either David or Natalie.

She wasn't hiding at the coffee shop, exactly; she was fortifying herself for the day ahead, which consisted of decorating the inn to the nines while simultaneously avoiding David and Natalie, either of whom was likely to destroy her carefully manufactured composure.

She was trying to think happy, positive thoughts when Russell Cade, her attorney, called her cell. She punched the talk button, and Russ's gruff but kindly voice came over the line. "Willow, it sure looks like someone up there doesn't like you."

So much for the power of positive thinking.

"What?" she said in an acid tone.

"The Department of Health and Human Services let us know late yesterday that they aren't going to pursue the case against Restero."

"But why?"

"Who knows? It could be budget cuts. It could be someone in a high place who doesn't want Restero touched. It could be that the lawyers over there don't think we have a good case. I can't tell you what goes through their minds. But this changes nothing."

"Except there's no way to send Corbin to jail now."

"Well, there is that. But it was unlikely that anyone was going to get nailed with criminal charges. Let's just make 'em pay. And the good news is that if we win this case, we'll get one hundred percent of the penalties instead of thirty percent. So it's a lot more money now."

She propped her elbow on the table and rested her head in her hand. "Russ, this has never been about money to me. You know that, don't you?"

"I understand that, but keep in mind that if you nail a corporation hard enough in the pocketbook, it can change behavior."

"Yeah, but until I win the case, they are out there telling the world that I'm just doing this for the money. They make me look crass and mean and..." She let her voice trail off as memories of Pam Lyndon's vitriol from last night replayed through her mind.

"Courage, Willow. You're not the first whistle-blower to have their reputation trashed. And I've never once met a whistle-blower who cared about the money, either. It takes a certain kind of person to stand up against a giant corporation like Restero. Just remember that."

"Yeah. I guess. A totally crazy person."

"Not so crazy. A moral person," Russ said in his gravelly voice. "So, are you ready to go it alone?"

"Yes," she said. "I have no other choice."

"Good for you. I think our case is strong. We're going to win this thing, but it's going to get ugly before we do."

"I know." All that ugliness would give Pam Lyndon more fuel for her fire. But it couldn't be helped. If Willow walked away now, what was to stop Restero from doing something like this a second time? If she walked away, she'd never clear her name.

"Look, there won't be much action between now and the first of the year. I'll give you a call in a few weeks. In the meantime, have a happy holiday, okay? And stay strong."

She pushed disconnect, squared her shoulders, and told herself that she was doing the right thing. But this wasn't a choice she could impose on Natalie or David. That was very clear.

She just needed to get through the next week and a half, until the wedding, and then she could figure out what came next. She'd have to find a real job and give up her dream of buying Eagle Hill Manor and becoming, of all things, a wedding planner.

She dawdled over her coffee and then spent the morning following up with the baker and the florist, so it was after ten by the time she got back to the inn. The place was deserted. David was at work, of course. And Natalie was at school. But Mrs. M was nowhere to be found.

Willow went straight to work on the tree, hanging lights, draping the gold bead garlands, and putting up ornaments. When that was finished, she moved on to draping pine roping on the banisters of the grand stairway. She tied yards and yards of bows and strung miles of twinkle lights. Mrs. M finally checked in after lunchtime to say that she would be out and about all day doing un-

specified errands, which included picking Natalie up after
school and taking her to her semiannual dental appointment. So Willow worked on alone, and the more holly she
hung, the less jolly she felt.

By late afternoon she needed to get away from the red
and green. She bundled herself up and strolled out to Laurel Chapel. It was windy up on the hill, so she took refuge
in the ruins of the church.

Mrs. M had once said that she felt close to Shelly
out here, and Willow understood exactly what she meant.
There weren't any ghosts out here, of course, but Shelly's
memory haunted this place.

"Here I am, Shelly," she whispered, self-conscious to
be speaking aloud to a feeling. "I'm trying to be strong,
but, you know, I feel like a character in one of your
Gothic romances. Someone who's brokenhearted and
takes to long, frozen walks on the moors."

She leaned against an empty window frame and
laughed in spite of herself. "Listen to me. Brokenhearted.
Did you ever think? No, I don't guess you did. Especially
not me and David, anyway."

She let go of a long breath that steamed in the chill,
waiting to feel something like guilt, but it didn't come.
She wasn't guilty about David. She had this strong sense
that Shelly wasn't interested in holding on to David from
beyond the grave.

Willow pulled her cashmere coat closer around herself,
raising the collar against the cold. It was starting to get
dark; the days were so short this time of year. She really
ought to be heading back to Serenity Farm.

She turned toward the door, but before she reached it,
David came striding through.

His cheeks were ruddy from the cold, and the wind had blown his hair across his brow, making him look a lot like one of those Gothic heroes Shelly loved so much. His dark eyes sealed the deal. He was wrapped in a single-breasted charcoal-gray overcoat that fit his broad shoulders as if it had been made for him.

"You decorated the tree," he said in a slightly annoyed tone as he stopped in the doorway, blocking her escape.

Of all the things she expected (or wanted) David to say, this wasn't it. In fact, coming from him—a stand-in for Ebenezer Scrooge—this comment was downright nonsensical.

"Um," she said, "I thought we were in agreement that decorations were needed for the wedding. And it's sort of my job to see that the inn is ready for Jeff and Melissa's big day."

His lips thinned. "Natalie will be disappointed. Did you even think about that? She wanted to help."

Damn. He sure knew how to cut right to the heart. "Uh, no, I guess I didn't. I'm really sorry. I just needed to do my job today. You know, what you're paying me to do." Her voice quivered.

He closed his eyes and drew in a deep breath. He had such amazingly thick, dark eyelashes. He opened his eyes. "You're fired."

"What?"

"I have to fire you, because you know, we've got a thing going. And I really thought the whole Christmas tree was about doing something together and not about Jeff and Melissa's wedding. I'm tired of hearing about Jeff and Melissa's wedding."

"Wait a sec. Do we have a thing? Because as far as I'm

concerned, whatever thing we had is officially over and done with."

He stepped forward, his hands jammed into his coat pockets. "Look, I'm sorry about what Mother said last night. I don't agree with her point of view."

A lump the size of a walnut swelled in her throat. He was so handsome it almost hurt to look at him.

"Come here," he commanded, but she stayed put. Touching him would weaken her resolve. And she needed to be strong, especially if he wasn't going to be.

She shook her head. "Look, I know you don't share your mother's views about me, but unfortunately, a lot of other people do. So it's kind of a no-brainer, you know. We don't belong—"

He stepped up to her, pulled her into his arms, and kissed her right into silence. The touch of his lips, slightly cool on the outside, hot on the inside, made the world spin in crazy circles. She wanted this. She wanted him. She fell into his kiss and might even have made a little moan that told him everything she was trying to hide.

He finally pulled back, but not until he'd thoroughly warmed her from head to toe. "This is how it's going to be," he said in that take-charge voice of his. "We're going to date exclusively. And we're going to do it in public."

She almost laughed. "Date? Really? Does anyone really date anymore?"

His grip on her shoulders firmed. "You know exactly what I mean. Do I have to spell it out for you? I want us to be friends with benefits."

Lovers. But he hadn't used that word. She shook her head. "No, David. It's not going to work."

"Of course it's going to work. We just need to give it time. I even told my political consultant to take his concerns and shove them in an unmentionable place."

"His concerns about me?"

David nodded. "It's all that crap about Restero. But I changed his mind. Look, all you have to do is drop your private suit and let the government do its thing. Once you aren't in the mix, most of the problems go away."

"What?" She took a step back, her heart suddenly racing a mile a minute. "Why would I do that?"

"Because if you walk away from your private claim, then no one can say you're doing this out of some kind of profit motive. It really weakens what the opposition is going to hit us with. And besides, the government will take up the case. I'm sure of it."

"The opposition? Who is that, precisely?"

He stabbed his hand through his hair. "Look, Bill Cummins is going to challenge me in the primary. And he's just the kind of guy who will use this stuff to suggest that I have poor judgment or something. And, of course, it will come up again in the general election, but I'm less concerned about that. We can deflect the downside. All you have to do is walk away from the lawsuit."

She took another step back, feeling as if she'd fallen into a trap that she should have seen from the start. Hadn't Corbin used exactly the same words when she'd come to him with her concerns about the defective hip replacements? "We can deflect the downside," he'd said, "just keep your mouth shut."

And if she'd done that, she just might have moved from being friends with benefits to being Mrs. Corbin Martinson. Corbin had been hinting about a deeper commitment. But, of course, she had to get in line and behave in order to win that particular prize.

This is how the world worked. You didn't get loved unless you behaved.

"No," she said.

"No, what?"

"No, I'm not walking away, David. I'm not getting in line, or behaving the way your campaign handlers want me to behave. Damn. I should have known. Mom even warned me. David, this is who I am. Your parents despise me, your campaign people think I need to be managed, and you just want me to keep my mouth shut and behave. This isn't what I want."

She walked right past him, her heart shattering into a million pieces. She had thought, maybe foolishly, that David Lyndon was ready to care about her—maybe even love her—for who she was, not what she did or how she behaved.

"Well, what the hell *do* you want?" he asked from behind.

She stopped and squeezed her eyes shut. He didn't really get it, did he? Not even after all those beautiful words he'd said on Wednesday morning. "If I have to explain that, David, then it's best if we part ways right now."

She turned and faced him. "Am I still fired?"

"What? Yes, you're fired. I can't date an employee."

"I don't want to date you. Haven't I made that clear?"

"Yes, abundantly."

"So, am I still fired, or do you want me to continue to help you with the wedding?"

"Jesus, Willow, why are you being so difficult? Shelly was like this too."

"Yeah, I bet she was. I just need to know whether you want me to finish what I started or not."

"Christ, of course I want you to finish what you started."

"Okay. Fine." She turned and stalked away into the woods.

He followed her. "Willow?" he said when they finally made it back to the inn. It was almost dusk, and he had the nerve to sound confused about what had just happened. "Stop. We need to talk."

She turned around. "No, we don't. And in case you're confused, here is precisely what I'm thinking right now. Go run for Congress, David. It's what you were born to do and what you want. You'll make a good politician. But don't try to turn me into a shadow of myself just to please the voters or your family or your campaign manager. It won't work. I will disappoint you. And last night's meltdown should be warning enough of what's in store. Do you really want to put Natalie through all that? Because, here's the thing, David: I love your daughter, and I sure as hell don't want another episode like last night's. And if I become your friend with benefits, that's exactly what's going to happen."

She turned away again, ran to her car, and peeled out of the driveway before he could see that he'd once again reduced her to tears.

Chapter 17———————————

For a few days in early December, David had managed to ignore the advent calendar in his head. But when Willow walked away from him, he awakened from his foolish dreams, took a look at the date on his Movado watch, and realized that he was coming up hard and fast on the two-year anniversary of Shelly's death.

And this year he felt more alone than ever.

Which was odd, because he didn't mind being alone.

Last year the weather had turned warm, and he'd spent the day alone out on the run with his fly rod and a bottle of Maker's Mark. He hadn't landed any trout, just a killer hangover. But at least he hadn't spent the day having to accept people's condolences. He hated that more than anything.

There wouldn't be any fishing this year. A Canadian high had swooped down on Shenandoah Falls, providing endless blue skies and sending daytime temperatures plummeting into the twenties. He also didn't have the luxury of crawling into a bottle somewhere private.

This year, the anniversary of Shelly's death fell on the day before Jeff and Melissa's wedding, so David's attendance was required at the Presbyterian church for the rehearsal and then at the big rehearsal dinner Mother and Nina had planned at Charlotte's Grove. With all the excitement, he wouldn't be the center of attention this year. People had probably forgotten that it was the anniversary of Shelly's death.

Which was fine. He would remember. Let everyone else go celebrate and leave him alone. He was better when people left him alone, anyway.

The rehearsal was scheduled for five in the afternoon, which gave him just enough time to pick up Natalie from school.

"Will Miss Willow be at the party?" she asked as he pulled away from the school pickup area.

"No," he said, as he took the turn onto Washington Avenue. He glanced in the rearview mirror just in time to see the sadness in his daughter's dark eyes.

Damnit. Willow said she had Natalie's best interests in mind, but it was hard to see how that was the case. For a solid week Willow had managed to avoid both of them while still fulfilling her contract with him. The public spaces of the inn never looked better. There was Christmas crap draped over every inch of the inside and the outside. The lawn had been mowed, the overgrown bushes trimmed, the kitchen polished and shined.

In fact, the inn showed so well that Bryce Summerville had just made an offer on the place that was only a few grand below asking price. David hadn't accepted the offer yet. He'd made a promise to Willow that he wouldn't sell the inn until after the wedding, and he aimed to keep that promise.

He was hoping she'd find an investor. But according to Gracie, Willow had all but given up looking for one. No doubt Gracie had imparted that piece of information in order to make him feel guilty. Grace seemed to be on a one-woman mission to change the town's opinion of Willow, but he was already a believer.

Willow was the one who didn't believe.

He made the turn through the stone gates of Greenwood Cemetery and glanced in the mirror again. Natalie sat up straighter. "Are we visiting Mommy?" she asked.

A lump formed in his throat. "Yeah," he said. "It's December eighteenth. Two years ago today Mommy went to heaven."

"Oh. I didn't remember."

"I know. It's okay. It's my job to remember for you."

He drove up the gravel drive to a sloping spot under a stand of cedars. He opened the door for Natalie and then pulled the small Christmas wreath from the back of the SUV.

"That's pretty," Natalie said. "Mommy will like it. She loved Christmas."

"Yeah." He took Natalie's hand and they walked up the hill until they came to the granite headstone with Shelly's name on it. The pot of mums that Poppy had probably put there last fall had died. He moved them aside and cleared the area of a few dead leaves before he put the wreath against the headstone.

They stood there in silence for a while, as he let his mind drift back to that day when he'd stood at the front of

St. Thomas' Parish in Washington, DC, and watched her come down the aisle, carrying orchids, wearing a veil and a dress with a killer neckline.

He'd been so in love with her that day. He'd expected to be with her for the rest of his life. But it hadn't worked out that way.

"Miss Willow." Natalie's voice pulled him out of his misery. He turned to find Willow, wearing her big winter coat, climbing up the hill. She had a bouquet of evergreen in her hand.

Natalie ran down the hill and tackled her, wrapping her arms around her middle. One of Willow's hands came to rest on Natalie's head, and she closed her eyes tight, as if she were drinking in the child's hug.

Damnit. Why were they not together?

He knew the answer. Standing here by Shelly's grave, he understood. He wondered, sourly, if the epitaph on his tombstone would read: "He was a Lyndon; he made sacrifices."

Willow squatted down to be on Natalie's level as she spoke with his daughter. David couldn't hear what she said, but Natalie's head bobbed up and down and a serious, almost sad, look stole over her face. It broke his heart.

He turned and strolled away from Shelly's grave, angry and alone and powerless to change the course of his life.

He gave Willow and Natalie a few more minutes before he called Natalie. She gave Willow another big hug before she came down the hill to the car.

"Daddy," she said, as she climbed into the backseat. "Miss Willow didn't forget about Mommy. She told me that Mommy would be watching me tomorrow from heaven and that she would be proud of me."

He nodded. "Miss Willow is a very wise person." He shut the car door and looked up the hill where Willow stood, shoulders straight, hands jammed into her pockets, head bowed. He wanted to walk up that hill and pull her into his arms.

But he couldn't do that. Everything she'd said to him last week made sense. It would never work between them, not if he ran for Congress.

The rest of his life beckoned. He ought to get on with living it.

Alone.

It had been sheer bad luck running into Natalie and David at the cemetery. But if Willow had thought things through, she would have visited the grave in the morning, when David was at work and Natalie was at school.

But she'd been so busy this morning with the final details of the wedding. At the inn, she and Dusty had set up the table rounds, and then she and Mrs. M had draped them all in creamy linens and old lace. The evergreen and red rose centerpieces would be delivered tomorrow morning. Antonin, the longtime chef at the inn, had arrived two days ago and taken care of getting all of the dishes and silverware washed and all of the food purchased. Tomorrow morning he would arrive early with a group of handpicked sous chefs, all of whom had worked for Mrs. M over the years. Later in the day a group of former waitstaff would arrive to set the tables and set up the bar. Every i had been dotted, every t crossed. There would be no drama tomorrow at the reception.

Willow had also spent a lot of time over the last few days with the Presbyterian altar ladies because the decorations for Melissa's wedding would serve double-duty on Christmas Eve. The altar was now flanked by two ten-foot Douglas firs that had been freshly cut at the Snicker's Gap Christmas Tree Farm not far away. The trees had been hung with large white, silver, and gold stars. Baby's breath tucked between the branches gave the appearance of snow, while vintage chandelier crystals at the ends of the branches shimmered like icicles.

Tomorrow evening those crystals would sparkle in the candlelight. Dozens of candles would be placed on the Communion table, fat column candles in glass lanterns would line the aisle, and twelve four-foot wrought-iron candleholders would be placed around the sanctuary. In addition, every wedding guest would be given a small candle to light at the appropriate time.

When Jeff and Melissa said their vows, the sanctuary would be bathed in romantic candlelight.

But right now the church was relying on electricity, as the members of the wedding party arrived for the rehearsal. Willow tried to stay in the background as much as possible, deferring to Reverend Gladwin, who had officiated at hundreds of weddings.

She was fine hanging back in the narthex where she'd be stationed tomorrow evening, making sure that everyone who was supposed to get down the aisle did so at the right moment.

For now she was trying hard to avoid members of the Lyndon family, most especially David. Seeing him and Natalie at the cemetery had ripped her apart. The next twenty-four hours or so were going to be ridiculously hard. And then she could walk away and figure out her next steps. She had a couple of job interviews lined up next week—for glorified secretarial positions.

Pam Lyndon came into the church with her husband and another man who looked enough like Senator Lyndon to be one of his brothers. Willow could recognize Charles and James Lyndon on sight, so this guy must be Thomas. Jeff's dad.

Well, now she knew where he got his height from. Nina Talbert was in the next wave of guests. Followed by Melissa, Courtney, Arwen, and Jeff—the first friendly faces to arrive. The girls surrounded her with happy smiles, each of them giving her a big hug and thanking her for all her hard work. Jeff hung back, staring down into the sanctuary where his parents were waiting for his arrival.

"Into the fray," he muttered.

Melissa snorted and took his arm. "Relax. It's going to be fine," she said as she tugged him down the aisle. If only Willow were as brave as Melissa. If only David were as independent as Jeff.

But neither of those things were true. And besides, Jeff and Melissa didn't have to worry about an eight-year-old child or a congressional career.

Willow was thinking hard about Natalie when Gracie Teague arrived, still wearing her waitress uniform under her coat. "God bless," she said, huffing and puffing. "I didn't think I was going to ever get away from the diner. Anna was late, as always. I had to decide which would be the bigger embarrassment, showing up in my uniform or being late."

"Don't be ashamed of your uniform, Gracie."

Gracie stopped before she headed down the aisle and turned toward Willow. "Girl, why are you hiding back here?"

"Because I'm the wedding planner. And, to be honest, those people down there at the front of the church don't like me much, and I don't want to make a scene on Melissa's big day."

"I hear you, and I understand. But sooner or later someone needs to make a scene. Honey, that man has been walking around the last week looking like the end-times are upon us and he's not getting a ticket to heaven."

"Which man?"

Gracie gave her one of those matronly looks. "You know good and well who I'm talking about. And if I'm not supposed to be ashamed of my uniform, then you shouldn't be ashamed of what you've done—standing up for a bunch of old folks who got crappy hip replacements. Hon, in some quarters that makes you a hero."

"Thanks."

"Yeah, well, I'm not done with you yet, you hear?" She turned and headed down the aisle with her head held high. Melissa greeted her with a gigantic hug. Nina Talbert and Thomas Lyndon gave Gracie the expected superior looks.

"Where in the name of heaven is my son?" Pam said in a worried voice.

Oh great, David and Natalie were still missing. After ten minutes of waiting, Melissa finally came sprinting back to the narthex. "We can't do this without the best man. Can you give him a call?" She didn't wait for a response but turned and sprinted back down the aisle.

Great. David was the last person on earth Willow

wanted to call. But she whipped out her cell and hit the speed dial. The call went to voice mail. She left a message and then sent him an urgent text, followed by an e-mail. Then she forced herself to walk down the aisle as everyone on the Lyndon side of the church looked at her. She approached Pam and said, "I've left a message for David. He didn't pick up when I called."

"Where could that boy be?" Pam said, throwing her hands into the air.

"Chill," the senator said in a firm voice, and Willow kind of wanted to give the man a hug. She didn't think anyone ever told Pam Lyndon to chill. But apparently Mark Lyndon wasn't cowed by his wife. Good for him.

"Do you know where he is?" Pam demanded.

"Uh, no. I saw him about an hour ago out at Greenwood Cemetery. Natalie was with him. She wasn't dressed for tonight, though."

"He went to the cemetery?" Pam asked. "Doesn't he know we're trying to put on a wedding?"

"Uh, well, um, maybe you forgot, but today is the two-year anniversary of Shelly's death. I don't know for certain, but I'm pretty sure he's not having a real good day."

There was a collective in-drawing of breath. Had all of these people forgotten? She wanted to yell at them, but that would be a career nonstarter, so she turned and headed back to the shelter of the narthex.

Behind her the minister said, "Well, why don't I get started and we can fill him in when he gets here."

"But the flower girl is with him," Melissa said in a slightly panicky voice. "And it's really important that Natalie gets to run through this at least once. You know, she's only eight, and I don't want her to freak out tomorrow during the ceremony."

Reverend Gladwin had a lot of experience dealing with panicky brides. He gave Melissa a gentle smile. "Don't worry. It will all work out, and Natalie will be fine."

Five minutes later David and Natalie arrived with expressions on their faces that said it all. Father and daughter were not speaking. Natalie looked as if she'd been crying, and David's jaw was set, his eyes dark and angry.

Natalie saw her standing in the narthex and rushed right into her, just like she'd done at the cemetery earlier that afternoon. She buried her head into Willow's midsection and set off a cascade of emotions that knocked Willow for a loop. She truly loved this little girl, and it slayed her to see her so unhappy on a day that should have been joyous.

"Natalie," David said in a curt voice. "We're already late." He gave Willow a look as sharp as his words.

Willow squatted down. "What's the matter?" she asked softly, ignoring David's impatience.

"I hate my dress."

"The dress for the wedding?"

She shook her head and opened her jacket to reveal a red velvet and royal Stewart plaid dropped-waist party dress. It was an unflattering silhouette for the little girl and definitely not Natalie's best color. "Grandmother bought it for the party tonight. Daddy said I had to wear it even though I wanted to wear the green dress I wore on Thanksgiving." She turned and gave her father a mutinous scowl.

"Natalie," Willow said, gently turning her around. "I know you don't like this dress, but your grandmother bought it for you, and her feelings would be hurt if you didn't wear it."

"But—"

"I know. It's not your favorite color. But maybe your dad could find a way to explain to your grandmother that you really don't like red dresses." She glanced up at David. He looked down at her, his jaw twitching.

"And even though you don't like the dress all that much, you need to think about Melissa and Jeff. They're counting on you to be the best flower girl ever. And they don't want to see a sad face tonight, okay? Tonight is when you practice being a flower girl. You don't want to upset Melissa, do you?"

She shook her head.

Willow gave her as big a hug as she could. "You'll do great. And I'm sure you'll have a fabulous time at the party. Just pretend you're wearing your magic green dress. And think about the wonderful dress you get to wear tomorrow. Okay?"

She nodded, even if the pout on her face remained.

Willow stood up and met David's stare. It burned through her like a laser, right to her heart. She wanted to give him a big hug too. She wanted to get right up in his face and tell him he needed to get his mother to stop putting Natalie in dresses she hated. But hugging him or yelling at him would be inappropriate—especially with his family watching.

She expected him to retreat down the aisle, but instead his gaze melted a little and then he said, "Thank you," in a barely audible voice.

He turned away and guided Natalie down the aisle, where his family awaited him.

The casual buffet Mother had planned for the rehearsal dinner was anything but casual. Everyone dressed up for the event, and the tension between Jeff and his parents was so in your face that it was hard for anyone to have a good time, no matter how many bottles of Bella Vista Cabernet were consumed.

David decided early on that crawling into a bottle wouldn't make him feel any better tomorrow. Nor would it change the facts of his life, the first one being that, as always, the Kopps had been invited to this party. So the managing partner of the firm was there with both of his children, Roxanne and her brother Brandon. And even though everyone knew that he wasn't interested in Roxy, Mother continued to find little ways of throwing them together.

It was infuriating.

The final straw dropped when Roxanne said, "You know, David, once Natalie gets a little older, we can fix the problems. A little hair dye and some makeup would go a long, long way. Just you watch. We'll transform her."

"Transform her into what?" he said in an angry voice just about everyone heard.

"David. Honestly, I can help. Really."

He got right up into Roxanne's face "I. Don't. Want. Your. Help. Especially if you can't see that Natalie is a beautiful gift from God."

He pulled away from her and stalked right out of the family room, through the French doors, and out onto the terrace, where it was no more than twenty degrees. He didn't feel the cold. He was hot, inside and out. He wanted to punch someone. He wanted to yell out his rage. He wanted . . .

Shit, he didn't know what he wanted. Not anymore.

A moment later, the French doors opened, and Uncle Jamie, the family peacemaker, came strolling out.

"Geez, David, we're going to freeze our balls off out here."

"No one asked you to come out here," he said.

"That's debatable. I nominated myself when your mother made a move for the door. You can thank me later. Or now." His words made plumes of steam in the patio lights. "I did bring some refreshments." He held up a bottle of bourbon and stepped forward to give David's shoulder a squeeze. "And I think there's a space heater in the garage. C'mon, let's go get drunk."

"I don't want to get drunk."

"That's a start. Let's go have a quiet woodshed talk, then."

"I don't want to talk."

"No surprise there."

His uncle draped an arm around him and half guided, half dragged him off to the old barn that had been converted into a four-car garage. They found a couple of lawn chairs, fired up the electric space heater, and passed the bottle a couple of times, all without speaking.

For a woodshed talk, this was taking a while to get off the ground. The silence stretched out, and David had to stomp on the urge to break it, until Jamie finally said, "Love's a bitch," and then lifted the bourbon to his lips.

"It's been eight years since your aunt Debra died," he continued, once he'd swallowed down the liquor, "and I still need to crawl into a bottle when the anniversary rolls around. 'Course, the truth is, Debra and I were not very happy together, so it's always a surprise when I feel the need to drink myself into oblivion."

This was such startling news that David didn't know what the hell to say. So he kept his mouth shut.

"We didn't agree on how to raise the kids," Jamie said after another pull on the bottle. "She spoiled all of them. Spent money like it was water. She lived to shop. It was all she ever thought about—material stuff. It got so that I couldn't ever have a meaningful conversation with her. And, a long time ago, I cheated on her. She never forgave me for that, which only made things worse."

"Uh, Uncle Jamie, I thought we came out here so you could give me some sage advice about dealing with my anger, not so you could make a confession. I don't really—"

"The woman I slept with—I loved her."

"Um…"

"But I decided that I needed to sacrifice love for the good of my family. This woman I loved, she wouldn't have met with anyone's approval. Not just because we had an affair, but because she wasn't the kind of woman that your grandmother would have approved of. You don't remember Grandmother, but she's the one who handpicked your daddy's wife for him. And let's just say that Mother and Pam were cast from the same mold. Both of them were governor's daughters, born and bred for the political life."

"Okay," David said, standing up and starting to pace. If he didn't move, he might try to punch something—not Uncle Jamie, but a wall or something. And he didn't want to break his hand, and a primal scream would probably scare all the wedding guests. "I get it. I know what I'm supposed to do, Jamie. It's been drilled into me since I was a baby."

Jamie let go of a big breath. "And that, right there, is the problem."

David stopped pacing, turned, and stared at his uncle.

"Sometimes you give the impression that you're just going along to get along. You know, like you're drifting in your life. Everyone's given you a little time because of Shelly's death, but it seems to me that you're still drifting, David."

"I'm planning to run for Congress. That's hardly drifting."

Jamie settled back in his chair and propped his feet on the fender of Mother's Land Rover. He offered the bottle. David shook his head and waited for Jamie to say something. He didn't say anything. He just took another sip of bourbon.

"I am running."

"Why?"

Because it's expected of me. The words formed in David's mind. They weren't a good enough reason. His brain kicked in and he came up with a dozen additional reasons, all of which were acceptable. But they all lacked one thing: passion.

"See what I mean?" Jamie said, offering the bottle again. This time David snatched it and took a big gulp.

"Now, you see, if Heather was here and we were talking about her running for Congress, I don't think she'd have trouble coming up with reasons for why she wants it. I mean really wants it. And, David, I hope you take this the right way, but I don't for one minute think you have the personality to be a good politician. Heather, on the other hand, has the knack. People naturally like her. You know what I mean? She's social, and you're not. She's good in a crowd, and you're not. She'd have no problem making cold calls to raise campaign contributions, and I just don't see you doing that."

David passed the bottle back to his uncle and sat back down. "If I don't run, what the hell do I do with my life?"

Jamie had the temerity to laugh out loud. "Boy, you are confused."

He glared at his uncle.

"I wouldn't presume to tell you what to do. But let me point out a few things. First, there's always fly-fishing. A man can never get enough of that, and being a congressman is going to cut into your fishing time. Second, there's that beautiful redheaded daughter of yours. She's growing up, David. Fast. You'll be astonished how fast the kids grow up. If you give your time to politics, you'll lose your time with Natalie. You seem to be doing a better job of parenting lately. I approve." Jamie paused a moment to wet his whistle.

"And there are a couple of other things that come to mind. You could champion hopeless causes. You seem to have developed a talent for that. I'm impressed by the way you've stood shoulder to shoulder with Dusty McNeil, even though I deeply disagree with your position on that one. I hear that you solved a long-standing problem with a teacher down at Daniel Morgan Elementary with your negotiating skills. And then there is your crowning achievement: the end run that you orchestrated around Pam and Nina and their plans for Jeff and Melissa's wedding. Bravo on that one. Without you, we'd all be in New York celebrating this family occasion with two hundred deep-pocketed fund managers." He raised the bourbon bottle in salute and took another sip.

"You want me to become Don Quixote?"

Jamie laughed. "No. But you could try for George Bailey."

"Who?"

Jamie shook his head and looked heavenward. "It's a Christmas reference. Look it up on your smartphone when you get a minute. I think this town could use a George Bailey."

David refrained from digging for his iPhone right then. "Look, Jamie, I'm not a hero. I was pushed and prodded into all of those things."

Jamie nodded. "I know."

"You do?"

"Yeah, I do. But how did those things make you feel?"

Alive. The word came to David without any thinking. He didn't say the word out loud. But he did accept the bottle when Jamie passed it to him. He was beginning to feel a little buzzed.

And so was Jamie. His uncle leaned forward and put his hand on David's knee. "Kiddo, here's the main thing I wanted to say. Love is the only thing truly worth treasuring."

David found himself nodding, his eyes watering. "Today," he said in a gruff voice, "when I went out to visit Shelly's grave, I wondered if they would put the word 'sacrifice' on my headstone. It was a morbid thought, but it's the way I feel right now."

"You don't have to feel that way."

"Jamie, I'm not the one who walked away from Willow. She walked away from me."

Jamie frowned. "She did?" He truly sounded surprised. "Really? Are you sure about that?"

David nodded, but then suddenly the pieces of the puzzle rearranged themselves. Shit. Sure she'd walked out the night Mom came storming in, but that wasn't when he'd lost her. It had been in that moment out at Laurel Chapel when he'd asked her to give up her private action against Restero.

What an idiot he'd been.

The largest impediment between him and Willow wasn't his family. It was his decision to run for Congress—a decision he hadn't even really made for himself. And yet to save his so-called political career, he'd asked the woman he loved to walk away from a position that she regarded as the high moral ground.

"Damn, Jamie, I really blew it with her," David finally said, taking the longest pull yet on the bourbon.

"How?"

David hung his head. "I told her she had to behave according to my rules."

Jamie tipped back his head and laughed. "Yeah, that was a tactical mistake, son. You don't ever tell a Petersen woman to behave. They're likely to start painting signs and picketing your front lawn. Here, have a drink." Jamie shoved the bottle at David. He took a long pull and handed it back.

They stayed in the garage until the bottle was empty, and then they stumbled back to the party, where they endured Pam's disapproval with drunken dignity.

Chapter 18————————————

Willow got to the inn at the crack of dawn on Saturday, December nineteenth. Most of her work was finished, but she felt the need to hover and check off the items on her list.

She expected to run into David and Natalie and she quite literally didn't know what she would do or say, but Mrs. M explained that they'd ended up sleeping at Charlotte's Grove the night before. That news was oddly disappointing. She'd been avoiding them for more than a week, and yesterday had pretty much confirmed that her feelings for them ran deeper than she'd been willing to admit.

But did they run deep enough for her to give up her self-esteem to be with them?

The unequivocal answer to that was no.

So she threw herself into the issues at hand: the deliv-

ery and placement of the centerpieces, the arrangement
of candles and numbers on tables, the placement of the
guest book and table cards, a couple of crises relating to
the DJ's PA system, and at least one emotional outburst
from Antonin over the quality of the mushrooms available in the local market.

She also arranged for Melissa to pick up Natalie at
Charlotte's Grove for her hair appointment at Glamorous
You, the local beauty shop. This almost turned into a big,
honking disaster, because Pam insisted that Natalie was
too young for a manicure and pedicure, not to mention
that she didn't need a fancy hairdo. Thank God for Courtney, who, according to Melissa's telephone account, had
told Pam where she could shove her concerns and had literally pulled Natalie from the clutches of her overbearing
grandmother and whisked her off to a big-girl party at the
beauty shop.

Willow wished she could gate-crash the fun times at
Glamorous You, but her heart wasn't strong enough for
that. She had Courtney's assurance that Natalie would get
her mani, pedi, and a fabulous hairdo, which they both
conceded would probably last about five minutes, given
Natalie's talent for tangled hair. It wasn't so much about
the hairdo as it was about the kid's self-esteem. Courtney
understood. The bride and her bridesmaids were totally
on board with making Natalie feel like the most adorable
child in the world.

Which, as far as Willow was concerned, wasn't far off
from the mark.

With all that chaos, she was surprised when Jeff
showed up around lunchtime and pulled her into the library and closed the doors.

"What?" she said. "If you're here to tell me you've got cold feet, I will shoot myself."

He laughed. "No. No cold feet. I'm here to thank you."

She blushed. "You're welcome. It's been…" She paused a moment and looked around the library, freshly painted and newly staged with rented furniture that had already generated an offer from Bryce Summerville.

She took a big breath. "I guess you could say it's been a labor of love. Shelly would approve, you know. She had such big plans for the inn."

"Uh, well, that's kind of why I'm here."

She turned back. "What?"

"I still have your business plan, you know. And I've read it. More than once."

She said nothing as her heart started to pound.

"I've come to a decision, Willow, about a lot of things. I'm going to marry the love of my life today, in a smallish ceremony, in a pretty small town that I intend to make my home for the rest of my life. I've decided I don't ever want to go back to New York. And while helping Melissa run a used bookstore is fun, it's not really a big enough thing for me, you know. I mean, I have money to use, and I want to use it doing something important.

"I used to think that important stuff was what happened in New York or DC, but Melissa has opened my eyes. Important things happen here too. I think you understand that."

"I do," she said with a nod. "I used to think I wanted a corporate life. But these last few months I've come to understand that even a small business—like an inn—can be hugely important to a community."

He nodded. "Yeah. So here's the deal. I want to invest

in the inn. I'll put up the money under the terms you out-lined in your plan."

She stood there utterly nonplussed. "You will?"

He laughed. "Yeah, I will. And I'm going to look for other local business opportunities. I never saw myself as a businessman, you know. But I'm going to be living here, and I want this place to be more than it is right now. I suspect that means I'll be doing regular battle with Aunt Pam. Who knows? Maybe I'll join the Historical Society and oust her. What do you think?"

"I'd vote for you."

He laughed again, a truly wicked laugh. "Look, I know you're busy, but I just wanted to let you know that whatever Bryce Summerville's willing to pay for this place, I'll gladly match. The inn is yours, Willow. Merry Christmas."

She stood there for a moment, utterly speechless, and then she did something she never did. She gave Jefferson Talbert a crushing hug. "Thank you, thank you," she said in a rush. And she couldn't say any more because tears filled her eyes.

"I hope those are happy tears."

She nodded. "Thank you so much."

"It's an investment, Willow. I expect to see returns."

"And you'll get them. Now, get out of here. I have work to do. And you need to get ready."

He checked his watch. "I've got more than four hours before the ceremony. Maybe by that time David will be sober."

Her joy faded. "Is he all right?"

"He's fine. Uncle Jamie got him drunk last night. I guess we all forgot about the anniversary of Shelly's death...everyone but you, it would seem."

"She was my best friend. Until recently, I would say she was my only friend. But I guess I've made a few more now that I've come back home. It's funny I never thought I belonged here, but you and Melissa and Courtney and Arwen have made me feel as if I do."

"Don't forget Gracie and Poppy. Or Poppy's bridge club. You've got a boatload of fans among that crowd, you know."

"What about the bridge club?"

"They've been trying to rebrand you."

"What?"

The grin on his face was almost devilish. "Faye Appleby darkened my door the other day with a bunch of questions about how she should go about investigating you so as to clear your name. She was asking me professionally because of my journalism background.

"And someone got to Gracie with the idea of rebranding you. I have no idea where that term came from, but Gracie has been using her many business channels to spread the word that you are a fine, upstanding citizen who was motivated by your concern for Medicare patients who were harmed by Restero. Do you have any idea how many Medicare recipients live in Jefferson County? It's a substantial number. They see you as their champion.

"And I heard through the grapevine that Poppy has been all over Walter to get him to discourage Bryce Summerville. He can't do that ethically, but I've been told that Poppy has even resorted to using her body as an inducement."

"What?"

He snorted a laugh. "That was the way Gracie put it. I actually think that Poppy and Walter have a thing going."

"I guess I kind of knew that, after the way they were at Thanksgiving," Willow said.

"So there you have it, Willow. Poppy wants you to have the inn, and everyone seems to think that Poppy ought to get what she wants. And I just happen to have the means to make it happen."

"Thank you," she said.

He leaned in and gave her a kiss. As he drew away, he spoke again. "I think you might want to talk to David."

"There isn't any point. If I'm going to be an innkeeper and he's going to be a congressman, I don't see much of a future for us. He as much as told me that his campaign people see me as a problem to be managed. No woman wants to be told that."

"Yeah, I guess so. But I still think you two should talk. Promise me that you will."

"Okay. I promise. Now get out of here. Go feed David some coffee. I'll see you at the church."

Willow stood in the narthex of Grace Presbyterian Church and sent Natalie down the aisle. Her hair had miraculously not tumbled down from the curly updo she'd gotten at Glamorous You. The few sprigs of baby's breath in her hair looked like snow in the light of the candles.

She walked slowly and with a great deal of grace to the organist's rendition of "Jesu, Joy of Man's Desiring." She had a basket filled with rose petals that she carefully dropped on the white runner that ran down the aisle.

The moment had arrived. Willow opened the door to

the small room where the bride awaited. Melissa looked fabulous in her ivory taffeta, with the velvet cloak— exactly like the heroine in a fairytale.

"It's time," she said.

Gracie helped Melissa out into the foyer, arranging her train and veil. Then she took Melissa by the arm. "I wish your mom and dad were here," she said, tears glittering in her eyes.

"It's okay, Gracie. I have you." Melissa gave Gracie a big hug. "I can't think of anyone else I'd rather lean on as I make it down the aisle. I hope I don't trip on this ridiculous skirt."

They both laughed. The organist struck up the "Wedding March." The congregation stood, and Melissa headed off to marry Jeff, who waited for her, with his big brown eyes filled with love and the light of a hundred candles.

Willow stayed behind at the back of the church, where she allowed herself one hungry glance at David, standing beside Jeff, wearing a classic black tux, his hair just a little mussed and curling over his forehead.

And then, as her gaze lingered, he looked up from the approaching bride. Time seemed to stop as they stared at each other, but that was an illusion. As their gazes held, Melissa made her way down the aisle. And then the minister said, "God is love, and those who abide in love, abide in God, and God abides in them." Only then did David look away.

Willow allowed herself thirty seconds of self-pity before she turned her back on the wedding ceremony and headed for the exit. She had things to do.

Outside, Dusty was lining up the limousines and seemed to have everything under control.

"I'm going back to the inn to make sure everything is ready," she told him. "Thank you so much for helping. I couldn't be two places at once. If you need me, you have my cell."

She turned toward the parking lot. "Hey, Willow," Dusty called from behind.

She looked over her shoulder. "Yeah?"

"The next wedding you plan will be out at Laurel Chapel."

She stopped. "I didn't think about that. With Jeff's support, I can completely restore the chapel the way Shelly wanted it, can't I?"

"Yep. And I'm going to make a fearless prediction. When it's your turn to walk down the aisle, you'll be doing it out there."

She gave him the look she reserved especially for him. "I hate weddings. They make everyone so sappy."

He snorted. "Yeah, I can tell how much you hate weddings."

She turned and hurried to her car.

For the next two hours she was too busy to think about anything but making sure the wedding guests got through the receiving line, got their drinks and hors d'oeuvres, found their assigned seats, and had champagne for the toasts that would precede dinner service.

She was standing near the bar, having just delivered more lime wedges to the bartender, when the tinkle of silverware hitting water glasses signaled that the moment for toasts had arrived. The crowd quieted, and all eyes turned to the dais where the wedding party was seated.

David got to his feet holding a champagne glass and looking devastatingly handsome in his black tux.

"I'm wearing two hats tonight," he began. "First of all, I'm honored that Jeff chose me to be his best man. I have a lot of cousins—there are probably a dozen of them in this room tonight—but Jeff is the one who was always missing while we were growing up. And believe it or not, all of us felt his absence at family gatherings. So I cannot tell you how pleased I am—and I'm sure I speak for the rest of the Lyndon family—that he found a local girl."

He turned toward Melissa with a smile that actually showed his dimples. Oh, the man was hard to look at when he smiled like that. Willow's heart took flight, and she hated the fact that she still wanted him—heck, she loved him, even though he was beyond her reach.

"Melissa, thank you," he said, "for bringing our prodigal son back home where he belongs. And thank you for insisting that we hold your celebration here." He gestured to the room, which was filled with candlelight and Christmas lights and the aroma of evergreen and roses.

"Which brings me to my second hat. Eagle Hill Manor is my home, and since Shelly is no longer with us, I'm your host for this evening. The inn has been dark for a long time, but I think Shelly would be pleased to see the entire Lyndon family gathered here to celebrate this joyous occasion. So, Melissa, thank you for that too. You've brought life back into this place."

David's voice wavered, and he had to take a deep breath. Willow had to take one too. She remembered that day, weeks ago, when she'd gotten right up in David's face and told him how disappointed in him Shelly would be if he didn't step up and host this wedding. He'd listened. He'd made this reception happen, and if Shelly were here, she'd be beaming with pride for him.

"I'm not very good at speeches like this, but there is something I need to say, to both Jeff and Melissa and to everyone here," he continued, his voice a little gruff as his gaze wandered over the crowd of wedding guests until it found her and stopped.

He spoke again, and it was almost as if he was speaking right to her. "I remember the day I walked down the aisle. I can see that evening in my mind's eye like it was yesterday. I thought Shelly was the most beautiful woman in the world. And I thought I knew what marriage was about. But I didn't. Not really. In fact, I don't think I truly understood until it was too late."

His gaze shifted to the bride and groom, and Willow started breathing again. What was he trying to say?

"Jeff, Melissa, I don't have the words to express my joy for you both. But I also want both of you to remember that there are no guarantees in this life. So live your lives to the fullest every day. Hold on to each other like there's no tomorrow, but at the same time, you have to let go." His voice cracked, and his gaze found Willow again.

The lump in Willow's throat cracked open and the tears started flowing. She couldn't stop them.

He took another breath and spoke again, but he wasn't looking at the bride and groom. "You have to give each other space. You have to tell each other how you feel, even if it means showing your weaknesses sometimes. And you have to sacrifice.

"Now, that's a word that I learned at an early age, but I don't think I've understood its meaning until recently. Sacrifice doesn't mean doing something grudgingly because you have to do it. Or because it's expected of you.

Or because you're afraid of disappointing each other. Sacrifice shouldn't benefit one of you and harm the other. True sacrifice means doing something for love. And when you sacrifice out of love, it shouldn't be a burden but a joy."

He turned his gaze back on the bride and groom. "So, one day, many years from now, when you look back on today and the vows you made, I hope you feel as if those promises are still alive and fresh and new. I hope you work together to make each of you the very best that you can be. I hope you will have many, many years of happiness together. But most of all, I hope you have love for the rest of your time together. And not the kind of love that you fall into and that fades over time. But the kind of love that needs your attention and your commitment and your hard work. Every day.

"Jeff, Melissa, congratulations, and may you have a long, long life of happiness together."

He raised his glass, seemingly unaware that there wasn't a dry eye in the room, including Willow's.

Melissa got up and threw her arms around David and gave him a kiss on the cheek. Her mascara was running. David looked supremely awkward in that moment.

Jeff stood and gave him a man hug, which David accepted with a small smile.

Senator Lyndon dashed a tear from his manly cheek, stood up, and said, "Hear, hear."

Poppy openly wept into Walter's handkerchief. The Realtor had his arm around her.

And then Thomas Lyndon stood up, raised his glass, and started talking about Jeff when he was a kid. He talked on and on about how Jeff was a disaster at fly-fishing, which seemed sort of incongruent after David's emotional speech about love and commitment.

Willow wiped the tears from her eyes and made a quick escape before she, also, created an embarrassing scene. She headed for the kitchen to make sure the food service was ready to go, and with every step she wondered how a man could give such a deep and insightful speech about love and marriage and still behave like such an idiot.

A best man couldn't just disappear. Not until the toasting was done, and since there were a boatload of Lyndons in the room and they all thought they had a gift for oratory, the toasting went on for a long, long time.

Uncle Thomas spoke longer than anyone and managed to say less in the process. David put his champagne aside, avoided the wine, and sipped his water as the toasts went on. He was itching to leave the room and find Willow. He needed to have that talk with her that he should have had days ago.

But once the toasting was finished, the photographer demanded time. Then there was dinner, and he couldn't go missing then.

So it wasn't until the dancing started that he finally found a moment to slip away. By then it was a challenge just to find her. She wasn't in the kitchen. She wasn't on the terrace. She wasn't in the solarium or the library or the dining room.

If it hadn't been almost eleven o'clock and only thirty-five degrees, he might have gone traipsing out to the old chapel to look for her. But he knew she wasn't out there in the cold.

There was only one other place she could be. So he headed upstairs, where he found her standing in the dark at the corner windows of the Churchill Suite, staring up at the clear winter sky and a bright full moon.

She startled when he opened the door, a wedge of light from the hallway spilling into the darkness. "I need to talk to you," he said, closing the door behind him and plunging the room back into darkness.

His eyes needed time to adjust. The moonlight definitely gave a luster to the room—not quite the luster of midday, but enough to turn Willow into a silhouette against the windows and spark like silver in her hair. Enough for him to see her square her shoulders as if she was preparing to do battle with him.

He deserved that.

"Uncle Jamie made me watch an old movie today," he said. "Maybe you know it—*It's a Wonderful Life*."

She leaned back on the windowsill and crossed her arms. Her face was in shadow, but her body language said it all. He was going to have to grovel to get through her defenses. "How could you have never seen that movie?" she asked.

He shrugged. "I'm a failure at Christmas. I think I always have been. Even before Shelly died, I never could quite see what the fuss was about."

"Poor little rich kid," she snarked in the same tone she sometimes used with Dusty. "Guess when you have everything, Christmas presents lose their appeal."

"I like presents just fine. But Christmas at Charlotte's Grove was about much more than presents. Grandmother, oh my God, she insisted that Christmas run on a schedule like the military. She sucked most of the joy right out of it for me. Mother is a lot like Grandmother, to tell you the truth."

"Well, you got turkey for Christmas dinner. I got to eat Tofurky and brussels sprouts. Yuck. But I still managed to enjoy the day."

He laughed. "We usually had prime rib, actually."

"See. You have nothing to complain about. So why did your uncle make you watch this movie?"

"Last night, when we were tying one on, he told me that if I wanted to I could become George Bailey. I had no idea what he meant by that."

She didn't say anything to this, and he couldn't read her face in the dark. So he blundered ahead. "It's kind of amazing to think I could be like the guy in that movie. I mean, he makes one sacrifice after another. I've done that, too, but the difference is that he made all his decisions out of love. I always made my sacrifices out of obligation.

"And every sacrifice I made over the years hurt someone. Shelly. Natalie. Poppy. You."

"David—"

"Hush, let me finish. After that photo of us was published, my family and my consultants—everyone—told me that I needed to give you up. I told them all no, but then I tried to make this deal with Hale Chandler, my political consultant. I figured it would be better for you to sacrifice your case against Restero than it would be for you to sacrifice the potential for a wonderful relationship. I figured you'd be willing to do that. For me.

"I missed the point. I missed the fact that, if I love you, maybe I should be willing to sacrifice something. Like running for Congress."

"But you—"

"I know. I know. It's what I'm supposed to do. And that's the point. I never actually decided to run for Congress. I mean, I never questioned the idea that this was my fate. And maybe that's because I was just plain scared. Scared that if I didn't do what everyone expected of me, then my life would have no meaning at all. But I was wrong. And Uncle Jamie helped me to see that."

"By making you watch a movie?"

He shrugged. "Well, sort of. He pointed out that I could have a meaningful life living right here in Shenandoah Falls doing the right things instead of the expected ones. Like standing up for Dusty. Like hosting Melissa's wedding. Like taking Natalie to her swim trials instead of dancing to my mother's tune. Or like standing beside you and supporting your quest to bring Restero to justice. Or…well…like loving you, Willow. Loving you would be the right thing to do, even if it's not what is expected of me. I'd like to change those expectations. And I meant what I said tonight. I want to work at love this time, not just accept it as a given.

"So, the first thing is that I've decided not to run for Congress. I'm going to stay here and be an innkeeper's boyfriend, and maybe, in time, something more."

"Oh, David." Her voice broke, and he crossed the room to take her in his arms. "You can't do that."

"Yes, I can. I don't want to be a congressman. I hate campaigning. I always have. And I'd rather spend my free time fishing with you and Dusty than going to town hall meetings or dialing for dollars. I don't want it. It's a joy to sacrifice it, especially if it means I can be with you."

She rested her head on his shoulder. Holding her was

like coming home. "I don't think you're something that needs to be managed," he said against her hair. "And I love the fact that you make trouble. Seems to me that all the trouble you've made these last few months has been the good kind. And I have this feeling that we're going to have lots and lots of trouble in our lives from this moment forward. But I also think we're going to get through it all and maybe even have some fun at the same time."

He stroked her hair and tilted her head back so he could kiss her. He put his heart and soul into that kiss. She melted in his arms and even made a little inarticulate noise that pretty much blew his mind.

He nibbled his way down the column of her neck and then over to her ear. "I want you," he whispered, "not because we're friends with benefits. I just need you, Willow."

She wrapped her arms around his neck and gave him a hungry kiss. She didn't need words to let him know her answer. Her body was surprisingly eloquent.

Epilogue———————————————

One Year Later

The string quartet played the Bach beautifully as Courtney leaned down and whispered something into Natalie's
ear that Willow couldn't hear. The nine-year-old's brown
eyes lit up, and she turned toward Willow, who stood to
one side of the tiny foyer at Laurel Chapel.

"See you down there," Natalie said with a wink.

Her goddaughter looked adorable in her green moiré
taffeta dress with a big skirt, puffy sleeves, and just a hint
of crinoline showing at the hem. Her beautiful red hair
was piled up on her head and covered with baby's breath,
and Courtney had given her just a tiny bit of blush and
mascara.

Courtney had mad skills when it came to planning
weddings, which was why Willow had offered her a job
as the director of special events at Eagle Hill Manor.
Courtney, who had all but burned out as a nurse, had
jumped at the chance, and now she and Courtney worked

together every day, marketing the inn as the premier wedding destination in Northern Virginia.

The music swelled in the small confines of the Laurel Chapel, which had been thoroughly decked out with period-accurate Christmas decorations. Holly and ivy dripped from the beams and edged the windows and the altar.

The antique wood pews had been installed less than two weeks ago—after a year-long project that included consultations with historians and archaeologists from Williamsburg to make sure that the restoration was as historically accurate as possible. Just a week ago, Reverend Weston, the minister at St. Luke's, had reconsecrated the sanctuary.

Now the small church was lit up with dozens and dozens of candles.

"It's time," Courtney said, taking Willow by the hand and pulling her toward the center aisle. Willow would be making this walk alone. She didn't need anyone to give her away, and besides, she was learning to stop being embarrassed by the fact that her father had been a drugged-out rocker who had never been in the picture.

Courtney adjusted the tulle of her ball gown dress and made sure her tiara and veil were in place. Willow felt like Sleeping Beauty on her wedding day.

The string quartet finished the Bach and struck up the Wagner. Everyone stood up and turned toward her. Willow took her first step down the aisle, her gaze finding David's. He was devastatingly handsome in his tuxedo, with Dusty McNeil standing at his elbow. That had caused a minor furor in family circles. David choosing his friend instead of one of his male cousins had been tantamount to blasphemy or something.

Pam wasn't all that thrilled about Juni either, who stood on the left side of the altar wearing her own green taffeta gown with a big smile on her face. Last night, at the rehearsal dinner at the Jaybird Café, Juni had shocked the entire Lyndon clan when she'd stood up and told the world that David's and Willow's auras indicated strong sexual compatibility, which usually meant that they'd be having lots and lots of babies. Soon.

Willow had almost choked on her cheeseburger when her little sister made that announcement. Even if Juni was right about the whole sexual thing, Willow didn't see herself ever having lots and lots of babies. She had an inn to manage. But that sultry look in David's dark eyes never failed to ignite her body. It was having an impact right this minute, as she reached the end of the aisle and took his hand.

It was warm, slightly rough, and had become so familiar over the last year. She had no doubts, no concerns, no worries about this decision. She belonged with this man, and he belonged with her.

He was her prince. He'd awakened her with a kiss. He'd rescued her from a dungeon. And he'd slayed every one of the dragons that stood in the way of their love, chief among them his own family's expectations. Pam was still a little bit unhappy about the way things had turned out, but all that effort she'd aimed at David had found a new target—his sister, Heather.

A month ago Heather Lyndon had become the first female member of the storied Lyndon family to win a seat in Congress. She sat in the front row, the representative-elect for the twelfth congressional district. Mom had even campaigned for Heather, which had blown everyone's mind.

The minister began the service with the Bible verse that she and David had especially picked for this day. She looked up into his eyes, feeling light and happy and sure. The words the minister said were perfect, and if they were a lot like the ones David had spoken a year ago at Jeff and Melissa's wedding, well, that was not entirely by accident.

> ...*Love is patient and kind; love is not jealous or boastful; it is not arrogant or rude. Love does not insist on its own way; it is not irritable or resentful; it does not rejoice at wrong, but rejoices in the right. Love bears all things, hopes all things, endures all things...*

Privileged Amy Lyndon needs the one thing
she has never had before—a job.
Dusty McNeil is going to give her the one
thing she never expected—love.

A preview of *A Small-Town Bride* follows.

Chapter 1 ───────────

Amy Lyndon's first clue that something was amiss came at eleven forty-five on a sunny Friday, the last day of March, when Daddy stormed into her room without knocking. Daddy always knocked, so this was something new. Luckily, Amy, who had just gotten out of bed, was wearing her bathrobe, or there might have been an embarrassing father-daughter moment.

"I've had it up to here with you," Daddy said, gesturing wildly. His face was as red as a glass of Bella Vista Vineyards Pinot Noir.

"What's the matter?" Amy kept her voice low and calm. She'd learned this trick from Mom, who had been an expert at handling Daddy's sudden, but infrequent, rages.

"What's the—" His words came to a sputtering stop as a vein popped from his forehead. Uh-oh. The vein thing was a bad sign. And his complexion had turned almost purple, closer to the color of Malbec than Pinot Noir.

"Daddy, calm down. You'll give yourself a stroke or something."

He took a big breath and spoke again in a voice that rattled Amy's bedroom windows. "Get dressed. Then get out."

"What?"

"You heard me. I want you out of this house by..." He looked at his wristwatch. "Noon. That gives you fifteen minutes. And if you're smart, you'll run straight to Grady Carson. I understand he's proposed. Congratulations."

"But how did you know he proposed? I mean—"

"I'm done trying to teach you the value of work. If you want to be exactly like your mother and live in the lap of luxury without lifting a finger, then marry Grady."

Amy said nothing. Grady Carson was the last man she would ever marry. She'd told him that to his face last week at Tammy's wedding, when he'd popped the question right out of the blue. But she hadn't breathed a word about Grady's proposal to anyone.

"And then there's this." Daddy waved a piece of paper in front of Amy's nose. It looked a lot like an American Express bill.

Daddy pulled his reading glasses down from their resting place above his bushy eyebrows. "You spent twelve hundred dollars on shoes? Really?"

"They were Jimmy Choos, and I—"

"I don't give a rat's ass who made them. Amy, your credit-card bill last month was more than ten thousand dollars."

"Oh, really? That much?" She was bad with money,

just like Mom had been. Most of Daddy's rages were precipitated by the arrival of credit-card statements. This was a known fact.

"You're twenty-eight, still unemployed and living at home. This can't go on any longer. Either accept Grady's proposal or move out. Today." He turned and stalked out of her bedroom.

She followed him out into the hallway. "You can't make me go," Amy said to his retreating back. "And you can't force me to marry someone either."

He turned, one eyebrow arched in that classic angry-daddy look. "Wanna bet? Now get your things out of here before noon."

"But the Z4 won't hold all of my stuff." The sports car held two people, barely.

"Oh...that's too bad. Guess you'll have to learn to live with less." Daddy took a few steps down the hallway, then turned and said, "Or marry Grady."

They stood with gazes locked for a moment. "I'm not marrying Grady. He's an idiot."

"No, he's not. He's made a fortune as a fund manager. And, sweetie, you need a rich husband." Daddy turned and continued his march down the hallway.

Maybe she did need a rich husband, but not Grady Carson. She didn't love him. Hell, she didn't even like him.

She returned to her room and stared at the clothes in her giant walk-in closet. She'd give Daddy a couple of hours to calm down about the credit-card bill. That's how Mom had always handled him. Tomorrow he would be his normal, happy self.

In the meantime, she needed to get out of the house.

She threw on a plain white tank top, a pair of Rag and

Bone boyfriend jeans, her new Isabel Marant sneakers, and the black Burberry biker jacket that had most definitely contributed to the size of her Amex bill this month. But, really, Daddy needed to understand that she only went shopping in New York twice a year. It wasn't as if there was any place to buy clothes in Jefferson County, Virginia. And besides, she'd had to go shopping— Tammy, one of her sorority sisters, needed someone to help her pull together her honeymoon wardrobe, and Amy had a killer eye for fashion.

She heaved a sappy sigh at the thought of Tammy and Evan off together on a three-week honeymoon tour of Paris, Rome, and Athens. Paris in April would be fabulous.

She headed out to the circular drive and fired up the BMW Z4. Fifteen minutes later she took a seat at the Red Fern Inn, a two-hundred-year-old taproom and restaurant in downtown Shenandoah Falls. She waited a surprisingly long time before Bryce Summerville, the inn's owner, came over to the table, wringing his hands.

"Miss Lyndon," he said in a deferential tone, "I'm sorry to ask this, but how do you intend to pay for your lunch today?"

"What?"

"Well, this is sort of embarrassing, but your father called not five minutes ago and told me not to accept your credit card."

"He did what?"

"He called me—"

"I heard you. I'm just having a hard time believing you. How did he know I was getting lunch here?"

"You get lunch here quite frequently."

That was true.

"He told me he's canceled your card," Bryce said with a painful-looking frown on his face.

Amy's heart rate jumped. Daddy wouldn't really cut her off, would he? "I'll pay with cash, and I'd like the eggs Benedict." She wasn't sure she had the appetite for them now, but she couldn't just get up and walk out. Not with Viola Ingram and Faye Appleby sitting at the adjacent table, listening in like the notorious gossips they were.

Amy waved at Viola. "Hey, Ms. Ingram, how are you doing today?"

"Just fine and dandy," the senior citizen said in a chipper voice. "I heard that you and Grady Carson are about to make a big announcement."

This was bad. Very bad. Someone had let the cat out of the bag. "No, Mrs. Ingram, no big announcements are pending."

When her brunch finally arrived, she managed to choke down two or three bites before giving up on the whole food idea. When the check arrived, she used the last of her cash to cover it.

She strolled down to the Bank of America branch on Liberty Avenue, where she visited the ATM only to discover that the machine wouldn't give her any money. The bank said she was overdrawn.

Which was impossible. Just last week Daddy had deposited some money...

Oh, crap. He wouldn't. Daddy was a joint signer on the account, and what he could transfer in he could just as easily transfer out.

She was angry now.

She drove back to the house she and Daddy shared. It sat up on the ridge not far from the vineyard. She stormed up the front walk, but when she tried to open the front door, it was locked, which was odd because Daddy's office was in the house and he was always in his office. Always. Besides, Lucy, the housekeeper, was always around too.

She dug for her keys, but when she tried to open the door, the key wouldn't fit.

She stood there dizzy for a moment as her pulse raced out of control. She reached for her cell, looking for reassurance, but the darn thing wasn't getting a signal; up until this moment she'd always gotten four bars of service up here. Daddy wouldn't have shut off her cell phone, would he?

And that's when she panicked. Bella Vista Vineyard's headquarters was a short way up the drive, but she was out of breath when she arrived, having run the distance. Ozzie Cassano, Daddy's chief winemaker, was hanging out in the front drive, as if he'd been waiting for her.

"Where's Daddy and Lucy?" she asked in a shaky voice.

"Lucy is on vacation."

"Since when?"

"Since this morning. And your father isn't here either." Ozzie's lilting Italian accent failed to calm her.

"What do you mean? Daddy's always here unless he's at home or at Charlotte's Grove."

"I'm sorry. He told me to tell you that he's taking a vacation too."

"Holy crap, not with Lucy, I hope."

Ozzie shrugged. "I don't know, miss."

"But the house is all locked up and my key doesn't work. Do you have a key?"

Ozzie had the good sense to look slightly uncomfortable. "I'm very sorry, Miss Lyndon, but your father, he told me that you were not to be let into the house under any circumstances. He also told me you were getting married soon." Ozzie flashed his gold fillings. "Congratulations."

Amy had fallen into a nightmare. Without a working cell phone or money or a place to sleep, Daddy was counting on her to say yes to Grady. And if there'd been a pay phone in town, she might have done exactly that. But pay phones were like dinosaurs, utterly extinct in Shenandoah Falls, Virginia.

She might also have driven to DC and thrown herself on Grady's mercy, but the Z4 was running on empty and she had zero money for gas. So she parked in the town lot and sat there thinking for most of the afternoon.

Daddy expected her to take the easy way out.

Well, screw that idea. She'd show Daddy. She would sleep in her car.

The Z4 had two bucket seats with a console between them, and neither of the seats reclined enough to make sleeping easy. Plus the sunny March day was turning into a bitterly cold March night. Could a person die from exposure when the temperature was forty degrees? She would have asked Siri if her iPhone had been working. Which, in a way, was a saving grace. She probably would have called Grady if the phone had been working.

Instead she toughed it out. And when the sky began to turn pink, it was as if she'd won a moral victory, even though it was hard to feel morally victorious when you were starving and had to pee and didn't have a bathroom handy.

But luckily Gracie's Diner had a bathroom and it was a short walk away.

Amy had never set foot in the diner before eleven in the morning, so she was surprised when she opened the door and discovered she was the first customer of the day. She hadn't been counting on that. She'd been counting on Gracie Teague being busy with other customers.

Instead, Gracie greeted Amy from her post near the coffee machine. "'Morning, Amy. Boy, you sure are here early. You want the usual?"

So awkward. She hadn't thought this through. It would be rude to use the diner's bathroom and not purchase anything. But Amy didn't have any other choices. "Uh, I'm on my way out of town," she lied, "but I needed the restroom."

Gracie cocked her head and gave her a once-over. Amy hated to think what she must look like after trying to sleep in a small car, so she brazened it out by turning her back and walking to the ladies' room with her shoulders straight.

She was a Lyndon. She came from a wealthy and influential family. She wasn't going to beg for the chance to pee in a toilet instead of somewhere outside. The thought of peeing in the woods left her trembling. How did a girl do that, anyway? And what about toilet paper?

The diner's bathroom was basic but clean. She did her business, washed her hands and face, and gave her hair a quick comb. She felt much better.

Hungry, but better. Still, she lingered in the bathroom for a long time, trying to figure out how to leave the diner without humiliating herself. She was running various scenarios in her head when the truth descended like an atom bomb.

She was homeless. And penniless (almost—she had fifty cents in her purse). And unless she said yes to Grady Carson, she would have to sleep in her car again tonight. Not to mention the fact that she would go hungry.

Someone knocked on the door.

Her time was up, and she didn't have a plan and didn't know what to do next, unless it was driving up to Charlotte's Grove and throwing herself on Aunt Pam's mercy. That would be the same as calling Grady, since Aunt Pam was the one who'd set her up with him, way back a year and a half ago.

She didn't want to marry Grady.

"Hon, are you all right?" Gracie called from the other side of the bathroom door. "You've been in there a while, and I…"

Amy opened the door. "I'm fine." Her voice wobbled.

"No, I don't think so. You come out and have your eggs and bacon."

Oh crap. What was she supposed to do now? Tears filled her eyes.

"I…I…don't. I mean, I can't…" She let go of a long, trembling breath. "Daddy locked me out of the house yesterday and told me I had to marry Grady Carson. Then he took all the money out of my checking account." She didn't wail the words or yell them. They came out in a terrible whisper.

She expected Gracie to get angry and bawl her out for using the bathroom without having any intention of buying food. Instead Gracie draped her arm over Amy's shoulder. "Come on, get your breakfast. You can pay me for it later, after you sort things out with your father."

Gracie led Amy to the counter, where a plate of eggs and bacon was waiting for her. She downed them like a starving person and allowed Gracie to refill her coffee cup several times while the usual Saturday crowd arrived for breakfast.

Pippa Custis, the owner of Ewe & Me, the yarn shop in town, came in for a bowl of oatmeal. Walter Braden, the owner of Braden Realty, came in with his old-fashioned paper copy of the *Washington Post* and occupied the corner table while he ate his toast and drank his coffee. Alicia Mulloy, the hygienist at Dr. Dinnen's office, ordered three different kinds of donuts. Amy wondered if Dr. Dinnen was aware of Alicia's sugar habit.

Not that Amy was judging anyone this morning, especially since everyone who arrived at the diner pretended that she wasn't there at all. And then Dusty McNeil strolled through the doors with an athletic grace that made every woman in the place, including Amy, turn and look. Somehow, Dusty always managed to look like a badass biker boy even when he wore crisply pressed khakis and a golf shirt. And he sure did fill out his Eagle Hill Manor shirt with six feet of pure muscle and sun-brown skin.

Gracie was right there with a cup of coffee and plate of eggs and bacon for him. He gave Gracie a smile full of laugh lines and dimples and white teeth. And then he turned toward Amy.

Unlike the other customers in the diner, he didn't try to pretend that she was invisible. Oh, no. He gave her a long, assessing gaze that made Amy's pulse jump. Dusty McNeil had a reputation ten miles long. He'd carved a lot of notches on his bedpost over the years. And no wonder—all that golden-blond hair, sharp, chiseled features, and a deep, soulful look in his brilliant blue eyes. The guy didn't have to say a word.

In fact, for a long, crazy instant, Amy wondered if she could throw herself on his mercy. Spending a night with him wouldn't be much of a sacrifice. And it would probably be way more fun than sleeping in the Z4.

Or sleeping with Grady, for that matter.

But no. She had chosen to sleep in her car instead of falling back on a man. So falling into bed with Dusty McNeil wouldn't be a step in the right direction. She looked down at her coffee mug and tried to actually figure out what her next step ought to be.

She came up with nothing.

"Y'all seem to be really busy up at Eagle Hill Manor these days," Gracie said to Dusty, and since Amy didn't have anything better to do, she eavesdropped.

"Yep," Dusty said in his mountain accent. "Ever since that article in *Brides*. Willow's hiring another event planner. Know anyone who might be interested?"

Gracie shook her head. "No, but I'll keep my eye out."

Event planner? Now, that sounded like a job description Amy might be able to fit. In fact, becoming an event planner at Eagle Hill Manor sounded way more fun than becoming Mrs. Grady Carson. And even if Amy didn't have any real work experience, she had tons of experience planning sorority events, not to mention her sorority sisters' weddings.

She could surprise Daddy. She could get a job.

And this particular job was in the bag because Willow Lyndon, Eagle Hill Manor's owner, was Amy's cousin by marriage.

About the Author

Hope Ramsay is a *USA Today* bestselling author of heartwarming contemporary romances. Her books have won critical acclaim and publishing awards. She is married to a good ol' Georgia boy who resembles every single one of her Southern heroes. She has two grown children and a couple of demanding lap cats. She lives in Virginia, where, when she's not writing, she's knitting or playing her forty-year-old Martin guitar. Visit www.hoperamsay.com/mailing-list/ to join her mailing list for information about upcoming releases and book signings.

Fall in Love with Forever Romance

MERRY CHRISTMAS COWBOY
By Carolyn Brown

No one tells a cowboy story like *New York Times* bestselling author Carolyn Brown. So grab your hot chocolate and settle in because this Christmas, Santa's wearing a Stetson. Fiona Logan is everything Jud Dawson thought he'd never find. But with wild weather, nosy neighbors, and a new baby in the family, getting her to admit that she's falling in love might just take a Christmas miracle.

A CHRISTMAS BRIDE
By Hope Ramsay

USA Today bestselling author Hope Ramsay's new contemporary romance series is perfect for fans of Debbie Macomber, Robyn Carr, and Sherryl Woods. Haunted by regrets and grief, widower David Lyndon has a bah-humbug approach to the holidays—until he's shown the spirit of the season by his daughter and her godmother Willow. Paired up to plan a Christmas wedding for friends, David and Willow will discover that the best gift is the promise of a future spent together...

Fall in Love with Forever Romance

CHRISTMAS COMES TO MAIN STREET
By Olivia Miles

It's beginning to taste a lot like Christmas...or so Kara Hasting hopes. Her new cookie business is off to a promising start, until a sexy stranger makes her doubt herself. Fans of Jill Shalvis, RaeAnne Thayne, and Susan Mallery will love this sweet holiday read.

Fall in Love with Forever Romance

A HIGHLANDER'S CHRISTMAS KISS
By Paula Quinn

In the tradition of Karen Hawkins and Monica McCarty comes the next in Paula Quinn's sinfully sexy MacGregor family series. Temperance Menzie is starting to fall for the mysterious, wounded highlander she's been nursing back to health. But Cailean Grant has a dark secret, and only a Christmas miracle can keep them together.